Bite Club

Books by Laurien Berenson

A PEDIGREE TO DIE FOR
UNDERDOG
DOG EAT DOG
HAIR OF THE DOG
WATCHDOG
HUSH PUPPY
UNLEASHED
ONCE BITTEN
HOT DOG
BEST IN SHOW
JINGLE BELL BARK
RAINING CATS AND DOGS
CHOW DOWN
HOUNDED TO DEATH
DOGGIE DAY CARE MURDER
GONE WITH THE WOOF
DEATH OF A DOG WHISPERER
THE BARK BEFORE CHRISTMAS
LIVE AND LET GROWL
MURDER AT THE PUPPY FEST
WAGGING THROUGH THE SNOW
RUFF JUSTICE
BITE CLUB

Published by Kensington Publishing Corporation

Bite Club

LAURIEN BERENSON

KENSINGTON BOOKS
www.kensingtonbooks.com

KENSINGTON BOOKS are published by

Kensington Publishing Corp.
119 West 40th Street
New York, NY 10018

All Kensington titles, imprints and distributed lines are available at special quantity discounts for bulk purchases for sales promotion, premiums, fund-raising, educational or institutional use. Special book excerpts or customized printings can also be created to fit specific needs. For details, write or phone the office of the Kensington Special Sales Manager: Kensington Publishing Corp., 119 West 40th Street, New York, NY, 10018. Attn. Special Sales Department. Phone: 1-800-221-2647.

Kensington and the K logo Reg. U.S. Pat. & TM Off.

Library of Congress Control Number: 2019932229

ISBN-13: 978-1-4967-1836-5
ISBN-10: 1-4967-1836-4
First Kensington Hardcover Edition: July 2019

ISBN-13: 978-1-4967-1842-6 (ebook)
ISBN-10: 1-4967-1842-9 (ebook)

10 9 8 7 6 5 4 3 2 1

Printed in the United States of America

Bite Club

Chapter 1

It started as a joke. After all, who would name a friendly book club Bite Club? Well, we did. First, because we were all dog lovers, some of whom had met as fellow dog show exhibitors. And second, because when we formed the group we decided to concentrate on reading mystery novels. Books with bite.

Plus, we all liked the idea of belonging to a club that sounded as though Brad Pitt might stop by on occasion.

Especially Terry Denunzio. Terry always has plenty to say—and all of it is entertaining. He didn't back down when the rest of us told him that he was barking up the wrong tree because Brad Pitt wasn't gay. Instead, Terry just sat there and smiled like he knew something we didn't.

It wouldn't be the first time. Terry is one of my best friends and I've seen him in action. I'm pretty sure if anyone could change Pitt's preferred orientation, Terry would be the one to do it.

You might be wondering what all that had to do with books. Truthfully, not much. We weren't even halfway through our first meeting when it occurred to me that maybe the books were just a good excuse for us to get together and enjoy each other's company.

And drink a little wine while we were at it.

The idea for the book club had arisen from my own love

of reading. I'd envisioned spending a few evenings a month with a small group of like-minded people. Good friends coming together to share stories and swap reading recommendations.

I'd begun by recruiting my former neighbor, Alice Brickman. She and I had met years earlier when our older children were infants. The shared trials and tribulations of motherhood had brought us together, then quickly solidified our bond. Since I'd remarried and moved to a different part of town, Alice and I didn't see nearly as much of each other as we used to. This seemed like a wonderful opportunity to reconnect.

Next I'd called Claire Walden Travis, a family member by virtue of being married to my ex-husband, which also made her stepmother to my older son, Davey. She'd been delighted to become part of the group. An organizer by nature and profession, she'd brought a list of potential book choices to the first meeting to get us started.

Then I'd asked Terry to join us. He's the longtime partner of professional dog handler Crawford Langley. He's also the best looking man I've ever met. I'd like to be able to tell you that Terry's flashy exterior conceals hidden depths, but not really. With Terry, what you see is what you get. He's exuberant in his love for dogs, for his friends, and for cozy mysteries. In other words, he was a perfect addition to the club.

It was about that time that my Aunt Peg found out about my plans. And overnight my little reading group suddenly became a Big Deal. That tended to happen whenever Margaret Turnbull got involved with anything. For decades she'd been one of the country's premier breeders of Standard Poodles. Now she was a much-in-demand dog show judge. Aunt Peg was accustomed to having her opinions matter.

She also had a habit of bossing people around. Especially her relatives. Most especially me. Is it any wonder that she hadn't been among the first people I'd called? Apparently that made no difference. Aunt Peg simply assumed that she would be included. And unfortunately none of us were brave enough to dispute that assumption.

True to form, Aunt Peg first wanted to iron out a few details.

"Why are you forming a book club?" she wanted to know. "Aren't you busy enough already?"

"Well, sure. But I always make time to read."

Aunt Peg looked dubious. She was already approved to judge the Non-Sporting and Toy Groups. Her idea of reading for entertainment probably meant perusing the breed standards of new dog breeds she planned to add to her repertoire. Either that or the *Encyclopaedia Britannica*.

"Books?" she asked.

"Of course, books. Mostly mystery novels."

Aunt Peg blinked twice. And remained mute. That was a first.

Over the years, she and I had been involved in the solving of more than a few mysteries ourselves. Surely my choice of reading material made perfect sense.

Aunt Peg still didn't look convinced by the wisdom of my idea. Or maybe she just wanted to continue arguing. There's nothing she enjoys more than a good verbal sparring match. I'm pretty sure she thinks vocal confrontation should be a national pastime. Like baseball games and eating junk food.

As for me, I wasn't even sure why we were having this conversation. After all, no one—least of all me—had invited her to join the book club. Nevertheless, I felt the need to justify my decision. Yet again. For some reason, Aunt Peg always had that effect on me.

Well, on everybody really. We all did our best to shape up when Aunt Peg was around. Being related to her was like living with my own personal cyclone. Or maybe runaway train.

"Reading is fun," I told her. "It's educational. It reduces stress."

"Of course, it's fun. I do it all the time. You're not the only one who enjoys a good mystery novel." Then she thought about what I'd said and stopped. "*Stress?* Why on earth would *you* feel stressed?"

Plenty of reasons. And I probably didn't have to point out that the first one was standing right in front of me—trying to hijack my book club idea and turn it into something she liked better.

But beyond that, I lead a busy life. I'm a wife, a mother of two wonderful sons, and a special needs tutor at a private school. I also have a houseful of Standard Poodles. Five to be exact, plus a small spotted mutt named Bud.

Sometimes I wondered if there would be enough hours in the day to get everything done. Then I stopped wondering and started doing. Every mother knows how that works.

I narrowed my eyes at Aunt Peg. It was difficult to produce a full-on glare since I'm five and a half feet tall and the person I wanted to intimidate towered over me by more than six inches. Aunt Peg was nearing seventy. She had the posture of a ballerina and shoulders that would do a linebacker proud. It was a formidable combination.

"Do you want to join or not?" I asked.

"I'm considering. . . ."

I sighed under my breath. "Considering what exactly?"

"Whether or not I want to let other people dictate my choice or reading material."

"You're right," I agreed—probably too quickly. "That sounds like a terrible idea."

Aunt Peg wasn't fooled by my easy acquiescence. "You're trying to get rid of me."

"Not at all. I'm simply enabling you to make the responsible choice."

"I'd be delighted to join your little group," she decided abruptly. "Can we hold the meetings at my house?"

And already she wanted to be in charge.

"You can hold some of them at your house," I said. "Everyone will take turns hosting. We'll meet twice a month, every other Tuesday night."

Aunt Peg nodded. I was pretty sure she'd stopped listening to me. "I might have some other ideas for new members. . . ."

And that was when things began to spiral beyond my control. Six people had attended the first meeting, held at my house. Seven had shown up at Alice's home two weeks later. Now it was the night of our third meeting, scheduled to take place at Aunt Peg's. Judging by the glee with which she'd volunteered to serve as hostess, I suspected she might be planning on a crowd.

Not for the first time when it came to my dealings with Aunt Peg, I wondered what I'd gotten myself into.

Aunt Peg lives in the back country area of Greenwich, Connecticut. Her house has clapboard siding and a wraparound porch, and once served as the family home for a working farm. Forty years earlier, Aunt Peg and her husband, Max—then newly married—had purchased the property to found their Cedar Crest Kennel. Over the ensuing decades it had been home to dozens of champion Standard Poodles.

My car window was open to admit the warm, early July breeze when I turned into Aunt Peg's driveway. Max had been deceased for a decade now, and the kennel building behind the house had burned to the ground the previous summer. For a moment I imagined that the scent of that long-gone smoke still lingered in the air.

Glancing in that direction, I squinted toward the descending sun and saw nothing but a wide stretch of uninterrupted lawn where the building had once stood. Of course, the thought had been fanciful. I quickly dismissed it and parked the Volvo toward the rear of the empty driveway.

The meeting was scheduled to start at seven. Fifteen minutes early, I was obviously the first to arrive.

Visitors to Aunt Peg's house were met with an effusive canine greeting—offered in the belief that if you minded being mobbed by her Standard Poodles, she probably didn't want to know you anyway. By now I was accustomed to the onslaught. Her dogs and I were old friends. Not only that, but each of them was related to the Poodles I had at home.

The four adults were first to come flying down the front steps to say hello. All were black in color, and all were finished champions. They sported the easy-to-maintain kennel clip with their faces, feet, and base of their tails clipped short, and a trim blanket of curls covering the remainder of their bodies. The two bitches, Hope and Willow, led the way. The males, Zeke and Beau, brought up the rear.

Coral, the only puppy in the group, remained standing in the doorway at Aunt Peg's side. Coral was nine months old and just starting her career in the show ring. She already had two points toward her championship, and my teenage son, Davey, was going to be handling her in some summer shows.

Coral's dense, black coat was longer than that of the other Poodles. It was carefully shaped to leave a profusion of hair on the back of her neck and over her shoulders. The puppy's topknot hair was banded into ponytails on top of her head and her ear hair was wrapped in brightly colored plastic paper.

Until Coral won the coveted fifteen points needed to attain her championship, her coat—which had been growing from birth—would need to be cosseted and protected at all times. For that reason, she usually wasn't allowed to join in the older Poodles' rough-and-tumble play. Now, however, Aunt Peg released the big black puppy from her side and

Coral came skipping down the steps joyously. When I knelt down, she threw herself into my arms.

"You're early." Aunt Peg followed her canine crew down the stairs. "Don't think I'm going to let you dive into the pupcakes before everyone else arrives."

"Me?" I managed an innocent look.

Okay, so maybe I'd skimped on dinner in anticipation of the goodies I was sure to find at Aunt Peg's gathering. Her sweet tooth was legendary. And over the years I'd spent in her company, I'd developed my own lust for sweets by osmosis. I knew there would be pastries from the St. Moritz Bakery waiting inside. Pupcakes—vanilla cupcakes whimsically frosted to resemble a puppy's face— were a special treat.

"Yes, you," Aunt Peg replied sternly. "I'm expecting a full house tonight. I would hate to run out of refreshments."

"A full house." I tried not to sound annoyed. "How did that happen?"

Aunt Peg snapped her fingers. The Poodles immediately stopped racing around the front yard. They ran up the steps and through the open door into the house. She and I followed.

"Oh, you know," Aunt Peg said blithely. "One thing led to another."

"You do realize this was supposed to be a small group, right? Just some friends getting together to talk about books."

"Yes, of course. But there's the problem. I have so many friends."

Aunt Peg ushered me in the direction of her living room. The two chintz-covered loveseats that had flanked the fireplace were now angled to face a grouping of assorted chairs gathered from the dining room and library. At a quick glance, I counted more than a dozen seats.

The refreshments were set out on a sideboard. There was a pot of tea, and several bottles of wine, along with appropriate china and stemware. A tray of pupcakes was sitting beside a large dish of chocolate and macaroon Sarah Bernhardts. The entire display looked heavenly.

"Like . . . how many?" I asked.

I sidled over toward the buffet and reached for a Sarah Bernhardt. Aunt Peg slapped my hand away.

"Wait for the guests to arrive," she said.

"I'm a guest."

"Since when?"

There was that.

I turned away and sat down on the edge of a loveseat. Hope walked over and placed her head in my lap. I ruffled my fingers through her topknot and ears. Hope was littermate to my beloved Faith. I was sure she could smell her sister's scent on my clothing.

"How many?" I repeated.

"They're a lively cross-section of exhibitors. You probably already know some of them. Or at least you've seen them at shows. I'm sure you'll like them once you've met them."

Note that once again she'd dodged my question.

"Do they read books?" I asked.

"I should hope so. I did tell them this was a book club."

I supposed that counted for something. "Do they have names?"

"Oh pish," said Aunt Peg. "Of course they have names. Felicity Barber, for one."

I frowned briefly. After a moment, a vague image of the woman's face swam into view. I was pretty sure she had a toy breed. We're dog people. We identify everyone by their breed affiliation.

"Japanese Chin?" I guessed.

"That's right." Aunt Peg looked pleased. Apparently I'd turned out to be a better student than expected.

"Marge Brennan," she said next.

"I know her. She has Bulldogs." Marge was a fellow Non-Sporting Group exhibitor. She was easy to picture. Short and squat, she also had the pendulous cheeks and perpetual scowl of her chosen breed. "Who else?"

"Jeff Schwin."

I shook my head.

"Tall? Skinny? *Greyhounds.* You know."

"No, I don't."

And just like that, my approval rating dipped again.

Aunt Peg rushed through the rest. "Toby Cane. He has Welshies." Welsh Springer Spaniels for the uninitiated. "And Rush and Vic Landry breed Belgian Tervurens. There, you see? That's all."

"That's six new people," I pointed out unnecessarily.

Alice had arrived at our first book club meeting with a neighbor named Evan Major, who'd recently moved onto her block. She'd confided that she'd brought him along because she felt sorry for him. A small, unassuming man in his forties, Evan had been shy in our boisterous company and had mostly kept his thoughts to himself. He didn't volunteer any personal information, but he did describe himself as an avid reader.

At our second meeting, held at Alice's house, another neighbor had shown up unexpectedly. Bella Barrundy came through the door with a smile on her face and a pot full of homemade macaroni and cheese in her hands. She informed us that Evan had invited her to join the group, though he appeared surprised to hear that. But Bella had read the book we were discussing and she joined our conversation with enthusiasm. So we accepted her into the fold.

At the time I'd thought that seven people seemed like a fine size for the book club. It was large enough to offer room for differing opinions, yet small enough to keep things cozy and copacetic.

And now it seemed that our numbers had nearly doubled.

Thank you, Aunt Peg, I thought somewhat murder-
ously.

"You're welcome," she replied.

Oh Lord, I hadn't said that *out loud*, had I?

The doorbell rang and Aunt Peg went to answer it. The
Standard Poodles leapt up and ran after her, the five of
them eddying around the closely grouped furniture like a
fast-flowing canine stream. A moment later, a chorus of
new voices filled the front hall.

Ready or not, I thought. *Here we go.*

Chapter 2

"Where did all these people come from?" asked Terry.

Only minutes had passed, but the living room was already packed with a lively crowd. I'd given up my perch on the loveseat to claim a spot by the wall from which to observe the new arrivals. Fortunately the corner I'd staked out was next to the dish of Sarah Bernhardts. When Terry cut through the group and joined me there, I'd just stuffed a second one into my mouth.

Since I was briefly unable to speak, Terry took up the slack. "This crowd is unexpected, isn't it? I'm glad I dressed for the occasion." He peered around the room. "Is that Rush Landry? I wouldn't have pictured him as a novel reader. Automotive magazines, maybe. Or possibly porn . . ."

I swallowed hastily and slapped him on the arm. "Stop that!"

"Stop what? Saying out loud what you know perfectly well you're thinking?"

"I am *not*," I replied. "And what is that you're wearing anyway?"

Terry was in his thirties but he could easily pass for a decade younger. For some reason, he'd decided to come to the meeting dressed in a velvet smoking jacket with a cream-colored cravat knotted around his neck. His blond hair was slicked back off his face and his nails were perfectly manicured. He looked like an extra in a British period film. All he needed to complete the picture was a pipe and a valet.

"Do you like it?" Terry spun in place. Though it was evening, the temperature hovered around eighty degrees. Dressed like that, I would have been sweltering. Terry looked cool as a cucumber. Or maybe a cucumber sandwich. "I found the ensemble online. It seemed like just the thing to wear to this convivial gathering."

"If we were on *Downton Abbey*, maybe," I retorted. "In February."

"It may not be Highclere but we are at Aunt Peg's house. For all I knew, the dress code might be formal."

"We're here for a book club meeting," I told him. "*My* book club. It's casual. You wore shorts to my house last month."

"You held your shindig in the backyard. Shorts were appropriate."

At my house, we'd sat out back on the deck and sipped sangria. We'd held our discussion with the Poodles and Bud cavorting in the yard around us.

At least that part was the same, I thought, as Claire Travis stepped through the doorway and gave Zeke a friendly pat on the head. Aunt Peg's Poodles were mingling happily with the guests.

"Last time there were just half a dozen of us," Terry said. "You know, a friendly gathering. Tonight this place is jammed. What happened?"

"I'm surprised you even have to ask." I nodded toward the hallway where my aunt was holding court. "Aunt Peg happened."

"Did she invite the entire dog show world?"

"I sincerely hope not, but don't hold me to it."

"Who's that?" Terry pointed toward a tall man with

black-framed glasses and a long, slender nose. "He looks familiar but I can't quite place him."

"Aunt Peg acquainted me with the guest list before you got here. I'm guessing that's Jeff Schwin. She said he has Greyhounds."

"Of course," Terry said with a nod. When you've been to as many dog shows as we have, the entire dog community begins to look like someone you probably know.

Alice entered the room, spotted me, and immediately waved. She cut through the throng of people between us and made her way to my side. Alice's husband, Joe, was a partner at a law firm in Greenwich. Her son, Joey, was thirteen like Davey, and the two of them were best friends. Daughter Carly, a budding ballerina, was three years younger. Alice worked part-time as a paralegal at Joe's firm.

We both missed the easy intimacy we'd enjoyed when we were young moms and neighbors. Sharing babysitters and swapping kid-friendly recipes, we'd supported each other through highs and lows. No matter what transpired, Alice would always have my back, just as I had hers.

She and I shared a quick hug. Terry poured her a glass of Pinot Grigio. Both part of the original book club group, they'd known each other for almost a month.

"What's with the crowd?" Alice asked. She gulped down a swallow of wine as if to fortify herself. "Did I come on the wrong night?"

Claire was heading our way too. She arrived just in time to hear Alice's question. "Ditto that for me," she said.

Claire was sleek as a cat. She had shiny, dark hair and honey-toned skin. An event planner by trade, she was very good at managing things. And people. Now her hand lifted, long fingers pointing gracefully toward the side-board. "And ditto on the wine too, Terry, if you wouldn't mind?"

"Not at all," he replied. "In fact, I'll pour for all four of us before the horde descends on this spread like locusts."

"Horde indeed." Claire caught my eye and frowned. "This is Peg's doing, isn't it? I should have known our amiable little group was too good to last."

Claire was a relative newcomer to the family. She and Bob had been married for just eighteen months. Unlike most people, Claire wasn't intimidated by Aunt Peg. Of course when they'd met, Claire had suspected that Peg might be guilty of murder. The two women were friends now, but Claire had no illusions about the kind of mischief Aunt Peg was capable of causing.

"You know Aunt Peg," I told her. "The bigger the production, the better. I'm not surprised she wanted to add to the group. But what I can't figure out is how she managed to dig up so many book lovers among the dog show crowd so quickly. It's not as if anyone stands around at the shows and talks about what they're reading."

"What makes you think they're all book lovers?" Alice asked skeptically.

We all looked around the room. People were gathered in small groups, chatting with one another. Most seemed to be discussing the previous weekend's dog show results. Two were comparing pictures on their phones. No one was holding a book.

"Well, for one thing . . . they're here." I might have sounded a little defensive. "And for another, Aunt Peg says they are."

"Oh please." Terry sniffed. "Peg is the sneakiest woman I've ever met. Since when have you believed everything she told you?"

Ummm. He had a point.

Terry tilted his wineglass to point toward a plump, middle-aged woman on the other side of the living room. She had beautifully styled blond hair and an Hermès scarf wrapped around her throat. Unlike everyone else, she wasn't talking to anyone. Instead, she was standing by herself, surveying the other book club participants with a calculating expression on her face.

"That's Felicity Barber," he told us. "She's been showing dogs since Crawford was in short pants and she's one of the toughest competitors on the circuit. Felicity would sell her own mother to get in the good graces of a judge as powerful as Peg."

I huffed out a breath. "Well, that's disappointing."

Claire didn't think so. She seemed to be enjoying herself. "Five dollars says Felicity didn't read this week's book."

"Ten dollars says she doesn't even know the title," Alice shot right back.

"Done," said Claire. The two women shook on it.

I winced and looked away. Some people had put in an appearance tonight to gain favor. Others were placing bets. My friendly little book club was morphing into something unrecognizable right before my eyes. And I was powerless to prevent it.

I chugged the glass of Pinot Terry had handed me and poured myself another. He glanced at me and smothered a grin. Terry doesn't miss a thing.

I suspected it was going to be a long night.

Aunt Peg stepped into the middle of the room. As hostess for the meeting, it was her job to take charge to the proceedings. "Can I have everyone's attention, please?"

Conversation died down. People put their phones away. We all turned politely in her direction.

"I'd like to welcome all of you to tonight's gathering. Bite Club," she said with a smile. "Please don't take the name literally."

Most people laughed in appreciation. Marge Brennan, seated on a loveseat, emitted a loud guffaw. Apparently Felicity Barber wasn't the only one who'd joined the book club in order to suck up to Aunt Peg.

"Thank you." Aunt Peg dipped her head in gracious acknowledgment. "There are refreshments on the sideboard. I hope you will all help yourselves to a drink or a snack. Then please take a seat so we can call the meeting to order. Has anyone counted noses? Is everybody here and ready to get started?"

People were making their way toward our side of the room. Drinks already in hand, Alice, Claire, Terry, and I moved out of their way. I was considering the best place to find a seat when Alice spoke up.

"I don't see Evan," she said. "I know he was planning to be here tonight. I'm sure he must be on his way."

Aunt Peg was a stickler for punctuality. She made a show of looking at her watch—a clear warning to anyone who might contemplate tardiness in the future. "I suppose we can wait a little longer before beginning."

Ten minutes later, Evan still hadn't arrived. The selection on the sideboard had been depleted. Dog-related conversation had resumed.

And Aunt Peg was growing increasingly restless. She hated it when things didn't go to plan. I was about to ask Alice to give Evan a call when the Standard Poodles jumped up and ran to the front door.

"It's about time," Aunt Peg muttered under her breath. She followed the dogs out of the room.

"I am *so* sorry to be late." Evan's apology was audible from the front hall. A moment later he appeared in the doorway. "I hope I haven't inconvenienced everyone."

Aunt Peg was right behind him. "As long as you don't make a habit of it . . ." Her voice trailed away as Evan stepped into the light. "My word, that looks awful. What happened to you?"

Evan Major was slight of build and diffident in demeanor. With his pale eyes, receding hairline, and slightly hunched shoulders, he'd struck me as a person who never wanted to stand out in a crowd. Now he had no choice.

Everyone in the room was staring at him. Specifically we all were staring at the bruise—swollen, red, and starting to turn purple—that was blooming on the side of his jaw.

Evan's hand rose self-consciously to his face. "Oh, this."

At six feet tall, Aunt Peg towered over him. She leaned in for a closer look. "Yes, *that*. It appears you must have taken quite a wallop. Would you like me to fetch you an ice pack?"

"No, thank you. I'm fine. Really." Evan started to shake his head, then evidently thought better of it. "Please don't go to any trouble on my behalf. It's bad enough that I've delayed the meeting."

Bella Barrundy stepped forward. She guided Evan to a nearby chair. "None of us minded waiting. And it looks as though you had a very good excuse."

A rumble of assent came from others in the room. It was followed by a weighty silence. Mystery readers are curious people. It was clear that everyone was waiting for Evan to explain himself.

He looked pained by the necessity, but finally mumbled, "I got in a car accident on the way here."

"You poor thing." Bella patted his back solicitously.

Claire gathered a handful of ice from the bucket on the sideboard. She wrapped it in a linen napkin, then crossed the room and handed it to Evan. "This will help the swelling," she said briskly. "And take ibuprofen for the pain. Are you injured anywhere else?"

"No. At least I don't think so." Evan shrank down into his chair. "It was just a fender bender. I rolled through a stop sign and hit a guy's bumper. Nothing to get excited about."

"You might think that now." A man separated himself from the crowd. He had a muscular physique, strong features, and a piercing gaze. "But then lawyers get involved

and everything goes south. It sounds like you were the one
at fault?"

"No, I . . ." Evan glanced up uncertainly. "I'm sorry,
who are you?"

"Rush Landry. New book club member." He grabbed
Evan's hand and pumped it up and down. "Just trying to
help."

"Thank you." Evan managed a small smile. "I appreciate your concern." He looked at the rest of us. "That goes
for all of you. You're very kind to worry about me. But it
was nothing. Please, let's just go on with the meeting."

"If you're sure . . . ?" said Aunt Peg.

Evan nodded. "The other driver and I exchanged information. Our insurance companies will take care of everything. I'd really rather just put the whole episode behind
me. So on a totally different subject—did anyone happen
to read a good book this week?"

Aunt Peg knew how to take a cue. "Good question!"
she agreed. "Let's take our seats, shall we? Margaret
Maron is a wonderful writer. I know we'll all have plenty
to say about *Bootlegger's Daughter*. And I'll begin by saying that I think the title is genius. Who wouldn't want to
know more about Deborah Knott after a tease like that?"

The conversation that followed was fast and furious.
People chimed in with opinions from all corners of the
room. When they were too impatient to wait their turns,
they simply talked over one another. Aunt Peg tried to
moderate the discussion, but the choice of the debut novel
in Maron's southern mystery series had proven so popular
that even she could barely get a word in.

Those among us who hadn't previously been acquainted
with Judge Knott were now planning to dive in and read
the rest of the series. Those for whom the book wasn't
new had been happy to revisit it. The only complaint came
from Toby Cane, who grumbled about the choice of a

book that was first published in the previous century. He was quickly overruled by consensus.

As for Felicity Barber, she had not only read the assigned book, she gave it a rave review—causing both Alice and Claire to lose their bets. Neither woman seemed to mind. When the meeting ended, they left arm in arm, still arguing companionably over who had placed the better wager.

As the exodus began, I bid adieu to Aunt Peg's Standard Poodles, who acknowledged my good manners with bright eyes and wagging tails. The line to pay my respects to Aunt Peg was considerably longer. I decided to slip out the door, but before I could make my escape, I was hailed by Evan. He was standing at the sideboard, replacing the linen napkin Claire had given him earlier.

"Alice recommended that I have a word with you," he said as I approached.

"Oh?" My gaze dropped to his jawline. The swelling might have gone down a little but the bruise was even uglier than when he'd come in. "Are you feeling all right? Do you need me to do something?"

"No, I'm okay. I wanted to ask you about something else entirely. I know you have lots of dogs. . . . I saw them last month when we met at your house."

I nodded. "Yes, we have six. Sometimes it feels like a lot."

"The thing is . . . I recently got divorced. That's why I moved to Stamford. I guess you might say I'm starting over."

"I can understand that." I smiled encouragingly, wishing he'd get to the point.

"I didn't realize how lonely it would be, living by myself with no one to talk to. So I decided to fix that." Evan's expression brightened. "I went out and bought a puppy. He's a Bulldog, three months old. And he's great. But the problem is, he doesn't *know* anything."

"Puppies are like that," I said. "They're a blank slate. That's why it's so important to start them right with proper training."

"That's what Alice told me you would say." Evan paused, then added hopefully, "She also said you might be willing to help me with that. She said you know *everything* about dogs."

The thought made me laugh. "You have that wrong. That's Aunt Peg, not me."

"Your aunt is a formidable woman," Evan replied seriously. "I wouldn't dream of asking her to spend her precious time dealing with my problems."

I was pretty sure there was an implied insult in there about *my* precious time, but I decided to ignore it. I must have looked annoyed, however, because Evan gestured toward the exit. "I didn't mean to hold you up. Let me walk you out while we finish our conversation."

We skirted around the last of the stragglers—Aunt Peg's dog show cronies who were still paying court—and let ourselves out the door. In a courtly gesture, Evan took my arm to guide me down the darkened steps.

"I'm the white Prius," he told me. Last to arrive, he'd still managed to find a spot near the house. "So what do you think? Bully's awfully cute. But he and I need proper guidance from someone who knows what she's doing. Will you help me get him off to a good start?"

Of course I agreed.

Evan shook my hand and thanked me profusely. His gratitude seemed so out of proportion to the favor he'd requested that I wondered if he'd expected me to turn him down. Maybe when I was finished showing Evan how to train his puppy I'd work on finding a way to shore up his self-esteem.

After we'd made a plan to get together later in the week, Evan got in his car. When he started the engine, his headlights flicked on. They illuminated the Prius's grill and fender. My gaze slid over the front of the car, looking for signs of damage. To my surprise, the white bumper looked pristine.

That was odd. Even if Evan hadn't been wearing a seat belt, it was hard to imagine how he'd ended up with such a big bruise without acquiring so much as a scratch on his car. I would have asked, but Evan was already backing away down the driveway.

I stood and watched him leave. Thanks to his new puppy, I'd be seeing him again soon. There'd be plenty of time to find out then.

Chapter 3

The drive from Greenwich to my home in North Stamford took only twenty minutes on the Merritt Parkway. Stamford is a thriving city on the Connecticut coast in lower Fairfield County. Like much of the area, it had once served as a haven for New York commuters. Since that time, however, the city has grown in both size and opportunity. Stamford now possesses more than enough commerce to be a destination in its own right.

I lived with my family well north of downtown on the other side of the Merritt Parkway. Fortunately our suburban neighborhood remained mostly untouched by the rapid expansion that characterized much of the city. We had wide streets lined by mature trees and houses situated on comfortable two-acre lots. Children can play outside and ride the school bus to local schools. It was a great place to raise a family.

I'd barely entered the house when a delighted shriek filled the air. "Mommy's home!"

My younger son, Kevin, four years old, and turbo-powered by boundless energy and exuberance, came flying down the hallway. He launched himself into my open arms.

Following just behind him were five big, black Standard Poodles—each hoping to offer a greeting of his or her own. I straightened and swept Kev up in the air as we were mobbed by the oncoming dogs. The Poodles scrambled, then ducked and bobbed, as I swung my son around in a circle. That led to more shrieking. And even a bark or two.

My favorite kind of welcome.

Standards are the largest of the three Poodle varieties. They're smart and athletic, and they know how to tell a joke. When they're happy—which is most of the time—they bounce straight up in the air, springing skyward from all four feet at once. Poodles also possess a natural sense of empathy and a strong desire to please. They're a perfect companion for just about any activity—or no activity at all.

As the mayhem continued, Faith, dog of my heart and the oldest member of our Poodle posse, flattened her ears against her head and gave me a reproachful look. It wasn't that she objected to boisterous play, just that at her advanced age of almost nine she sometimes felt obliged to stand upon her dignity.

And perhaps to try and remind me of mine.

Faith was the first pet I'd ever owned. She had come to me as a gift from Aunt Peg when she was just a puppy, and she'd quickly taught me all the pleasures of dog ownership. Over the years we'd spent together, she'd enriched my life in more ways than I could count.

So when Faith registered a rebuke—even a mild one—I listened.

After the second swoop around, I stopped and set Kevin down on the floor in front of me. He wobbled briefly on his feet, then looked up and cried, "More!"

"No. No more." I blew out a breath. That child was getting heavy. "I'm worn out. Look what time it is. I thought you'd be in bed by now."

"It's summer vacation," Kevin informed me. As if I didn't know.

And let's face it. We were talking about vacation from half days of preschool.

"You still need your sleep," I told him.

"Nope." Kev shook his head. "I'm not tired."

"It's after nine o'clock." I headed toward the kitchen. The patter of many feet followed behind. "Where's everyone else?"

"Outside catching fireflies!" Kevin slithered around me and ran on ahead.

As I turned the corner, I saw that the back door leading out to the deck was wide open. The light in the kitchen was serving as a calling card to every bug in the neighborhood. I flicked off the switch and the Poodles and I followed Kevin out into the fenced backyard.

It was a beautiful midsummer night. Though still warm, the air was clear and fresh. Looking up, I felt like I could see a thousand stars in the wide sky. Then my gaze returned to earth and I saw my own personal star heading toward me across the darkened yard.

Sam isn't just my partner, he's my best friend. We've been married for six years. He and I support each other and we complement each other's flaws. We always seem to be able to find something to laugh about. And I never get tired of looking at his smile.

When Sam stopped in front of me and pulled me into his arms for a hug, I leaned into the embrace and sighed. It was good to be home.

"How was book club?" he asked.

"Interesting." I dropped my arms and stepped away.

"Oh? Not all book chat and pupcakes?"

"Hardly." I laughed. "The meeting did take place at Aunt Peg's house, after all."

Abruptly all five Standard Poodles went flying past us. Somewhere in the back of the yard a rabbit must have poked its head out of a hole. I doubted that the dogs would catch it but they would certainly enjoy the chase.

Tar, an impressive adult male and Sam's former specials dog, was leading the charge. Augie, Davey's Poodle who'd recently completed his championship, raced alongside him.

Two bitches, Faith's daughter, Eve, and Sam's Raven, scrambled to keep up. Faith trotted along sedately in the rear.

It was the first time in several years that we didn't have a dog "in hair." With no show coat to protect, we didn't have to monitor the Poodles' play. Bud could jump up and yank on Augie's ear and the only one who would yell at him for that was Augie. It was nice to be off duty for a change.

"Kev said something about fireflies," I said. "Where's Davey?"

Sam pointed toward the big oak tree in the middle of the yard. "He's up in the tree house."

Hearing his name, my older son leaned out a window. I could barely see him through the leafy branches. "Hey, Mom," he called. "Look what we have."

Davey held out a mason jar that appeared to be lit from within. When I walked closer, the soft glow inside the wide glass bottle separated itself into a dozen twinkling lights.

"I hope you poked holes in the top," I said.

"Of course." Davey sounded miffed. He was thirteen and ready to start high school in the fall. As a consequence, he knew everything. "Besides, we're letting them go at the end of the night anyway."

"That's right," Kevin agreed with a solemn nod. "I wanted to put them in my room but Dad said it would be mean to keep them just because they look nice." His voice dropped to a horrified whisper. "They could *die*."

I crouched down in front of him. "That's nice of you to want the fireflies to live a long, happy life even though that means you can't enjoy them in the house. How come you were inside when everyone else was out here?"

"I was looking for Bud," Kev told me. "He disappeared."

I glanced up at Sam, who said, "Bud was out here with us earlier but he seems to have gone missing."

Now that they mentioned it, I realized that I hadn't seen

the little spotted dog since I'd arrived home. Usually he hung out with the other dogs.

"Gates both closed?" I asked.

"Yup," Sam replied. "I checked."

"He hasn't been digging any new holes, has he?"

"Not that I'm aware of. My guess is that he found some kind of treasure out here and dragged it inside to hide behind the couch."

For Bud, a *treasure* could mean anything from one of Davey's smelly gym socks to a medium-sized Halloween pumpkin. The chubby little mutt was a pack rat. His obsession with gathering portable objects and storing them in his self-styled den verged on hoarding.

Bud had been with us for a year now. All we knew about his past situation was that it had been bad. When we'd picked him up from the side of the road the previous summer, the little dog had been skinny, wormy, and covered with sores. That was long behind him now, but Bud still wolfed down his food like he was afraid it might disappear. And his obedience training continued to be a work in progress.

"I'll track down Bud if you put Kev to bed," I told Sam. My younger son's eyes were already drooping. I was pretty sure he'd be asleep in minutes. "Unless it turns out that whatever Bud brought in the house was once alive and is now dead. In that case, I reserve the right to switch jobs."

Sam grinned. I figured that meant we had a deal.

He picked up Kevin. I called the Poodles. Davey came swinging down from the tree house. We all watched as he opened the jar and released the fireflies back into the night.

"Pretty," Kevin said drowsily. He lifted a hand and waved good-bye.

Sam and Kevin went upstairs. Davey washed and dried the mason jar and put it away—all without being asked. That was kind of miraculous. Then he spent the rest of the evening in a more predictable teenage fashion—locked in his room, talking to his friends on the phone.

I found Bud behind the couch in the living room gnawing happily on a stick. "You could have done that outside," I told him as I pried the prize out of his mouth.

Bud wagged his stubby tail. The black patch over his eye gave him a piratical air. *It's more fun this way!*

Faith looked at the spotted dog and rolled her eyes. She'd probably told him much the same thing I had.

Wood chips were scattered everywhere. I swept them up into a dustpan, deposited them in the garbage can, and counted myself lucky. At least Bud hadn't brought in something really gross.

Half an hour later, Sam and I met up in the living room. We sat down on the couch and put our feet up on the coffee table. Bud was upstairs, asleep on Kevin's bed. Four of the Poodles draped themselves over the furniture around us. Faith was wedged in beside me on the couch.

That's about as cozy as it gets around here.

Sam turned on a TV show that was lacking in logical plot but featured plenty of honking horns and screeching tires. As far as I could tell, the program had been created for the sole purpose of serving as background noise. So I proceeded to tell him about the book club meeting.

Sam enjoyed a good book as much as the next person. But the idea of having to discuss what he'd read reminded him entirely too much of school. He'd declined to join the club, but was happy to hear about what was going on with the people who had. This time there were twice as many people to tell him about.

I thought Sam would be surprised to hear that.

He wasn't.

I sat up straight and stared at him. Faith lifted her head inquiringly. She'd thought we were settled in for the night. I massaged her withers with my fingertips and she lay back down.

"*You knew?*" I said to Sam.

He just shrugged. "Peg and I talk."

Aunt Peg and I talked too. But she hadn't mentioned anything to me about doubling the membership of my book club. Visions of a hostile takeover flitted through my brain. Then I got real. This was a neighborhood reading group we were talking about, not WarnerMedia.

"Peg called and asked if I thought you would mind if she added a couple more people to the group," Sam mentioned.

"And you said?"

"That she ought to be asking you that question, not me."

I muttered something uncomplimentary under my breath.

"I gather that means she didn't?" Sam's gaze slid back to the television screen. A woman in a tight red dress was slithering out of a low-slung car.

I was tempted to say, "Hey, I have a tight dress too," but then it occurred to me that I didn't. At least not *that* tight. And definitely not that red.

"No," I said grumpily. "She didn't."

Smart man, Sam turned his thoughts back to the topic at hand. "Were they at least nice people?"

"I guess. Mostly."

"Only mostly?" That earned a smile from Sam. "Then boot 'em out. It's your book club."

"It used to be my book club," I grumbled. "Now it's a democracy."

Sam's eyes skimmed back to the television. It looked like an arrest was imminent. For what, or why, I had no idea. "At least Peg isn't in charge."

"Try telling her that," I muttered.

I waited until after the perp had been stowed inside the police car and the officers had shared a round of high fives. The only one who didn't look happy about the outcome was the woman in the red dress. There was a cautionary tale for you.

Then I said, "There's something else."

Once again, Sam didn't look surprised. Considering the way my life goes, he would probably have been more shocked to hear that there wasn't something else.

He picked up the remote, clicked off the TV, and asked, "What?"

When I hesitated, he tried again. "Who?"

"Evan Major. Remember him?"

In June when the meeting had been at our house, Sam had greeted the book club members, then made himself scarce. At that point, Evan was the only participant he hadn't previously known.

"The guy who came with Alice? The one who looked like he wished he could fade into the wallpaper?"

"That's the one. Evan bought himself a puppy. He asked for my help with some basic training."

"That sounds like a good idea," said Sam. "Is there a problem?"

"Maybe." I chewed on my lip. "I'm not sure. He showed up late to tonight's meeting, and arrived with a big bruise on his face. He said he'd been in a car accident on the way."

"Nothing serious, I hope?"

"That's the thing. He and I left the meeting together, and when we walked outside, I saw his car. A white Prius. It didn't have a scratch on it."

"Hurray for Toyota workmanship?" said Sam.

I reached over and punched his arm. "You're not taking me seriously."

"On the contrary, I think you might be taking things too seriously. Evan just moved into a house around the corner from Alice, right?"

I nodded.

"He's new to the area, probably still trying to get himself situated. Maybe for once, rather than letting your suspicions run rampant, you could just give the guy a pass."

"Rampant?" I lifted a brow. "Says that man who just

made me sit through a cop show where all anybody did was drive fast and shoot at everything that moved."

"It wasn't about the plot," Sam informed me loftily.

"Was it about the red dress?"

"You noticed that, huh?"

"Yes, I did." I got up off the couch and headed for the stairs. "But if you're nice, I might let you make it up to me."

Sam stood up to follow. "With incentive like that, I can be the nicest man you know."

He had that right.

Evan called the next day to confirm that I hadn't changed my mind about helping him with his Bulldog puppy. And also to give me directions to his house. GPS aside, the directions weren't necessary. I'd spent the entirety of my first short marriage—and half a dozen years after that—living in the same housing development.

Flower Estates was a subdivision built more than half a century earlier to provide affordable housing for homecoming World War II veterans and their families. It featured rows of snug, clapboard cottages that were designed for practicality and constructed side by side on tiny plots of land. The city of Stamford had grown up around it, but the neighborhood remained an enclave of small, reasonably priced homes that appealed to buyers who ranged from first-time homeowners to downsizing retirees.

I'd been living in Flower Estates when I married Sam. Due to the expansion of our families—both human and canine—we'd needed more room, and our current house had been the answer. But I was always hit with a pleasant rush of nostalgia when I visited the neighborhood where I'd spent many happy years raising Davey as a single mother, and finding my own footing as an independent adult.

Evan lived on Bluebell Lane in a house predictably similar

to the one I'd owned. Rather than block his short driveway, I parked the Volvo on the road. Evan had a tidy front yard and no curtains on his front windows. I didn't have to go inside to know that I would find a compact entryway and three rooms—living room, dining room, and kitchen—on the first floor. Upstairs would consist of two bedrooms separated by a small bathroom.

My house had been yellow with green shutters. Evan's was dove gray with white trim. Even so, the narrow walkway that led to the front door felt familiar beneath my feet.

I had to knock just once before the door drew open. I was wearing a T-shirt and shorts. Evan had on a long-sleeved button-down shirt, khakis, and loafers. Suddenly I felt seriously underdressed.

Evan didn't seem to notice. He greeted me with a smile. "Thanks for coming, Melanie. It's nice to see you again."

"And you as well," I replied.

The purple-and-yellow bruise still shaded his jaw, but Evan's face wasn't nearly as swollen as it had been two days earlier. He'd clearly been uncomfortable with the attention he'd drawn at the book club meeting. Now, if he didn't bring up the injury, I wasn't about to either.

Instead, I stepped inside the house. I glanced around the sparsely furnished rooms. *No wonder I hadn't seen curtains*, I thought. Evan barely had chairs.

The battered couch in the living room looked like it belonged in a college dorm. The wooden table sitting in front of it was scarred and pitted. In the dining room, I saw only a tall stack of packing crates, a folding card table, and a pair of plastic benches.

Evan had mentioned that he was recently divorced. It looked to me as though he'd needed a better lawyer. His ex-wife must have gotten custody of all the good stuff.

"Sorry about the condition of the place." Evan followed

the direction of my gaze. "As you can see I'm still working on getting settled in. In our other house, my wife took care of, well . . . everything."

I could tell.

"Divorce is hard," I said. "I've been through it myself. I know it takes a while to recover. And to start thinking of yourself as a single person again, rather than part of a couple." I paused, then added, "Or a family?"

"No, we didn't have any children. I guess that turned out to be a good thing in the end." He sighed. "I'd always thought we'd get a puppy when the babies came. Kids and dogs seem like a natural combination. But then that never happened either."

"I'm sorry," I said.

Evan shrugged. "Nobody's life is perfect. Things go wrong all the time. All you can do is deal the best you can and move on."

"Maybe that's one good thing about your new situation," I said. "Now you get to make your own decisions about how you want to live."

Evan managed a small smile. "I guess you're right. And I'm working on getting things back together. Both here and in other aspects of my life. But enough about me." He turned and headed toward the rear of the house. "Let's go out back and I'll introduce you to the newest member of my family. Bully is outside waiting for us."

Chapter 4

Bully was a pudgy, totally adorable, fawn-and-white Bulldog puppy. He had a broad head with a pushed-in muzzle and dark eyes. His body was covered with thick wrinkles of excess skin.

Evan had the puppy contained in an exercise pen in the middle of his backyard. As soon as we stepped outside, Bully jumped up and galloped toward the gate. His shuffling way of moving made him appear to roll from side to side.

"Oh my," I said. "I think I'm in love."

Evan unlatched the wire door and Bully came tumbling out.

I sat down in the grass and the puppy quickly scrambled up into my lap. He tipped his head upward, pink tongue reaching for my chin. I'd just started to scratch beneath his ears when Evan reached down and snatched Bully away.

"You don't have to let him do that. I'd hate for him to dirty your clothes. And besides, I read a book. It said you're supposed to show puppies who's the boss right from the start."

Arms stiffened, hands hooked beneath Bully's elbows, Evan held the Bulldog out away from his body. Bully's hind legs dangled in the air. The puppy began to wiggle unhappily. I didn't blame him. That had to be uncomfortable.

It looked as though I'd gotten there just in time.

"Your book is bunk," I said. "And everything I'm wearing is wash and wear. Plus, you're holding him all wrong. Come down here and sit next to me. And put Bully on the ground."

Evan hesitated. The puppy continued to wriggle back and forth. If I had to stand up and rescue him I would. But it would be better if Evan made the move himself.

"Is Bully your first puppy?" I asked.

"Yes," he admitted in a small voice.

"Then you were smart to ask for help." I patted the grass beside me. "Come on, let's talk. Bully can run around the yard."

Evan lowered himself gingerly to the ground. Spontaneity didn't seem to be his strong suit. Lounging in the grass probably wasn't something he did often. Or ever.

Once he was sitting cross-legged, Evan still continued to keep a firm grip on the puppy. I gave him a pointed look.

"The book said that he should be properly contained at all times," he told me. "Spoiling is bad for a puppy. And what if he runs away?"

"I'm going to burn your book," I muttered.

"Pardon me?"

"Nothing," I said as Evan grudgingly released Bully. The chubby Bulldog began to roll around on the lawn. "Showing affection to a puppy isn't spoiling him. Nor is paying attention to him. That's what you're supposed to do."

Evan started to object. I just kept talking.

"Bully's not going to run away. And if he did, we could easily catch him. Judging by how happy Bully was to see us, we're the most interesting thing that's happened to him all day. How long has he been out here by himself?"

Evan sidestepped my question. "The book said fresh air would be good for him."

I looked at the space enclosed by the wire pen and frowned. Now that the Bulldog had been removed, it was entirely empty. At least the ex pen was sitting in the shade. I supposed that was something.

"Did your book say anything about a puppy needing access to fresh water?" I asked.

"Umm . . ."

"Or maybe a couple of toys to keep him entertained?"

"Puppies should be raised firmly and with proper discipline." Evan recited the words as if he was holding the wretched tome in his hands. "At all times your dog should know that you are his master."

"Bollocks," I said.

Evan blinked. "Excuse me?"

We could discuss the problems with dominance theory later. Right now I had more immediate issues to attend to. "Snub nosed dogs don't handle the heat as well as other breeds. Did your book mention that?"

"I don't think so." He frowned. "But keeping him outside is just common sense. That way, he can't make a mess in the house."

"Bully's just a baby. He's not going to live outside," I said firmly. "Not now, and not when he grows up. You bought him for companionship, right?"

"Yes."

"So the only way that's going to work is if he's where you are. That's why we're going to housebreak him."

"I've read about housebreaking," Evan said uncertainly. "It sounds difficult. And what if he chews on my furniture?"

It wasn't as if he had much furniture to worry about, I thought. It would probably be rude to point that out.

"Then we'll teach him not to," I replied. "At his age, Bully still has everything to learn about being a good canine citizen. And step by step, we're going to educate him about what he needs to know."

"This all sounds a lot harder than I thought it was going to be."

"It's not particularly hard, but it is time consuming." I picked up the pudgy puppy and plopped him in Evan's lap. "But Bully's worth it, right? The two of you are going to be together for years."

"I guess." He still didn't sound convinced.

But Evan's hands came up to steady the Bulldog on top of his legs. And when his fingers began to stroke the chubby body, both man and puppy began to relax. The two of them looked good together. I was sure that with time and guidance Evan would eventually get things figured out.

"Where did Bully come from?" I asked. "Does his breeder live nearby? Did he or she give you any tips about Bulldog care before you brought him home?"

"No, there was nothing like that." Evan shook his head. "I found Bully through an ad on Craigslist. The breeder told me I was lucky to call before the litter was all gone."

So apparently his suitability to own a puppy hadn't been determined by a reputable breeder prior to the purchase. That meant we were starting from scratch.

"Tell me about your job," I said.

"My job?" Evan appeared startled by the question.

"Yes. How much time do you spend away from home each day? How long will Bully have to manage on his own when you're not here?"

"Oh, that." To my surprise, he almost sounded relieved. "It's not a problem. As you know, I just moved here. So at the moment, I'm between jobs. Bully and I can spend all day together if we want."

As long as the puppy wasn't locked up in the backyard, I thought. "That's good news. It will make his life—and yours—much easier."

Bully's head was drooping. His eyes were half closed. He'd also begun to pant. It was time to move inside.

I stood up and brushed off my shorts. "Bully looks ready

for a nap. Let's take him in and get him a drink of water first. Then while he's sleeping, we can go over some of the basics of puppy care."

Carrying the drowsy Bulldog in his arms, Evan led the way. He had several fans running, so it was cooler inside the house than it had been in the yard. That would help.

Tucked into a corner of the kitchen was a small, round dog bed that looked as though it had barely been used. A weighted dog bowl sat on a rubber mat nearby. The bowl was partly filled with tepid water. I picked it up and emptied it into the sink. After running the water until it was good and cold, I refilled the bowl and put it back down.

When Evan put Bully down on the tile floor, the puppy took a long drink. Then he climbed into his bed and curled up into a ball. Almost immediately he'd fallen asleep.

"Bully sleeps a lot," Evan said with a frown.

"He's a baby. Sleeping is normal. Other than that, does he act like a happy, healthy, puppy?"

"I guess so."

Definitely not the hearty endorsement I'd been hoping for.

"Did you have him checked out by a vet when you first brought him home?"

"No. Why would I do that?"

I answered his question with one of my own. "Did you get a schedule of the shots he's had from the breeder? Do you know when he was last wormed?"

Evan frowned again. He seemed to be doing that a lot. "I'm beginning to realize that dog ownership is much more complicated than I originally thought. Maybe you'd better have a seat. Do you want something to drink?"

A small rectangular table was pushed up against a wall. There was a chair at either end. I pulled one out and sat down.

Evan had opened his refrigerator and was looking inside as if he wasn't sure what it might contain. From where I was sitting, the shelves appeared to be mostly empty. I hoped that he was paying more attention to Bully's food supply than he was to his own.

"There's beer and diet Coke." Evan glanced back over his shoulder apologetically as he pulled out a can of soda for himself. "Not much of a choice, I'm afraid."

"How about a glass of water?"

"That's easy enough. Is tap water okay?"

"Sure."

Evan stared around the kitchen as if he didn't know where to find a glass. I waited a few beats, then got up and had a look myself. It turned out there were three glasses in the cabinet nearest the sink. I hoped Evan was paying attention. Some day he might also want to drink something that didn't come in a can.

"Baby gates," I said when we were seated across from each other at the table.

"What?"

Once again, I'd managed to surprise him. Apparently when it came to puppy care, that wasn't a difficult thing to do. Never having had children or dogs, the man was a neophyte when it came to babies and their myriad needs.

"Baby gates," I said again. "You can put them across your doorways to confine Bully to the kitchen while you're working on getting him housebroken. The process will be much easier if he isn't allowed to roam around the whole house." I paused, then added, "And it's even better if you never take your eyes off him."

"Never?" Evan gulped.

"Not for the rest of your life. Just until he knows stuff. Or you could use a crate to help with his training."

"No," he said quickly. "I wouldn't want to do that."

I sighed. Then I fortified myself with a sip of water. "Don't tell me. Your book doesn't like crates."

"It says they're cruel."

"Your book is wrong." Silently I added the word *again*.

"A crate is like a dog's house. His own personal den. A place where he can feel safe."

"Are you sure? Because the book—"

"Oh, for Pete's sake, Evan, your book is a crock. I don't know where it came from but just about everything you've told me about it so far is incorrect. Or backward. Or out-dated thinking."

"Everything?" He looked so forlorn that I began to regret my hasty outburst.

"Well, fresh air is a good thing," I conceded. "And you were smart to figure out a way to contain Bully when he's by himself in your yard. Although a fence would be a better long-term solution."

"I'm working on that part," he told me.

"That's great. And we'll work on the rest together. Don't worry about how much you don't know yet. We've all been there."

"Oh?" Evan looked up.

"Eight years ago, I'd never had a dog of my own. Or any other kind of pet. So when I got Faith, I had to learn everything there was to know about how to take care of her—just like you do."

"Who taught you?" he asked.

"My Aunt Peg. She's the one who bred Faith and gave her to me."

"I understand Peg is an accomplished dog show judge," he said with admiration. "That's quite impressive. Tell me about the rest of your family."

I cast a quick glance in Bully's direction. The puppy was still asleep in his bed. He had begun to snore softly.

"You probably don't want me to get started," I said. "It could take all day."

"Are there that many of you?"

"No. But we're a contentious bunch. And more often than not, something unexpected or wildly inappropriate seems to be happening."

Evan smiled. "That sounds like fun."

"I wish," I said with a laugh. "How about you? Where does the rest of your family live?"

Abruptly his gaze dropped. "I don't have any family."

"None?" Now he'd surprised me. I guessed that meant the ex-wife no longer counted. I'm still friends with my ex-husband but I've been told that's a rarity.

"No," he replied. "It's just me."

"I'm sorry."

"Don't be. I do all right. And now I have Bully. He's all the company I need."

It was clearly time to get back to business.

"Let's talk about the specifics of housebreaking," I said. "And I'd like to have a look at what you're feeding Bully. I'm also going to give you the name and phone number of my vet. It would be a really good idea for you to take him in for a new puppy checkup. After that, if you have any additional questions or concerns, we can take some time to address them."

"Alice was right," Evan replied. "You're just what Bully and I need to see us through this. We're both grateful for your assistance."

I spent the next twenty minutes talking. Evan mostly listened and took copious notes. He asked intelligent questions and listened carefully to my answers. He seemed open to taking direction, and eager to learn everything he could about dog ownership. All of which boded very well for Bully's future health and happiness.

As we were wrapping up our conversation, Bully awoke from his nap. He rolled out of his bed onto the floor, then stood up and stretched. We'd covered this in our discussion and Evan knew just what to do. He quickly picked the puppy up and took him outside for a potty break. Both of us then praised the puppy effusively.

Afterward, Evan and Bully walked me out to my car.

"This has been a great help," he said. "I can't thank you enough. Will you come again?"

"I'd be happy to," I replied. "Maybe next week? And feel free to call if you have any questions in the mean-time."

I paused next to the Volvo, struck by a sudden thought. Evan was new to the area. He didn't appear to have met many people yet. His schedule of activities probably wasn't full. Maybe he'd enjoy being introduced to my avocation.

"There's a dog show this weekend in Westchester County," I told him. "My son Davey is going to be show-ing a Standard Poodle puppy that belongs to Aunt Peg. She'll be there and so will the rest of my family. Other members of the book club will probably attend too. Maybe you'd like to join us if you don't have other plans?"

"No, I'm free," Evan said with interest. "Will there be any Bulldogs there?"

"I'm sure there will. Offhand I don't know how many, or what time they'll be judged. But I can check the sched-ule and get back to you."

"That would be great. It sounds like fun."

"Excellent." I opened the car door and got in. "I'll call you tonight with directions and judging times and we'll see you there."

As I drove away, Evan remained on the sidewalk with Bully in his arms. He watched until I'd reached the end of the block and turned the corner. He looked utterly solitary standing there, and more than a little sad.

Evan didn't have any family. He seemed to have few friends. Like Alice, I couldn't help but feel sorry for him. I hoped he'd have a good time at the dog show.

Abruptly the thought made me laugh. It was a dog show. Of course he'd have a good time.

Chapter 5

Saturday's dog show was sponsored by the Mount Kisco Kennel Club and located in Westchester County, not far from the New York–Connecticut state line. The drive from North Stamford took us well under an hour. Considering that most dog show exhibitors routinely traveled great distances to seek out the best judges, this event felt like it was right around the corner.

We got a leisurely start that morning. Standard Poodles weren't scheduled to be judged until early afternoon. Not only that, but for the first time in a long time, we weren't bringing a Poodle of our own to the show. Instead, Davey and Aunt Peg's nine-month-old puppy, Coral, would be making their show ring debut as a team.

From a care and preparation point of view, the ramifications of that were huge. Sam and Davey hadn't needed to spend the previous two days clipping, bathing, and scissoring. The puppy trim wasn't complicated, but like all the clips Poodles were permitted to wear in the show ring, it was labor intensive.

The process would start with Coral having her face and throat, her feet, and the base of her tail shaved to the skin. Then the dense black hair on her body would be bathed and meticulously blown dry. Finally her coat would be scissored to refine its highly stylized shape—long and full on the back of her neck, then tapering down to a flattened plane over her topline. Coral had rounded cylinders of hair on her legs, accented by a swooping outline behind that was meant to highlight her hocks and movement.

Grooming a Poodle for the show ring required both skill and precision. It was an art form that took most people years to perfect. Sam had the technique down cold. So, of course, did Aunt Peg. And since Coral lived with her, this week she would be in charge of the puppy's preshow grooming.

Sam and Aunt Peg must have coordinated their schedules because we arrived at the showground just in time to help her unload her minivan beside the handlers' tent. That tent was the place where exhibitors spent most of their time on show days. There, they readied their entries for the ring, hung out and chatted with friends, and celebrated or commiserated over the day's results.

On a typical day, an exhibitor with a single dog to show would be in and out of the ring in mere minutes. The time spent being judged was miniscule in comparison to everything else that was involved in making the entry happen. At many shows—especially the unsuccessful ones—the best part of the entire exercise was the interactions that took place beneath the grooming tent.

"Just what I needed." Aunt Peg appreciated our timely arrival. "Two strong, strapping men to help out."

Davey grinned, flattered to be included in that designation. "What do you want me to do first?"

Though he'd tried to hide it, I knew my son was excited to have an opportunity to handle a Poodle he didn't own. He and Coral had had several practice sessions at home before Aunt Peg had finally pronounced the pair ready to take their show on the road. He was looking forward to seeing what the two of them could accomplish together.

"You"—Aunt Peg pointed at Davey—"take Coral's grooming table. Sam?"

"Yes, ma'am?"

"Can you manage her crate?"

"Of course." With the practiced ease of someone who'd performed the maneuver many times previously, Sam swung the big wooden crate out of the back of the minivan.

"You." This time Aunt Peg's imperious finger pointed at me. "Scope out the tent and find us a convivial place to set up our gear."

"Convivial? Aren't you setting the bar a little high?"

Grooming tents were usually crowded. The professional handlers, with their large strings of dogs and the most work to do, arrived at first light. They staked out the best spots for their rows of tables and stacked crates. A single-dog owner who arrived hours later often found herself squeezing in her setup anywhere she could find a little bit of space.

"Not at all," Aunt Peg replied tartly. "I have every faith in your abilities. Go. Find me some nice neighbors with whom to spend my day."

Kevin had grown tired of listening to us talk and entered the grooming tent on his own. The place was packed. I wouldn't have been able to see him except for the fact that he'd apparently found Terry and Crawford's setup. I deduced that from the fact that Terry was holding Kevin up in the air so that my son could wave to me across the bustling expanse.

"Here we are, Mommy," he cried. "Over here!"

I headed in their direction, weaving an indirect path as I slithered between crates and chairs, and skirted around blow dryers and exercise pens.

"You might have hurried," Terry grumbled as I approached. He set Kev down on the ground at his feet. "How much does that kid weigh anyway? I thought I was going to get a hernia."

"His weight is just right," I replied as Terry and I air

kissed. Today he was dressed like a normal person. If Crawford won with two entries in the same breed, Terry might be called upon to take a dog in the ring. "Nobody asked you to pick him up and wave him around like a balloon."

"I did!" Kevin said gleefully. "I asked."

"Well then, I stand corrected." I laughed. "Terry, is there enough room for us to fit our stuff in next to you?"

" 'Morning, Melanie." Crawford was scissoring a silver Toy Poodle he had out on a table at the other end of the setup. He sketched me a quick wave. "You know perfectly well we saved you some space. Peg would never forgive us if we didn't."

I slipped between two tightly packed tables and reached up to give Crawford a hug. He had to stop scissoring while I briefly wrapped my arms around him—heaven forbid I mess up his line. Crawford acted as though the show of affection was an imposition, perhaps even an affront to his dignity, but I knew him better than to believe that.

"You know Aunt Peg would forgive you just about anything," I whispered when we were close. "And so would I."

Crawford and I had initially met as adversaries, and our current, cordial relationship had taken a while to evolve. Tall, perpetually tan, and sleek as a Vizsla, Crawford had been one of the top professional handlers on the East Coast for decades. Now in his sixties, Crawford hadn't lost a step. The talent and showmanship with which he presented his dogs still continued to dazzle judges and spectators alike.

Terry and Crawford had been a couple for almost as long as I'd had Faith. Flamboyant, carefree Terry and quiet, dignified Crawford couldn't have appeared more different from the outside. Yet their partnership worked on every level. Professionally, they made a formidable team. Personally, I was incredibly happy to count them as friends.

"Here we are," Aunt Peg said merrily. "I see the early birds have saved us a nice, cozy spot." She winked in Crawford's direction. "I do so enjoy having friends in high places."

Davey had the folded grooming table tucked under his arm. Sam was lugging the heavy crate. Aunt Peg was holding the end of Coral's leash while the puppy trotted beside her. Her other hand was empty. Someone, probably me, was going to have to go back to the minivan and retrieve the tack box and cooler.

"A friend of yours stopped by earlier," Crawford told Peg. He slipped on a numbered armband and picked up a Bichon Frise that looked ready to go the ring. "A guy named Evan Major. Terry knew him from your book club."

"*My* book club," I said under my breath.

Terry heard me and grinned. "Evan said you'd told him about the show. He got here early so he wouldn't miss anything. I told him you were on your way but he said he was just as happy to wander around on his own. I steered him in the direction of the Bulldog ring, even though they won't be judged for an hour. Last time I saw him, he was under the other tent drooling over a pair of Frenchies."

"Bulldogs, only cuter," Sam said with a laugh as Crawford left with his Bichon. "That makes sense."

"I'll track Evan down as soon as we're set up here," I said.

Davey was way ahead of me. He already had the rubber-matted grooming table unfolded and set up. Then he'd run back to the van to grab Aunt Peg's tack box and the rest of our gear. Now he took Coral's leash from Aunt Peg and hopped the puppy up onto the table.

"You should probably move your minivan from the loading zone," he told her. "Sam and I will start getting Coral ready."

Aunt Peg's eyes widened. In the sudden silence you could have heard a greyhound comb drop.

"We had a deal," Davey reminded her before she could protest.

"Yes, but—"

"You said you trusted me to show your puppy. And I can't do that properly if you intend to hover over me and critique everything I do."

"We're not in the ring now," Aunt Peg pointed out. "And you'll need my help with Coral's topknot."

And anything else Aunt Peg could get her hands on, I thought.

Davey had finished Augie's championship in the spring, doing most of the work by himself. The mature, male Standard Poodle had had twice the coat Coral did. Having dealt with Augie's towering topknot, Davey would find setting Coral's much smaller one to be a breeze.

"If I need help, I'll ask Sam," Davey said reasonably. "Right?"

Sam nodded.

Aunt Peg harrumphed under her breath. "And what do you expect *me* to do in the meantime?"

Terry leaned across into our small setup. Of course he'd been listening to our conversation. "I believe Davey would like you to go park the car."

He was playing with fire with that comment. Terry must have realized it because he quickly scooped a second Bichon off a nearby table and followed Crawford to the rings.

Aunt Peg glared at his departing back.

"Later," I said brightly, "you can pick up Davey's armband."

That was a job any idiot could do. As a result, it usually fell to Kevin and me.

"This is mutiny," Aunt Peg snapped. Her gaze swung my way. "Don't think I can't see what you're doing."

What I was doing was trying to secure Davey a little

breathing room. Pressure from Aunt Peg had ruined my son's initial experience as an exhibitor. As a result, Davey had taken several years off from the show ring. Now Sam and I were both determined that showing Poodles—no matter whom they belonged to—had to be something for him to enjoy, not dread.

I was pretty sure that wasn't what Aunt Peg was talking about, however. Her next words confirmed my suspicions.

"You're just jealous," she told me.

"Jealous?" My back stiffened. "Of what?"

Sam abruptly ducked his head and looked away. He busied himself with unpacking the grooming supplies and laying them along the edge of Coral's table. I got the distinct impression that he didn't want to meet my eye.

"It was perfectly obvious the other night," Aunt Peg said. "The Bite Club members would rather follow my leadership than yours."

Oh. I swallowed heavily. *That* was unfair.

"No," I replied evenly. "The problem is that Bite Club doesn't need a leader. Everyone has a say in which books we're reading and where we're going to meet next. Everybody is supposed to participate equally."

"That wasn't the impression I got on Tuesday. You seemed quite put out that I'd added a few new members to our group."

"Six is not a few," I growled. "You doubled the size of the book club."

"Which led to quite a lively discussion, if I do say so myself."

"Peg?" Sam straightened suddenly and turned around.

"Yes?"

"I think it's time for you to go park your minivan."

Aunt Peg opened her mouth. Then closed it. She spun on her heel and walked away.

"That went well," Davey said. He had Coral lying quietly on her side. Fingers working quickly, he was line brushing through the long hair.

"Aunt Peg bribed the book club members with Sarah Bernhardts," I said to nobody in particular. "No wonder they were happy to follow her lead."

It turned out Kevin was listening. He stuck his head out from under the table where he was playing with a trio of toy cars. "We have Sarah Bernhardts?"

I reached down and ruffled his hair. "Not today, sweetie. Sorry."

"There was an element of truth in what she said," Sam mentioned mildly. "The book club was supposed to be fun and it doesn't sound as though it's turning out that way. Everything between you and Peg doesn't have to be a competition, you know."

I sighed. Of course he was right.

"I'll stop, if she will," I said.

"Good luck with that." Davey smirked. He had Aunt Peg problems of his own.

"Look on the bright side," I told him. "As long as she's on my case, Aunt Peg will leave you alone."

Sam laughed at that. "If that's the bright side, we're all in trouble."

There was more than an hour until the start of the Standard Poodle judging. In the meantime, I went looking for Evan. I found him over by the food concession munching on a hamburger. I probably should have warned him about dog show food. His stomach might regret that meal later.

"Hi, Melanie!" he called out as I approached. "I'm so glad you asked me to come today. I never even knew that events like this existed. I'm having a terrific time looking at all these different dogs." His voice lowered. "Not to mention their equally interesting owners. This is the most fun I've had in a long time. I had no idea there were so many canine varieties."

"The diversity you'll see at most shows is pretty amazing," I agreed. "The American Kennel Club recognizes nearly two hundred breeds that come from countries all over the world."

"Wow," said Evan. "I never would have guessed. I thought about bringing Bully with me today—it *is* a dog show after all—but now that I see all these beautifully groomed specimens, I'm glad I thought better of it."

"I'm glad you did too," I replied. "Bully's too young to have had all his shots. Which means he's also too young to be exposed to this many strange dogs."

"Speaking of strange," he said, "I ran into Vic Landry earlier. You know, from the book club?"

That was an interesting segue.

"Yes, I know who she is. Was Rush with her?"

"No, but she was walking a big hairy dog on a leash. It looked quite fierce."

"That was a Belgian Tervuren," I told him. Aunt Peg had mentioned the Landrys' breed at the meeting on Tuesday.

"That's what Vic said. So I replied 'gesundheit.' She was not amused." Evan shrugged. "Maybe she didn't get it. Or maybe she thought I was insulting her Belgian dog by speaking German to it?"

"It sounds like you're overthinking things," I said with a laugh. "Vic was probably just concentrating on her dog. Maybe they were about to go in the ring. The judging can be pretty intense. Some people get pretty nervous."

"They do?"

"Sure. It's a competition, after all. Most exhibitors are trying to win points so their dogs will become champions."

Evan considered that. "How many points?"

"Fifteen."

"That doesn't sound too hard."

Once upon a time I might have said the same thing. Now I knew better.

"Don't knock it until you've tried it," I said.

"I wouldn't dream of it," Evan replied. "Didn't you tell me your son was showing a dog today?"

"Yes, a Standard Poodle puppy. We'll be in ring six at twelve thirty."

"Ring four is where I'm supposed to find the Bulldogs." He glanced down at his watch. "Their judging should be starting in just a few minutes."

I grasped his shoulders, turned him around, and pointed him in the right direction. "Bulldogs are always popular with spectators. You'd better go stake out a good spot so you don't miss a thing. When they're finished, come and find us at ring six. That's where the Standard Poodles are being judged. I'll be there with Aunt Peg and the rest of my family. When their judging is over, you and I can go and do some sightseeing."

"That sounds great," said Evan. "I'll see you then."

Chapter 6

Back at the grooming tent, Coral was just about ready. I was happy to see that Davey was looking pretty pleased with himself. That probably meant that Aunt Peg's interference had been held to a minimum.

The setup next door was empty, which wasn't surprising. Busy professional handlers spent dog show days on the run. According to Sam, Terry and Crawford had returned with their Bichons, then disappeared again with their Mini Poodle entry.

Kevin had the cooler open and he'd stuck his head inside. I was pretty sure he was hoping to find some Sarah Bernhardts in there.

I didn't see Aunt Peg anywhere. That was a relief, but her absence also made me leery. Aunt Peg had a way of popping up when I least expected it. I hoped we wouldn't have to continue our earlier conversation when she did.

"You won't believe it," Davey told me. "Aunt Peg went to get my armband."

He was right—I didn't believe it. "She did?"

"Would I lie to you?"

I hoped not. But he was a teenage boy, so I felt obliged to keep an open mind.

"I could have done that," I said.

"But you didn't." Davey grinned. "Luckily Aunt Peg volunteered."

"I think she feels bad for yelling at you earlier," Sam told me.

"That would be a first. Aunt Peg yells at me all the time. Usually it makes her happy."

"Maybe she's mellowing in her old age."

Davey looked at Sam and me. "Or maybe she just wanted to make herself *useful*."

That made us all smile. Useful people were Aunt Peg's favorite kind.

The conversation must have conjured up her presence, because suddenly there she was. "What's everybody doing standing around talking?" Aunt Peg bellowed from the edge of the tent. "Chop chop! The Standard judging is about to start."

I gestured toward the setup next door. Crawford's Standard Poodle entry, a class dog and a bitch special, were waiting patiently on their tables. "Crawford and Terry haven't taken their dogs up yet."

"That's because they're late," Aunt Peg said briskly. "And so are we."

After spending more than an hour on top of her table, Coral was eager to get down and stretch her legs. Sam set her on the ground and she bounced in place. Then she shook the length of her body from her nose to the tip of her tail. When the puppy was still again, Davey smoothed everything back into place with a comb.

Now we were ready to go.

As we left the tent and started across the grassy expanse that led to the rings, Crawford and Terry came running by. "The judge stopped for pictures, so we did too," Terry said as they hurried past. "But now Puppy Dogs are already in the ring and we have an entry in Open. Don't let them start without us."

There wasn't much possibility of that, especially since Crawford had already picked up his armbands—so the ring steward knew he was on his way. And indeed as the Open class was being called, there was Crawford back at ringside with his white Standard Poodle dog at his side. The dog looked perfect and Crawford wasn't even out of breath. I wished I could manage my own mishaps with such seemingly effortless grace.

Breed competition began with the regular classes, which were divided by sex and open to dogs who had yet to complete their championships. Males would be judged first, followed by bitches. Seven different classes were offered, but at most shows only two or three drew an entry.

Once the individual classes had been judged, the class winners would return to the ring to compete for the Winners Dog and Winners Bitch awards. Those two entrants were the only ones who would earn points toward their championships. The number of points—between one and five—was based on the amount of same-sex competition beaten.

As I'd told Evan, a dog needed to compile a total of fifteen points to become a champion. But along the way, it also needed to achieve at least two "major" wins—meaning that it had to earn at least three points at a single show. The intent was to insure that an inferior dog couldn't complete its championship by piling up single points against equally inferior competition.

Coral was one of four entrants in the Puppy Bitch class. We stood near the gate and watched as Crawford presented his Open dog to the judge. There were only two dogs in the class, and Crawford's white Poodle won handily. A Puppy Class winner returned to the ring to compete for Winners, but it was all over in a minute as the judge quickly summoned Crawford's dog to the winning marker.

"Look sharp." Aunt Peg gave Davey a pointed poke between the shoulder blades. "You're up next. I expect you to make me proud."

"Oww." Davey flinched. "Was that really necessary?"

"I just wanted to make sure you were paying attention." Aunt Peg was unrepentant. "Now in you go."

Her hands propelled Davey and Coral toward the gate. The steward had called for the three puppy bitches in the class to line up in catalog order. Davey and Coral were at the end of the line.

"Good," Aunt Peg said under her breath. "That will give him plenty of time to get her settled."

Sam had been standing beside me. Now he moved around next to Aunt Peg. "You watched him show Augie for two years," he told her. "You know he's good at this. Why not just relax and let him do his job?"

"Aunt Peg, relax?" I snorted. "I don't think so."

She turned to glare at me, but I'd leaned down to pick up Kev so he could see the ring better. Her expression of outrage passed harmlessly over my head.

"Davey's good at this," Kev repeated, nodding solemnly. "He's going to show my dog for me too."

Kevin's dog had mismatching ears and an imperfect bite. Bud was also the product of uncertain—but definitely mixed—lineage. So that was not going to be happening. But it also wasn't a conversation we needed to have right now.

"If you say so," I agreed easily.

Aunt Peg started to shoot me another glare. This time I simply directed her attention back to the ring.

The judge had made her initial pass down the line, checking out each of the three puppies in turn. With Davey's right hand positioned beneath Coral's chin, and his left holding up her tail, the puppy had maintained her balanced stack beautifully during the first look. Satisfied with what she'd seen, the judge asked the trio of handlers to gait their puppies around the ring.

Aunt Peg sighed happily as she watched Coral stride out freely at the end of a loose lead. I had to agree. The Poodle looked lovely. And Davey was doing a great job.

Terry edged closer. He was holding Crawford's Winners Dog, with his hand cupped around the Standard Poodle's muzzle. Crawford was attending to his specials bitch. Both Poodles would compete in the Best of Variety class when the bitch judging was finished.

Gazing at Coral, Terry said, "She's going to be special someday."

"She's special *now*," Aunt Peg replied.

"But still a baby," Sam pointed out. "It's not her time yet and you know it."

If I had said the same thing, Aunt Peg would have argued. But since the statement came from Sam, Aunt Peg remained silent. That was probably as close as she could come to conceding his point.

The first two puppies had their individual examinations from the judge and went to the back of the line. Now it was Coral's turn. Davey had the puppy stacked and ready when the judge looked her way. For a moment, it looked as though the hands-on exam would proceed according to plan. But as the judge approached and extended her hand to greet the puppy, Coral broke protocol.

As her nose nudged forward to sniff the judge's fingers, the puppy's tail began to whip back and forth. Then her body followed suit. Within seconds she was wriggling gleefully beneath Davey's hands. I saw the moment he realized he'd lost control of the puppy and I felt equally chagrined on his behalf.

Davey looked up at the judge. "Sorry," he said with a wince.

"Not at all. I would never fault a Poodle puppy for being too friendly." She stepped back, giving Davey a few seconds to reset Coral for examination. "Ready now?"

"Yes, I think so."

On the second attempt, Coral's tail continued to sweep lavishly from side to side. And she tried to lick the judge when the woman went to look at her bite. But the puppy remained still when the judge ran a hand over the rest of her body. And when the examination was finished, Coral once again moved around the perimeter of the ring like a dream.

The judge took another quick look at the three puppies, then motioned Coral to the head of the line. She sent the trio of Poodles around one last time. Davey and Coral remained in front and won the class.

Davey exited the ring with the blue ribbon clutched in his hand and a big smile on his face.

Aunt Peg met him just outside the gate. "Not bad. But obviously there are a few things we'll need to work on."

My son's happy smile faltered. I was about to say something I would surely regret when Sam inserted himself between them.

"Nice recovery." He clapped Davey on the shoulder. "For your first time with a new puppy, I thought you both did great."

"Thanks," Davey said gratefully. He looped a protectively arm around Coral's shoulders. "Watch out for her hair. Coral and I still have to go back in the ring."

The puppy didn't have a lot of hair to mess up. But we all got his point.

There were just two bitches in the Open class and the judge quickly sorted them out. When Davey and Coral returned to the ring to compete for Winners Bitch, the judge gave the pair due consideration. Then she awarded the points to her Open bitch.

Davey remained in the ring so Coral could be judged against the second Open bitch for Reserve Winners. This time the puppy emerged victorious. The award was mostly

honorary since it didn't confer any points. But Coral bene-
fited from the extra time in the ring and Davey was happy
to receive another ribbon.

"I suppose that was all right," Aunt Peg said when the
pair exited the ring for the second time.

"It was better than all right." I swooped in and gave
Davey a hug. "Well done."

He ducked his head sheepishly. "You don't have to over-
react or anything, Mom. It's not like we won."

"No, but you came close."

"It was a good beginning," Aunt Peg allowed. "You'll
do better next time."

"I'm sure you will too." I stared at her long enough to
be sure that Aunt Peg couldn't mistake my meaning. After
several seconds, her gaze slid away from mine and I felt a
brief spark of satisfaction. That was a first.

In the ring, the Standard Poodle Best of Variety class
was underway. Crawford had the only special. Terry was
in line behind him with the Winners Dog. The Winners
Bitch brought up the rear. Now that Davey's part in the
competition had ended, I could relax. I scanned the ringside looking for Evan.

After a minute, I found him at the other end of the ring.
I might have spotted him sooner except that while most of
the spectators were riveted by the Standard Poodle judging, Evan was staring down at his phone.

Seriously? It was time I took that man in hand and
showed him how to enjoy a dog show.

I turned to Sam. "If you have everything under control
here, I'm going to go grab Evan and give him a guided
tour."

He gave me a look. Of course he had everything under
control.

"Keep an eye on Aunt Peg, okay?" I said in a low tone.
"Don't let her wreck Davey's day just because Coral
didn't win."

"Don't worry," Davey piped up from behind me. "That's not going to happen."

I hadn't realized he was standing close enough to overhear. "I hope not. But with Aunt Peg you can never be sure."

"I'm sure about this," Davey replied. "I thought Coral did great in there. And if Aunt Peg didn't like the way I showed her, then I'm done. She can find herself another handler."

"That's perfect," I said with a laugh. Threats were a currency Aunt Peg could understand.

Davey just grinned. Thirteen years old, and he was already better at handling Aunt Peg than I was.

By the time I reached the other side of the ring, Evan had slipped his phone back in his pocket. He was observing the end of the Standard Poodle judging with the apathetic air of a man who didn't have a clue what he was watching or why it was important. I could fix that.

He looked up as I drew near.

"Poodles are great, aren't they?" I asked.

"I guess so. I saw Davey win a blue ribbon. Congratulations."

"Thank you. He was happy about it."

In the ring, Crawford's champion was leading the line of three Standard Poodles around the ring for the last time. Evan didn't look impressed.

"Those are three nice dogs you're watching," I told him. "Tell me what you see."

"Ummm . . . honestly?"

"Sure. Have at it."

"I think they look kind of silly."

I nodded. I'm a teacher. I like learning opportunities.

"Because of the way the Poodles are trimmed?" I asked. "Or is it something else?"

Now Evan had to stop and think. He squinted at the trio who were lined up near the gate, waiting to receive their ribbons. "I guess it's mostly the way the hair is arranged. The dog that Davey was showing earlier looked better than these do."

"Lots of people feel that way," I told him. "Coral is still a puppy so she shows in a different trim. When she turns a year old, she'll have to be clipped like those Poodles are. That's called a continental clip. It's actually based on a traditional German hunting trim."

Evan turned to look at me. "You're kidding."

"Nope. The big Poodles were originally bred in Germany to be used as retrievers. They needed a thick coat to keep them warm in the cold German lakes. But then their owners discovered that when all that hair was wet, it got too heavy and dragged the dogs down. So they clipped off any hair they thought was unnecessary."

Evan was paying attention now. He finally looked interested.

"The hair you see on those Poodles"—I gestured toward the ring—"is what remained after the hunters clipped their dogs. The big mane coat on the front of the body protected the Poodles' hearts and lungs in cold water. The bracelets on their ankles warmed their joints. The hip rosettes covered their kidneys. And the pom pon on the tail was meant to act like a flag, marking their place when the dogs dove underwater to retrieve a bird."

Evan wasn't sure he believed me. "Are you making that up?"

"No." I smiled. "It's true. I promise. And you know what else?"

"Tell me."

"Nearly every breed of dog you see here today at the show has a story about where it came from, and what it was originally bred to do, that's just as interesting as the Poodles' history is."

"I thought most of these dogs were bred to run around a show ring."

"Not even close. Bulldogs got their name because at one time they were used for bullbaiting. A totally horrible sport that thankfully no longer exists."

"I should hope not," Evan said with a frown. He turned in place and I saw his eyes skim from ring to ring. He was studying the dogs around us with renewed curiosity. "Tell me another one."

Together, Evan and I made our way around the show-ground. I paused whenever he saw a breed he thought looked interesting, or one that he wanted to learn more about. Evan was drawn to the bigger dogs and we watched everything from Great Danes and Kuvasz, to Irish Wolfhounds and Borzois.

After an hour, I told him that I needed to get back to my family. "They're hanging out in the grooming tent with Aunt Peg and Terry," I said. "You're welcome to come and join us."

"Maybe for just a few minutes," Evan agreed. "I've already been here for quite a while and I don't want to leave Bully alone. . . ."

Abruptly his voice trailed away. I glanced over and saw that Evan had gone still. His face was pale, his expression wary. Then I realized that his gaze was riveted on a man who was striding in our direction from the other end of the showground.

"Evan, what's the matter—"

"I'm sorry," he said shortly. "I have to go."

"Now? Is everything all right?"

"It's fine. Everything's fine." He sounded as though he was trying to convince himself. "I just have to leave."

There was no time to protest his hasty decision. Evan was already gone. He hurried across the open field, heading toward the parking lot.

Evan's precipitous change of plan did nothing to deter the man who'd been coming toward us, however. He simply veered in the new direction, moving to cut Evan off.

I heard the man hail Evan by name. Evan ignored him and kept walking. When the man drew close, he reached out a hand and grasped Evan's shoulder, forcing him to stop and turn around.

I was too far away to hear what they were saying, but even from a distance, I could tell that both men were angry. Their conversation was brief. Less than a minute passed before Evan shrugged off the other man's hold and strode away.

I stood and watched until he was gone. Evan never looked back once.

Chapter 7

When I got back to the handlers' tent, Coral had been brushed out and was relaxing in her crate. Aunt Peg and Sam were packing things up. Davey was entertaining Kevin with a video game they were playing together on his tablet.

Everyone appeared to have eaten lunch in my absence. There was only half a sandwich and an apple left in the cooler. I snagged both and hoisted myself up onto an empty grooming table.

"The strangest thing just happened," I said.

"Strange things are always happening to you," Terry said from the next setup. "That's nothing new."

Good buddy Terry, ever handy with an insult.

"Do you mind?"

"Not at all," he replied blithely. "It certainly keeps life interesting."

The group judging would be starting shortly. Non-Sporting was first and Crawford would be showing his Standard. Later, he had a Brussels Griffon in Toys. I figured we were going to stay and watch him show his Poodle, so I made myself comfortable.

"What was that?" asked Aunt Peg. She was tremendously fond of strange things. And if one of her relatives was involved, that made it even better.

"I was walking around the show with Evan Major—"

"I saw him at the Poodle ring," Aunt Peg said. "Sam told us you were showing him the sights. I thought you'd bring him over to say hello."

"I was about to. But then he saw this guy—"

"Who was it?"

That was the other thing about Aunt Peg. Sometimes she asked so many questions you could barely get a story told.

"I don't know," I said. "I'd never seen him before."

"Too bad Terry wasn't there." Davey looked up. "He knows everybody."

Terry was brushing the hairspray from the coat of Crawford's other Standard entry. They'd been too busy showing dogs to do it earlier. He had his back to us but I could tell that he was pleased by the compliment.

"Not more people than I do." Aunt Peg sounded offended.

Sam had been lining up the grooming tools in the tack box. He stopped and turned to face the group. "People, I think we've lost the thread of the story. Maybe we should just let Melanie finish?"

"Thank you." I inclined my head in his direction. "*Anyway*, Evan and I were on our way here when he saw a man walking toward us. He stopped dead in his tracks—"

"Dead?" Kev pulled his gaze away from the game. "How did he die?"

"Evan wasn't really dead," I told him. "It's just a figure of speech. Evan is fine."

When Kevin resumed playing his game, I turned back to the others. "But he looked really upset. Then he said he had to go and he just took off."

"With no explanation?" Aunt Peg lifted a brow.

"None," I replied. "And it didn't end there. The man Evan was trying avoid went after him. He grabbed Evan and made him stop. The two of them had an argument about something. Unfortunately, I don't know what. I was too far away to hear what they were saying."

"That is odd," Sam agreed. "Especially since Evan is new to the area and this was his first dog show. Aside from your Bite Club members, I wouldn't have expected him to run into anyone he knew."

"Much less someone he wanted to fight with," I added.

"Evan seems like such a quiet man," Aunt Peg mused. "But obviously there's more to him than we know. Perhaps he makes a habit of fighting with people. Don't forget, he arrived at my house on Tuesday looking as though he'd recently engaged in a brawl."

"That was from a car accident," Terry pointed out. He'd stashed the first Standard Poodle back in its crate and was now doing some last minute tweaking to Crawford's special.

"*Was it?*" Aunt Peg asked ominously.

I was about to mention the condition of Evan's car when Crawford came hurrying back into the setup. He slipped the Min Pin he was carrying into a crate, and dropped a purple Winners ribbon in the top of the tack box. Then he grabbed a bottle of water, twisted off the cap, and took a quick sip.

The day had grown progressively warmer and Crawford had shown the class Min Pin in his shirtsleeves. Now, in preparation for the group, he whipped his sports coat off a hanger that was dangling from the side of his tack box. When he had the jacket on, Terry ran a pair of rubber bands up Crawford's sleeve. Then he fastened the Standard Poodle's numbered armband in place.

The show announcer was calling the Non-Sporting Group to the ring. Crawford gave his bitch a quick inspection. As he'd expected, she looked terrific. Crawford snapped the rubber band holding her folded leash together, then unspooled the narrow leather strip into his palm.

The Poodle knew what that meant. She rose to her feet. Hands positioned carefully around the hair, Terry lifted the bitch and lowered her to the ground. Crawford waited for the Poodle to have a quick shake, then he took off for the ring.

Aunt Peg and Davey were right beside him. Automatically they moved into position on either side of the Standard Poodle, preventing her carefully coiffed hair from being jostled by the crowd. Sam took Kevin's hand. The two of them fell in behind.

To my surprise, Terry hung back. Not only that, but he blocked my way to make sure that I did too.

"I have to talk to you," he said in a low voice. Though the others had already moved on without us, it seemed as though he was afraid of being overheard.

"Sure," I said. "What's up?"

"It's private."

I almost smiled at that. Where Terry was concerned, *nothing* was ever private. But the expression on his face stopped me. Terry looked unexpectedly serious.

"Go ahead," I said. "I can keep a secret."

"There's this guy who's been hanging around Crawford."

He stopped and frowned. I waited expectantly. Terry and I have talked about things that would make a longshoreman blush. I had never seen him so reticent.

"It's been going on for several weeks," he continued finally. "At least that's how long I know about."

"Okay," I said. "Is that a problem?"

"I didn't think so at first. In fact, I didn't think twice about him. I figured maybe he was a potential client just, you know, checking things out. But that wasn't it."

Terry paused again. I wondered if he would ever get around to telling me what it *was*. Maybe an easy question would help.

"Does the man have a name?"

"It's Gabe Summers," Terry replied. "And he looks amazing. He's tall, and buff, and he has dark curly hair. Picture Michelangelo's *David*. Or maybe a Greek god."

No wonder Terry had noticed him hanging around. I was tempted to mention that Gabe sounded just like his type—but Terry didn't look like he was in the mood for a joke.

"He's been at every show we've gone to for the last month," he said. "And he's ringside every time Crawford shows a dog. You must have seen him. He was outside the Poodle ring earlier."

I shrugged. With more immediate problems of my own, I hadn't been paying any attention to the spectators.

"Okay, so we know his name and what he looks like," I said. "Where did Gabe come from? What's he doing here?"

"Making himself very much at home," Terry growled.

"So shoo him away if he's become annoying. Politely, of course."

"I can't. He and Crawford have become friends."

Aha. Now we were getting somewhere. Crawford had many friends. But this sounded like it might be different.

"Are you concerned about that?" I asked.

"Maybe," Terry replied. Then he amended his answer. "Yes."

"Why? You and Crawford have tons of friends."

"It's not the same. Gabe is clearly interested in Crawford, but he's made no attempt to get to know me. It's like I'm not even there. Gabe barely acknowledges my existence."

"That's not nice." I frowned. "What does Crawford say about that?"

Terry looked pained. "He just shrugged it off. When I called him on it, he gave me some bogus explanation about Gabe wanting to become a handler, so he was hanging around to see what the job entailed."

In the decade I'd known Crawford, the only other person I'd seen him take under his wing was Terry. Nevertheless it seemed as though reassurance was called for.

"There you go," I said. "That makes sense."

"It does not," Terry snapped.

I glanced across the field toward the big double ring where the groups were going to be judged. The Non-Sporting dogs and their handlers had already entered the enclosure. They were moving quickly into line. Everyone must be wondering where we were.

And I still wasn't sure what this conversation was about. "Talk to me, Terry," I said. "Tell me what's really going on."

"Gabe is . . . hot."

"So are you," I replied roundly.

"Yes, but I'm old news. Gabe is so new he's practically still shiny."

"You and Crawford have a *great* relationship."

"That's what I thought." A fleeting look of sadness chased across his face. "*Before*. Now I don't know what to think."

"Do you want to know what I think?"

"Yes."

"You and Crawford need to talk."

"I tried that."

"Try again. Try harder."

Terry grimaced. "You know what Crawford is like. He's an incredibly private person. He was in his fifties when we met. I'll never forgive you if you tell him I said this, but he comes from an older generation than we do."

I nodded. I got that.

"Things were different when Crawford was young. Even now there's a lot of stuff I still don't know about him. Things that he'd rather keep to himself."

"I don't care," I said firmly. "That was then, and this is

now. Make Crawford talk to you about Gabe. Tell him their friendship bothers you."

Terry's gaze narrowed. "You know it's not that easy. I remember what happened with you and Sheila."

Sam and I had been engaged to be married when his ex-wife had unexpectedly reentered his life. Next thing I knew, Sheila was doing her sneaky, underhanded best to win Sam back. I hadn't been afraid to speak up for myself, but my complaints about the situation had gone nowhere. And in the end, Sam and I had broken off our engagement. It wasn't a chapter of my life that I liked to revisit.

Terry had to have known that. So the fact that he'd brought it up was a sign of his uneasiness. And perhaps his desperation.

"Terry, you know I love you," I said. "But you and Crawford are as solid as any couple I know. I really don't think you have anything to worry about. But I'm always willing to be a sympathetic ear whenever you want to talk."

"I appreciate that," Terry replied. "But I want more."

Terry was a glutton at heart. Whatever was being offered, he always wanted more. But in this instance, I didn't see what else I could do.

"I need your help," he said. "I want you to find out what's going on between Crawford and Gabe."

"You must be kidding." I stared at him, horrified. "You want me to *snoop* on Crawford?"

"Well, I wouldn't have put it exactly that way, but . . . yes."

"You're crazy," I said flatly. "Crawford would never forgive me."

"I know it's a big deal. And I shouldn't ask it of you. But I don't have a choice. I need to know, Melanie."

Melanie. His use of my name touched me more than any plea he'd previously made. Terry almost never called me by name. "Doll," "babe," "hon"—the silly endearments rolled off his tongue in an impersonal, interchangeable stream. But *this* told me how serious he was about the request.

Even so, I couldn't acquiesce. Terry was my friend. Our relationship mattered to me. But my relationship with Crawford mattered too. And therein lay the problem. Suddenly it began to seem like no matter what path I chose, ultimately I was going to end up betraying someone.

A smattering of applause from the direction of the group ring drew our attention. The judge must have made his cut. The group judging was almost over.

"We'd better get up there or we'll miss the whole thing," I said.

"What's the hurry?" Terry sounded defeated. "I'm sure Gabe is keeping an eye on everything."

There was a bitter edge to his voice that I hadn't heard before. It made me want to give him a hug. It also made me want to run away and pretend that none of this existed, that the conversation had never even happened.

I started to leave the setup. I hoped Terry would follow. Instead, he said something that spun me back around to face him.

"You owe me."

The words hung in the air between us. In the spring, I'd asked Terry to help me out with a problem. He'd complied and I'd promised to return the favor someday. Ironically it was Crawford who'd warned me that was a dangerous vow to make. And he'd been right. Because now it looked as though the pledge that I'd tossed out so flippantly was going to be used against him.

"That's not fair," I told him.

Terry just shrugged. He didn't care.

A minute passed. Finally, against my better judgment, I said, "I guess I can ask around. But that's *all*. Then we're even, right?"

He nodded.

To my surprise, I realized Terry looked just as uncomfortable as I felt. *He deserved that*, I thought. Coercion ought to take a toll.

We walked over to the ring in silence and got there just in time to see the Tibetan Terrier win the Non-Sporting Group. Crawford's Standard Poodle placed second. Sam, Aunt Peg, and the boys were standing near the in-gate.

I was about to head their way when Terry motioned toward the other side of the ring. It wasn't hard to pick out whom he was pointing at. In a tight T-shirt and formfitting jeans, Gabe did look like he'd sprung straight from the pages of Greek mythology. Perseus come to life.

"You see what I'm up against?" said Terry.

I closed my eyes briefly. I couldn't think of a single good answer to that, so I said nothing at all.

"It turned out that the incident with Evan wasn't the only strange thing that happened today," I told Sam later that evening. We'd finished dinner and he and I were cleaning up. He was putting away the leftovers while I rinsed the plates and stacked them in the dishwasher.

Davey and Kevin were out in the yard kicking a soccer ball around. The Poodle posse had opted to join them. With summer's longer days, the whole crew could play outside until nearly bedtime. I really hoped that Tar—the only intelligence-challenged Standard Poodle I'd ever met—hadn't decided to play goalie.

Sam was leaning down to stow the placemats in a cabinet. He glanced at me over his shoulder. "I don't often agree with Terry but his comment earlier was spot on. There must be something about you that attracts unusual occurrences. What now?"

"Funny you should bring up Terry. The second one was about him."

Sam closed the cabinet and straightened. "There are times when I think almost everything about Terry is unusual. But go on."

"This was about Crawford and Terry together."

"What does that have to do with you?"

"Good question. That's just what I said to Terry." I closed the dishwasher and dried my hands on a towel. My mug of after-dinner coffee was sitting on the counter. I picked it up, walked over to the kitchen table, and sat down.

"When was this?"

"When the rest of you went to watch the group. Terry asked me to stay behind so we could talk."

Sam pulled out a chair and joined me at the table. "I wondered where you had disappeared to. What did he want to talk about?"

"He's worried about some guy named Gabe."

Sam searched his memory. "Doesn't sound familiar. Do we know him?"

"No. But Terry pointed him out to me later when he and I got to the ring."

"What's the problem with him?"

"Terry thinks that Gabe is interested in Crawford."

"Why not? Crawford's an interesting man." Then abruptly he stopped and thought about it. "Oh. You mean *interested.*"

"Precisely."

"So? Crawford's in a relationship. End of story."

"Terry doesn't think so. Apparently Gabe and Crawford have become quite friendly in the last month or so. Terry said Gabe is always hanging around now. He implied that maybe Crawford is encouraging him."

"Encouraging him?" Sam shook his head. He was every bit as perplexed by the idea as I had been. "It sounds like Terry and Crawford need to talk."

Apparently that conclusion was easier for Sam to reach when the problem didn't involve him. "Right," I said with a smirk. "Because that's what men do. They talk about their relationships."

"Point taken," he agreed. "But still."

"I told Terry the same thing. He said Crawford doesn't want to discuss it."

"So? What's the alternative?"

I hesitated. Sam stared at me across the table. He must have read my mind.

"No," he said firmly. "Absolutely not."

"Again, that's what I told Terry."

"You'd be crazy to even *think* of letting yourself get in between the two of them."

"I can't disagree," I said.

Sam sighed. "You're going to do it anyway, aren't you?"

"Terry didn't give me a choice."

"If your mind is already made up, I only have one thing to say. 'That way madness lies.' "

"Really?" I lifted a brow. "You're quoting Shakespeare now?"

"*King Lear* is a classic. And the reason Shakespeare's plays are still popular today is because he understood human nature." Sam stood up and walked over to the back door. About to go outside, he paused and looked back. "Consider this too—that's the play where everybody dies in the end."

Chapter 8

During the school year I work as a special needs tutor at a private academy in Greenwich. So summer vacation is supposed to be my time off too. But somehow with two kids in the house, it doesn't feel that way.

Previous summers, Davey had spent eight weeks at soccer camp. This year he was attending just one month-long session in August. During July, he was doing odd jobs around the neighborhood—anything from mowing lawns, to cleaning gutters, to weeding flower beds—to earn some extra spending money.

Being employed and having an income of his own made Davey feel very mature. It made his younger brother feel left out.

"I want a job too," Kevin said.

"That's great," I told him. "You can clean your room."

My four-year-old son thrust out his lower lip and glared up at me with all the indignation he could muster. "That's not a *real* job."

"When I have to do it, it feels like one to me."

"Davey gets paid for his jobs," he argued. "Nobody pays you to clean the house."

"More's the pity," I said.

Kev and I were still working on negotiating the details of his summer schedule when I got a chance to check in with Evan on Tuesday afternoon. We'd planned to meet up again this week and I hoped he'd be free the following afternoon.

"Bully and I are doing very well," he told me. "I think we're both figuring each other out."

"I'm glad to hear that." I was tempted to ask him if he was still reading his book, but I didn't dare. "Are you ready for another puppy training session? Tomorrow afternoon works for me, if you're free."

"That sounds fine," Evan replied. "I'm sure Bully will be glad to see you again. Sometimes I think he gets a little lonely with just me for company. Someone told me that it's better to have two dogs than one. That way they have a friend to talk to. What do you think?"

"I don't agree," I said. "For a first-time dog owner like you, two puppies would be a lot to train at once. Plus, you want Bully to bond with you, not with another dog. Let's get him settled first, before you think about adding to your household."

"You might be right." Evan didn't sound entirely convinced by the points I'd made. "We can talk more about it tomorrow."

"In the meantime, I wanted to ask you about what happened at the dog show on Saturday," I said. "You left rather abruptly. Is everything all right?"

"I'm sorry for running out on you. Especially after you'd taken the time to show me around, it was unforgivably rude of me."

"I'm not worried about that," I replied. "I just wanted to make sure you're okay."

"It was nothing. I just ran into someone I didn't want to talk to, that's all. I'll see you tomorrow."

Evan ended the connection without waiting for my reply.

"It didn't look like nothing to me," I said to an empty room. At least nobody disagreed with me.

* * *

The next morning, Kevin went storming around the house. Once again, my child was in a serious snit. I didn't recall Davey being this argumentative at four. But Davey hadn't had an older brother who got extra perks and had a lot more freedom to do what he wanted.

Then too, Davey hadn't been this age for nearly a decade. Looking back, I remembered him as a model child. Maybe I'd purposely repressed anything unpleasant about his early childhood.

Sam was in his office, working. It occurred to me that maybe he'd closed his door on purpose. I was upstairs in our bedroom, sorting clean laundry. Faith was lying on the chaise near the window, keeping me company.

I could hear my children arguing downstairs. The two of them were making more noise than all six dogs combined. As soon the laundry basket was empty, sorting out Kevin would be the next thing on my list.

Before I got that far, Davey came to me. He stomped up the stairs, then down the length of the hall. Faith and I had plenty of notice that he was coming. By the time he appeared in the doorway, we were both waiting for him.

Faith flapped her tail up and down in greeting. Davey didn't even notice. His gaze was fixed on me.

"He's *your* child." Clearly he was seething with frustration. "You have to do something."

"He's *your* brother," I pointed out. "You always told me you wanted a sibling. Now you've got one."

"Apparently I was wrong." Davey stalked over to the chaise and sat down. Faith moved over to give him room. Instead of taking it, he pulled the big Poodle into his lap.

Good, I thought. She would calm him down.

"What's the matter now?"

"Kevin wants to come to work with me."

I put the laundry aside and perched on the edge of the

bcd. "Obviously that's not going to happen. I assume you told him no?"

"I did." Davey nodded. "He cried. I hate it when he cries."

We all hated it when Kevin cried. The child had realized that early on and was not above exploiting it for his own purposes.

"Where are you working today?"

"At Mrs. Hunter's, around the corner. Yesterday I took down her shutters. Today I'll be scraping and painting them. Tomorrow, I'll be putting them back up. For some reason, Kev thinks that sounds like fun."

"Kevin thinks anything he does with you is fun," I mentioned.

Davey sighed. He wrapped his arms around Faith's neck and gave her a hug.

"He looks up to you."

"I know." Davey sounded resigned. "But Mrs. Hunter is counting on me. She's *paying* me. And I can't do my job and watch Kev at the same time."

"Of course you can't," I agreed. "Nobody expects you to. I'm just thinking maybe you could exercise a little more patience with your brother, that's all."

"I try. But he never wants to take no for an answer."

It wasn't hard to figure where he'd gotten that trait from.

"Let's go downstairs," I said. "I'll talk to him."

Davey grudgingly rose to his feet.

I beckoned to Faith. "You come too."

Kevin was standing at the foot of the steps. He must have raided the front closet because he'd put on a rain slicker over his T-shirt and shorts. He'd also pulled on his red rubber boots. I had no idea why. Maybe he thought that was a shutter-painting outfit.

"I'm going to work with Davey," Kev announced as we

reached the bottom of the staircase. He stamped his foot for emphasis.

The other Poodles and Bud had been milling around the hallway. But stamping feet was a new thing for them. They stopped and waited to see what would happen next. Faith trotted over to join her crew. Davey leaned on the newel post.

I crossed my arms over my chest and faced Kevin. "How come?"

My younger son stared at me suspiciously. He suspected a trap. "How come what?"

"Why do you want to work when you could play all day instead?"

"I like painting," he said.

"You like finger painting," I pointed out. "We have finger paints here."

"Finger painting is for kids. I want to do grown-up painting. With Davey." Kevin looked to his brother for confirmation. Davey just stared at the ceiling.

"I guess that means you're going to be gone all day?"

Kevin nodded.

"That's too bad. I was thinking that while Davey was busy working, you and I could take Faith and Bud out back and spend the morning playing dog show. But of course if you're not going to be here . . ."

Kev looked back and forth between Davey and me. Indecision was written all over his face. Then Bud decided to help our cause. He left the pack and sidled over to where Kevin was standing. The little dog jumped up and placed his front feet on Kev's chest. He wriggled his body back and forth.

Normally jumping up isn't allowed. This time I was all in favor.

"It looks like Bud knows which option he wants you to choose," I said.

Kev wasn't sure. He still wanted to negotiate. "Can we play dog show for a whole *hour*?"

"At least an hour," I confirmed.

"Can Tar play too?"

"If he wants to, sure."

Kevin pushed Bud down and started to unfasten his slicker. He must have been hot wearing that plastic jacket inside the house. In July. Not to mention the rubber boots. I was sweating just looking at him.

"I guess I'll stay here," Kev decided.

"Good choice," I told him.

"*Excellent* choice," Davey said. "And I'll be on my way. Hard work awaits."

"Followed by a paycheck," I reminded him.

Skirting past me on his way to the door, Davey gave me a quick hug. An *unsolicited* hug. From a teenage boy. I didn't even know such things existed.

"Thanks, Mom," he whispered in my ear.

"Don't mention it. It's all part of the job."

"Job?" Kev looked up.

"Playing dog show," I said as Davey quickly slipped out the door and closed it behind him. "Isn't that what we were talking about?"

Kevin tossed his slicker in the direction of the closet and ran to get the leashes. I guessed that meant we were starting now. The laundry was going to have to wait.

Just before one o'clock I handed Kevin off to Sam and left to go see Evan and Bully. There were days when just getting out of the house felt like my real vacation.

The drive to Evan's house took ten quiet, peaceful minutes. I even listened to some music. It was bliss.

On my first visit, Evan and I had spent the entire time talking about Bully. Now that we'd mostly covered the basics of puppy care, I was looking forward to discussing

other things too. Like the truth about his supposed car accident. And why he'd run from the man who'd waylaid
him at the show.

I had questions and I hoped Evan would have answers
for me. If he was in trouble, maybe I could help.

As soon as I turned the Volvo onto Bluebell Lane, I
slowed down. Flower Estates was a family neighborhood.
I wouldn't have been surprised to see kids playing in their
front yards or riding their bikes in the road.

I was approaching Evan's house when a sudden flash of
movement caught my eye. I lifted my foot off the gas pedal
and took another look. A neighbor had planted a low border of decorative bushes between his yard and the sidewalk.
As I stared at the small hedge, a blocky, fawn-and-white
head popped out from behind it.

To my shock, that head looked like it belonged to Bully.
I must be wrong, I thought. Why would Evan's puppy
be outside on his own, and especially here, right next to
the street?

I blinked and looked again. It was Bully all right.

Quickly I nudged the Volvo to the side of the road and
parked. Evan and I had talked about this. I'd been very
clear about the need to keep the puppy securely confined
for his own protection. And Evan had appeared to agree
with me.

I scrambled out of the car and knelt down on the sidewalk. I held out my hand enticingly. "Hey, Bully, come
here, boy."

The puppy's chubby body was still half shrouded by the
shrubbery. He gazed at me uncertainly.

"Come on, Bully," I crooned. "You remember me."

I dug into my pocket, hoping to find a treat. No such
luck. So instead I patted the ground in front of me invit-
ingly. "Come on out, Bully boy. Let's play."

That move did the trick. With a small *woof*, Bully came
bounding out onto the sidewalk. He pounced on my hand.

His sharp puppy teeth closed over my fingers. In a few months, that would be a problem. Now it was easy to pry his mouth open.

I gave the puppy a pat and scooped him up in my arms. Bully's short tail began to wag. I was betting he wasn't any happier about being on his own in an unfamiliar place than I was to have found him here.

"Evan needs to take better care of you," I said, scratching underneath the puppy's chin. "And we're going to go tell him so."

Evan's house was just two doors down. I half expected him to open his front door and step outside as Bully and I approached. When he did, I intended to read him the riot act.

Except that didn't happen.

With a frown I stared at the house. Maybe Evan had seen us coming and realized that I'd be upset about his negligence. Perhaps he was hoping to avoid a confrontation—or at least postpone it for as long as possible.

I climbed the two steps to the narrow stoop and rang the doorbell. As we waited for Evan to appear, Bully began snuffling my T-shirt and tickling me with his puppy breath. No doubt the Bulldog was enjoying a whole host of enticing Poodle smells.

Evan's front door remained closed. I rang the bell again. A minute later, I knocked. Thirty seconds after that, I pounded on the door with my fist.

Still nothing.

"That's odd," I said. Talking to dogs always seems like a good idea to me.

Bully didn't reply. It was too bad Faith wasn't there. She and I could have had a whole conversation about the problem.

I juggled Bully into my other arm and pulled my phone out of my pocket. I tapped in Evan's number and listened to it ring. He didn't pick up.

I didn't bother to leave a message. What was there to say? *I'm standing outside your front door. Stop being a coward and open up?*

Yes, I was annoyed. We'd agreed to meet and Evan was expecting me. What did he think would happen if he didn't open the door? That I would put his puppy down and leave? I hoped he'd believe better of me than that.

"Now what?" I asked Bully.

The question was force of habit. I'd already discovered that the puppy wasn't much of a conversationalist. Actually I should have already known that. Being a Bulldog, Bully was likely to be the strong, silent, type.

I carried him back to my car and picked up a leash. The loop fit snugly around the puppy's neck. Evan and I had been planning to work on leash breaking this week. But even untutored, the puppy was happy enough to follow me around.

Back at Evan's house, I tried the doorbell again. *Maybe Evan was asleep*, I thought. Or he'd been on the phone. Or he was running the garbage disposal and hadn't heard me the first time.

Or maybe I was running out of excuses.

Bully and I walked around the side of the house and peered in a window. I had a great view of the barely furnished dining room. A glance inside the garage revealed that Evan's white Prius was parked within. At the back of the small house, we were able to see through the panes of the half-glass kitchen door. That room was empty too.

I tried the knob. Of course it was locked.

"I'm out of ideas," I told Bully.

He didn't seem upset to hear that.

The ex pen was still set up in the backyard. I was pleased to see that it now contained a small bowl of water.

"I can't leave you there all by yourself," I said.

Bully tipped his head to one side. He didn't have much to say but at least he was listening.

By now I'd been at Evan's house for nearly twenty minutes. Wherever he was, whatever he was doing, I was ready to be done. I wasn't going to stand around and wait for him any longer.

I took out my phone one last time. This time I left a message. It might have sounded a little peeved. Maybe more than a little.

I told Evan I wasn't happy that he'd stood me up for our meeting. And that I'd found Bully by the side of the road and taken him home with me for safekeeping. I urged him to get in touch with me asap.

I settled Bully next to me on the front seat of the car where I could keep an eye on him. The afternoon's excitement must have tired the puppy out. He quickly curled in a ball and went to sleep.

I envied him that. It would be nice to be able to put my concerns aside so easily.

Chapter 9

I intended to head straight home, but since I was in the neighborhood I found myself driving around the corner to Alice's house. At one point in our lives, she and I had virtually lived in each other's kitchens. I knew Alice wouldn't mind if I dropped in uninvited.

And maybe she would have an idea where Evan was. That would be useful.

Everything about Flower Estates felt familiar to me. Driving around the subdivision was like coming home. The houses I passed—all fashioned from the same basic design—didn't vary much. The home that Alice shared with her family was a mirror image of the one that I'd previously owned just down the street.

These houses predated central air-conditioning, so I wasn't surprised to see Alice's front door standing open. A screen door was letting a much-needed breeze inside. I parked out front and was lifting the sleepy puppy out of the car when I heard a rumble of deep-throated barking.

Berkley, the Brickmans' Golden Retriever, had noticed our arrival. He was standing just inside the house with his nose pressed against the screen door. As I crossed the small lawn with Bully in my arms, Alice appeared behind him.

Her strawberry blond hair was gathered on top of her head in a casual bun, and her pale skin was dusted with summer freckles. Over the years we'd known each other, Alice had lost and regained the same ten pounds of "baby weight" half a dozen times. Now she was somewhere in the middle: five pounds up or five down, depending on your point of view. Either way, her husband, Joe, thought she looked great.

Alice saw me approaching and smiled. "Melanie, what a pleasant surprise. When Berks started barking I thought maybe you were the UPS man. But this is even better. Give me just a minute, and I'll put this maniac in the backyard. What is *that* you're carrying?"

She looped her fingers through the Golden Retriever's collar and tugged him away from the screen door. Berkley was a good boy. After casting a longing glance in our direction, he followed Alice away down the hall.

When I heard the back door open and close, I let myself inside. As Bully lifted his head and had a curious look around, Alice hurried to rejoin me.

"You know Berkley, he wouldn't hurt a fly. At least not on purpose. But even after two courses of obedience lessons, he still would have jumped all over you. Especially with a puppy in your arms." Alice leaned in for a closer look. "Oooh, adorable! But definitely not a Standard Poodle. Are you branching out? Good for you. Peg must be horrified."

She giggled at the thought. Easy for her to do. She wasn't a relative.

"This cute boy is Bully," I told her. "He belongs to Evan Major."

"Really? That's the new puppy?" Alice took another look. "I remember him saying he was getting one . . . but honestly, I was dealing with a million other things at the time and it mostly went in one ear and out the other. So what's he doing with you?"

"Good question," I said. "Do you have a few minutes?"

"Of course. Carly's at ballet, and I don't have to pick

her up until four. Joey's at a friend's house. So I'm at your service." She seemed delighted by the idea. "Let's pretend we're civilized adults and sit in the living room for a change. Bully must be heavy. He looks like he must weigh a ton. Don't you want to put him down?"

"Not in your living room," I said. "I can't guarantee that he's fully housebroken."

"Oh well." Alice shrugged. "Kitchen it is, then."

She spread some newspaper over the hardwood floor. I placed Bully in the middle of a double sheet, then Alice and I grabbed bottles of green tea out of the refrigerator. We sat down opposite each other at the small oval table.

She twisted her bottle open with a sharp flick of her wrist. "So what's going on with Evan? It's nice of you to step in, but how come he can't take care of his own puppy?"

"I don't know," I said. "I was hoping you could tell me."

"Tell you what?"

"Where he is. Evan and I had an appointment to meet at his house this afternoon. We were supposed to work on Bully's training. You told him to ask me about that, right?"

"I guess I did. I hope that was okay?"

I nodded. "Of course."

"You know what Evan's like. He's lived here a month but he hardly knows anybody. It seems like he barely leaves his house. I thought sending him to you might broaden his horizons. I figured if you were too busy, you'd just say no."

"I was happy to help," I replied. "And our first session last week was great. Evan even came to a dog show with us on Saturday. He looked like he was having a good time."

I stopped and frowned. "At least until the end."

Alice sipped at her tea. "What happened then?"

"He ran into someone he didn't want to see, and left.

But when I talked to him yesterday, he sounded cheerful enough. We agreed to meet at his house, today at one o'clock."

She glanced at her watch. "It's past one thirty."

I nodded. "When I got there, Evan wasn't home. And I found Bully wandering around outside by himself."

We both turned to look at the puppy. Bully had decided that the newspaper made a comfy bed. He had stretched out on the financial page and fallen back to sleep.

"That doesn't make sense," said Alice.

"I know," I replied. "Evan's car was in his garage but there was no sign of him. I rang his doorbell. I knocked on his door. I even walked around the house and looked in his windows."

"You didn't." She laughed.

"Did too," I admitted. "But it didn't help. So here I am, hoping you might have a bright idea or two. You know Evan better than I do. What's going on with him? Why do you think he stood me up?"

"I wish I knew," said Alice. "To tell you the truth, he doesn't seem like a guy who has much to do. So I'm shocked that he wouldn't have been there waiting for you. He didn't call to cancel?"

I shook my head.

"Text?" she tried hopefully.

"Nada," I said. "He told me last week that he's between jobs. So it's not as though something could have come up for work."

"And he's divorced with no kids," Alice pointed out. "So most likely not a family problem either."

"What else do you know about him?" I asked.

She sat and thought for a minute. "I'm pretty sure he lived in New Jersey before he came here. Maybe Fort Lee. But I don't know what he did when he was there. Or why he moved to Connecticut. Now that I think about it, I guess Evan and I mostly talked about practical stuff, like who's the best plumber to call after hours or where to go watch fireworks on the Fourth of July."

"You're no help." I chugged the remainder of my tea. Then I got up to rinse out the plastic bottle in the sink.

"Sorry," Alice replied. "I guess you'll just have to wait for him to get in touch with you. I assume you left a message?"

"Oh yes."

She joined me at the sink. When both bottles were clean, Alice tossed them in the recycling bin. "I hope you didn't sound too angry. You wouldn't want to scare him off."

"Oh, for Pete's sake," I said. "Evan's a full-grown man, not a spotted fawn. It's time for him to man up. Plus, I have his dog."

"Perfect." She grinned. "Make Evan pay. You can hold Bully for ransom until he apologizes."

"I just might do that," I said.

The idea seemed funny at the time.

The Poodles raised a huge fuss when I arrived home, dragged an ex pen out of the garage, set it up in the back-yard, and placed Bully inside. Tar, Augie, and Bud raced in big circles around the yard—yapping and leaping, and generally making fools of themselves.

I'd anticipated something like that might happen. It was why the puppy was in a pen. That way he could have a meet-and-greet with the rambunctious crew without being trampled by their enthusiasm.

The bitches' reactions were more restrained. They stuck their noses through the holes in the wire and gave Bully a thorough sniffing. Eve and Raven were delighted to make a new friend.

Faith just gave me that look. Canine queen of the house, it was up to her to pass judgment on all new arrivals. *Not again*, she was saying.

I couldn't blame her. Six dogs was already plenty.

I was in the process of explaining to Faith that Bully's stay was only temporary when the commotion brought Sam outside to see what was going on. I thought he'd be surprised to see the puppy, but apparently living with me has pretty much cured that man of being surprised by anything.

"Didn't we just get a new dog?" he asked, glancing at Bud.

"This one isn't ours," I said. "Think of him as a loaner. His name is Bully."

Sam knelt down, stuck his fingers through the wire, and waggled them back and forth. The puppy trotted over, jumped up, and gave him a friendly lick. "He's pretty cute. Then again, I've never seen a Bulldog puppy that wasn't. I'm guessing he belongs to Evan?"

"Yup."

"Any particular reason why he isn't *with* Evan?"

"That," I said, "is the sixty-four-thousand-dollar question. I don't know where Evan is."

Sam tipped his head to one side and gazed up at me. "And that made you angry enough to steal his puppy?"

"Not exactly." I smirked. "Bully was running loose outside next to the road. Meanwhile Evan's house was closed up tight and he wasn't anywhere to be seen. I couldn't just leave the puppy there by himself."

"No, of course not," Sam agreed. "Do we have a timetable on Evan's return?"

"I left a message on his phone so he would know where Bully is. I'm guessing we'll hear from him shortly."

"One can only hope," Sam muttered. He didn't sound convinced.

"Look on the bright side," I said.

"There's a bright side?"

Actually I'd been hoping he'd come up with one.

"I'm sure there is," I told him. "We just have to think of it."

The bright side turned out to be that Davey and Kev loved having a puppy to play with—even if he wasn't there to stay. The Poodles also thought our canine guest was highly entertaining. Even Sam and I were not immune to Bully's pudgy adorableness.

All afternoon, I waited for a call from Evan. None came. By ten p.m. I gave up and went to bed.

There was no message on my phone the following morning. Evan's phone went straight to voice mail when I tried calling him again.

Midmorning there was a knock on the front door. Davey was up the street rehanging Mrs. Hunter's shutters. Sam and Kev were riding their bikes around the block. Bully was crated in the kitchen. The Poodle posse had been keeping him company, but now they ran to the door. I was only a few seconds behind.

It's about time, I thought.

Except that it wasn't Evan Major who was standing on my doorstep. My face fell. The greeting I'd been about to offer—half relieved, half annoyed—died on my lips.

My first impression of the man in front of me was that he looked like someone I wouldn't want to cross. Heavyset, probably in his fifties, he had short, dark hair and thick eyebrows that matched. The tan summer suit he was wearing didn't flatter his chunky body. I doubted that he cared. We hadn't even met yet, and already the man appeared to be in a bad mood.

Before he said a word, I was afraid I knew what was coming.

"Melanie Travis?" he asked.

I really wished I could say no. I nodded anyway.

"I'm Detective Sturgill with the Stamford Police Department. May I come inside?"

"Umm . . ." I'd opened the door only a sliver. The Poodles and Bud were standing in the hallway behind me, hoping for a visitor to swarm. "Do you like dogs?"

"What kind of dogs are we talking about?"

"Mostly Poodles," I told him. "And Bud."

Sturgill frowned. "What's a Bud?"

As I leaned against the edge of the door, the opening widened. Tar slithered between my legs. He stuck his head out and had a look.

"What's this about?" I asked.

"I'd like to ask you a few questions." His eyes widened as he stared at Tar. I guessed he was expecting smaller Poodles. "You really don't want to do this on your doorstep."

I had a sinking feeling that the detective was probably right. I'd had more than my share of dealings with the police in the past and I'd rarely found them to be the bearers of good news. Based on previous experience, I knew that finding a police detective standing outside my door was one of those things just about guaranteed to ruin my day.

Unfortunately there wasn't much I could do about that. I stepped back and drew the door open wide. "The dogs are big but they're friendly. They may take a minute to settle."

Sturgill looked taken aback by the sight that greeted him. For a few seconds, he didn't move at all. He appeared to be counting noses. "Six," he said.

Technically seven, I thought. *If you counted Bully.* I didn't feel the need to issue a correction.

"All licensed?" he asked.

"Of course."

"What happened to that one?" He pointed at Bud, who clearly didn't match the rest of the canine crew.

"Someone dumped him by the side of the road. We picked him up."

Detective Sturgill walked inside and I closed the door behind him. The Poodle pack eddied around his legs, each hoping to be the first to draw his attention. When he ignored the dogs and kept his gaze firmly trained on me, their disappointment was palpable.

I have a bad habit of characterizing policemen by the

breed of dog they remind me of. With his black hair, wiry eyebrows, and thick build, Sturgill was a Scottish Terrier. Scotties are energetic, scrappy, and tenacious. I wouldn't want to get into a fight with one. That didn't seem to bode well for my relationship with the detective.

"Let's sit down in the living room and you can tell me why you're here," I said.

I took a seat in the middle of the couch. Sensing I might need her support, Faith immediately jumped up beside me. Eve scrambled up to flank my other side. Detective Sturgill watched that, then deliberately chose a narrow chair for himself. Bud scooted under the coffee table and lay down. The remaining three Poodles wandered back to the kitchen.

"You are acquainted with a man named Evan Major," the detective began. "Is that correct?"

"Yes. I've known him for about a month."

"He's a friend of yours?"

"Yes, although I don't know him well. He's a new neighbor of a good friend of mine. And also a member of our book club."

"Bite Club," he said with a frown.

"The name was a joke."

"Really." Sturgill did not look amused.

"How do you know about that?"

He ignored the question. Instead he said, "I'm afraid I have some bad news for you, Ms. Travis."

I didn't ask what it was. I didn't want to know. But at the same time I was more than a little afraid that I already knew.

"Evan Major is dead. He was killed inside his home. We believe it happened yesterday afternoon, although we'll have a better idea about that after the medical examiner has had a chance to do his job."

"Dead." The word seemed to stick in my throat. Hot tears pricked the backs of my eyes. "What happened?"

"Major was stabbed multiple times." The detective was watching my reaction closely. When I didn't comment, he added, "His body was found this morning by a neighbor."

"Oh no." I drew in a sharp breath. "Not Alice?"

"No. A woman named Bella Barrundy. That's why I'm here. She told me that you were the last person to see Evan Major alive."

Chapter 10

"**W**hat?"
My startled response made Faith draw her head back in surprise. She lifted a paw and laid it on top of my leg. As always, her instincts were spot on. I needed all the comforting I could get.

I repeated myself incredulously. "Bella said *what*? That's not right."

"Which part?" Detective Sturgill asked calmly.

"I'm hoping all of it, but that's probably too much to ask." He nodded.

"I haven't seen Evan since last Saturday."

"You were seen at his house yesterday in the early afternoon. At approximately the time we think he was killed."

"By Bella Barrundy," I said. It wasn't a question.

Sturgill nodded anyway. "She lives on the same block. Across the street, a couple houses down. We know you were there. Why don't you tell me what you were doing?"

"I wasn't doing anything," I said. "You're right, I was *at* Evan's house yesterday afternoon. But I wasn't *inside* his house."

"Can you prove that?"

I sat up straight. "Do I need to?"

"I'm hoping it doesn't come to that," he replied. "Right

now, I'm just trying to gather some preliminary information."

What had Bella been doing spying on Evan anyway? I wondered if Sturgill had asked her *that*. Even though I had no reason to want to harm Evan, just the fact that I found myself in the detective's crosshairs made me feel uncomfortable.

"I don't have any information about Evan's death," I told him.

"I'm sure you think that's true. But it doesn't mean something you know might not turn out to be important. Why don't you start at the beginning?"

I stared at him across the coffee table. "The beginning of what?"

"How did you two meet?"

"We were introduced by a friend. Alice Brickman." I hated dragging her into this but it couldn't be helped. I consoled myself with the knowledge that since she lived in Evan's neighborhood, the police would probably talk to her anyway.

"That's the Alice you mentioned earlier?"

"Yes. I used to live in Flower Estates and she and I have been friends for years. I came up with the idea to have a book club and I asked her to join. She brought Evan along with her to the second meeting."

"Why did she do that?"

"Alice is like a mother hen. She takes people under her wing. Evan was new to the area. He was kind of a shy guy, maybe lacking in social skills. She brought him along so he could meet some new people. I think she felt sorry for him."

"And did you also feel sorry for him?" Detective Sturgill asked. It seemed like an odd question.

"I guess, maybe a little. Anyway I didn't mind helping Alice introduce him around. And when Evan asked me to help him train his new puppy, I was happy to help out. I also told him about a dog show last weekend in Mount Kisco."

"A dog show?" Sturgill glanced around the room. "Is that why you have so many dogs?"

"Yes. Although the Standard Poodle my son was showing that day didn't belong to us. Her name is Coral. She won her puppy class." Now I was babbling. That was never a good idea when talking to the police. I clamped my mouth shut.

The detective changed the subject. "Tell me about yesterday."

"Evan and I had an appointment to meet at his house at one o'clock," I said. "That's the reason I was there."

"Like a date?"

"No," I corrected firmly. "It was nothing like a date. Evan had just gotten a Bulldog puppy. Bully was his first dog ever. Evan didn't know anything about training, so I was going to give him some pointers."

"Why would you do that?"

I frowned at the question. "Why not? Every puppy deserves a good start in life. Do you have a dog?"

"No. Two cats."

It figured.

"So you went to Evan's house to meet with him. . . ."

"I showed up at the appointed time. But Evan wasn't home. And I was shocked to see his puppy wandering around in his neighbor's yard."

Sturgill looked up. "Why did that shock you?"

"Because Evan and I had spoken about that. He knew how important it was to keep Bully safely contained."

He still looked bemused. The detective was a cat person, I reminded myself. Cats were different.

"Bully is just a baby," I explained. "It's dangerous for him to go running off on his own. He could get lost, or be stolen, or hit by a car."

"What made you think that Evan wasn't home?"

"Because I rang his doorbell and he didn't answer. I knocked a couple of times too. Then I tried calling his phone, but he didn't pick up. He was supposed to be there, but he wasn't."

"Did that make you mad?"

I almost laughed. Surely the detective wasn't asking if a missed meeting was enough to make me want to kill someone?

"I was annoyed," I replied mildly.

"What did you do after that?"

I had a sneaking suspicion Sturgill already knew exactly what I did next. I stated just the bare facts.

"I walked around Evan's house and looked in the windows. To see if I could see him."

"Maybe you tried the windows to see if they were unlocked and you could let yourself inside?"

Seriously? Where had *that* come from?

"No, I did not."

"Ms. Travis, I'm going to ask you a question and I want you to think about your answer very carefully. We have a team going over Evan Major's house right now looking for evidence. Will they find your fingerprints inside?"

Well, crap. I didn't even have to stop and think about that.

"Yes," I replied.

"Even though you've just told me that you didn't enter his house?"

"I told you that I didn't go inside his house yesterday. But I was there with Evan and his puppy the previous week. He showed me around and we worked with Bully. Evan and I had something to drink in his kitchen."

"Something to drink." Somehow when Sturgill repeated the words, he made them sound incriminating. "What was that?"

"I had a glass of water," I snapped. "Evan was drinking diet Coke."

"Did you happen to touch any of his knives?"

"His knives—?" I stopped and sucked in a breath. The detective had told me Evan had been stabbed. *With a knife from his own kitchen?* Yikes.

"No," I said quickly. Then I qualified my statement. "At least not that I remember."

"Not that you remember?" Once again, he seemed to find my answer suspicious.

"Yes." I looped an arm around Faith's neck and pulled her into my lap. The closer she was, the better I felt. "Not that I remember."

"Is there anything else you want to tell me about your visit yesterday?"

"No, I don't believe so."

Sturgill sat and waited. As if he was sure I would change my mind.

So I straightened my shoulders and said, "I do have some questions for you, however."

"Go ahead." He looked wary. "But be advised I may not be able to answer."

"You said that Bella Barrundy was the one who found Evan's body."

The detective nodded.

"How did that come about?"

"Ms. Barrundy lives nearby. From her front window, she can see across the street to Evan's house. She happened to notice you snooping around there yesterday afternoon."

"I wasn't snooping, I was attempting to keep an appointment." I frowned. "In fact if anyone was snooping, it would have been Bella. She told you she stood in her living room and watched what Evan was doing?"

"I wouldn't quite put it that way," Sturgill said impassively. "But she did seem to be aware of his usual comings and goings. Apparently she hadn't seen him at all yester-

day—and then you showed up. She thought you were acting suspiciously. She was afraid something bad might have
happened while you were there."

Something bad had happened, I thought. *Bella had be-
haved like an idiot.*

"When she still hadn't seen any sign of him by last
evening," Sturgill continued, "she went over and had a
look for herself."

"She looked in his windows?" I arched a brow.

"No, she said she knew where Major kept his spare key."

That was interesting.

"Because he had told her where it was, or because she
spied on him?"

"We did not get into that."

And yet he'd wanted to know whether *I'd* ever touched
any of Evan's knives. Bella had been the one who'd found
Evan's body—then she'd turned around and thrown me
under the bus. And somehow the detective seemed to be
on her side. *What was wrong with this picture?*

"It was lucky for us that Ms. Barrundy decided to go
and check on Evan Major." Sturgill paused and took another look around the room. "She said you stole his dog."

"I did no such thing."

First Bella had implied that I was a murderer. And now
she'd called me a dognapper. That was the last straw.
When Tuesday came, I was going to eject that woman
from Bite Club.

"So you didn't put Evan Major's Bulldog in your car
and drive away?"

"Oh, sure," I said. "I did that. But I wasn't stealing
Bully. I was looking out for him. Keeping him safe until
Evan could come and get him. I thought I'd hear from him
last night."

We both pondered that for a moment. Bully would
never be going back to his owner now.

"Everything I did yesterday—everything Bella Barrundy saw or thinks she saw—was perfectly innocent," I said firmly.

Sturgill nodded. "I've heard your explanation. And much of it makes sense. But I'm still going to need you to come down to the police station so we can take your fingerprints."

My stomach dropped. "You don't believe me."

"This early in the investigation, it doesn't matter what I believe or don't believe. You've told me that your fingerprints can be found in Major's house. And possibly at the crime scene too—we'll have to see about that. If nothing else, we'll need your prints for comparison."

Sturgill rose to his feet. I lifted Faith and set her aside so I could stand up too. I started to walk toward the door. I hoped the detective was following. Not that I was in a hurry to get rid of him or anything.

When we reached the front hall, I turned to face him. I had to make one last attempt to establish my innocence.

"I just met Evan Major a month ago," I said. "I barely knew him. What motive could I possibly have had for wanting to kill him?"

"You don't know who Major was? You'd never heard his name before?"

I thought briefly, then shook my head. "No. Should I have?"

"How about Northeast Wealth Management, do you know anything about them?"

I thought some more. Still nothing.

"No. Who are they?"

"It wasn't a huge case, took place in New Jersey. But it made the New York news. NEWealth was an investment company that went bankrupt eighteen months ago, right before the holidays. Took quite a few people's money with it. It turned out that the partners were running some kind of Ponzi scheme."

I stared at him in surprise. "And Evan was a partner there?"

"No, not exactly. Something smaller than that. But he was involved. According to some, he was lucky not to end up in jail." Sturgill paused near the door. "You never heard any of this before? Major didn't mention anything about it?"

"No, nothing," I said with a frown. "All Evan told me was that he was between jobs."

The detective smirked. "Between jobs, that's a good one." Then his gaze narrowed. "One last question, since you were acquainted with the guy. The ME said that Major had an old bruise on the side of his face. Do you happen to know where it came from?"

"Evan told us he'd been in a car accident, a little fender bender. It happened on the way to our last book club meeting." I considered mentioning Evan's pristine bumper, then thought better of it. Sturgill would have access to Evan's car. He could see for himself.

Instead I said, "On Saturday at the dog show, Evan ran into a man whom he was clearly trying to avoid. The two of them got into an argument."

"About what?"

"I don't know. I couldn't hear what they were saying. But they seemed pretty angry."

"Who was the man?"

"I'm afraid I don't know that either."

Detective Sturgill looked skeptical. Like he suspected I might have made up the story to deflect attention away from myself.

"We'll look into it." He pulled a card out of his pocket and handed it to me. "If you think of anything else we should know, give me call. And if you can, this morning would be a good time to take care of those fingerprints."

The statement sounded more like a demand than a request.

"I'll see what I can do," I told him.

As soon as Detective Sturgill was gone, I went straight to Bully's crate in the kitchen. I hadn't meant to leave him confined for so long. Even though I'd mentioned the puppy, the detective hadn't asked about his whereabouts. That being the case, I'd seen no reason to remind him that I was currently in possession of Evan Major's property.

I put all the dogs outside in the yard. Then I grabbed my computer and went to join them. No surprise, it turned out that the World Wide Web was a good deal more conversant with Evan Major's past life than I had been.

I began by searching for information about the murder. There wasn't a lot of violent crime in Stamford, but so far the *Advocate* Web site had only a small article about a body having been found in a home in the Flower Estates development. The cause of death was listed as "suspicious" but was not otherwise described. Evan was not identified by name, pending notification of his next of kin. The *Advocate* promised to update its readership with new details about the crime as they became available.

I was ahead of the curve there.

Next I did a search for Northeast Wealth Management. That turned up more than a page of results. Some were from nearly two years earlier when news about the SEC investigation into the small company's business practices had first become public. Later articles discussed the resulting financial fallout, and then NEWealth's subsequent filing for bankruptcy.

The *New York Times* called the downfall a clear case of monetary malfeasance. Managing partner Wellington Cooke was referred to as a "mini Madoff." The five-man company had lured investors by guaranteeing impossibly high returns. The NEWealth partners then used new money being brought in to pay out "profits" to existing clients. The scheme had unraveled when several large clients requested their returns and the partners were forced to admit that the company lacked the necessary assets to make good.

NEWealth's four-man management team had subsequently been indicted for financial fraud. Two were now serving jail sentences. The other two currently had their cases under appeal. The fifth company employee was Evan Major. His name only appeared briefly in two of the articles. Described by his attorney as "an IT guy who had nothing to do with the company's handling of money or its investments," Evan had professed his innocence of the wrongdoing that surrounded him. Eventually he'd pled guilty to a lesser charge and received a suspended sentence and community service.

"Wow," I said out loud.

It had been too warm for the dogs to run around for long. While I'd been staring at the computer screen, the pack had returned to the deck and flopped down on the floor around me. When I started talking to myself, the Poodles lifted their heads. If there was going to be a conversation, they wanted to be part of it.

Not Bud. He was busy chewing on a piece of braided rope.

"I never would have expected this," I told them. "Evan seemed so timid. Like he couldn't hurt a fly. You guys aren't going to believe what he was involved in."

The Poodles listened eagerly. They'd met Evan at the first Bite Club meeting, which had been held in their own backyard. So they felt entitled to know what was going on. And unlike Detective Sturgill, they didn't ask too many questions.

When Bully started to pant, I picked him up and headed toward the house. There was a bowl filled with cold water inside.

"And then we'll have peanut butter biscuits," I told the others.

Bud, the only dog who hadn't seemed to be paying any attention to me at all, jumped up and beat us to the door. It figured.

Chapter 11

Alice called while we were in the kitchen. I finished handing out the treats before picking up the phone. I had my priorities straight.

"Did you hear the news about Evan?" she asked. "I can hardly believe it."

"Me either," I said. "Detective Sturgill from the Stamford PD was just here."

"You rated a visit from the police? That doesn't sound good. Come on over and let's talk. Claire is here too."

Spending time with good friends sounded like exactly what I needed. "I'll be there in half an hour," I told her.

I put Bully back in his crate, handed out another round of biscuits—what can I say, I'm a soft touch—left a note for Sam on the kitchen counter, and hit the road.

My first stop was at the police station to get fingerprinted. The process was interesting. And also a little creepy. Just the knowledge that my fingerprints were now on file somehow made me feel guilty. As soon as I'd washed the black ink off my fingers, I couldn't wait to get out of there.

Alice and Claire had originally met through me. But having become neighbors when Claire married my ex-husband, Bob, they were now friends in their own right. I liked that they got along so well. I disliked that the two of them were not above ganging up on me when they thought a situation warranted it.

It was kind of like having sisters, I supposed. Growing up with only a younger brother, I'd always longed for a sister. But now I had wonderful women friends and that was even better.

On my previous visit, Alice's front door had been standing open. Now, with a recent murder in the neighborhood, it was closed and locked. Alice and I don't stand on ceremony. I usually let myself into her house. This time I had to ring the doorbell.

"Melanie, is that you?" Alice called from the back of the house. "We're out in the yard. Come and join us."

I crossed the driveway and walked around the house. Through the fence, I could see Alice and Claire sitting on a couple of lawn chairs. Their bare feet were dangling in a blue plastic wading pool that sat in the grass between them. Berkley, the supposed watchdog, was asleep in the shade. Even when I opened the gate and entered the small yard, the Golden Retriever didn't wake up.

"Some security," I said. "What if it wasn't me? What if you'd just invited an ax murderer to come and find you?"

Abruptly I stopped. I stared at the two women in horror. "Sorry," I said. "That wasn't funny."

"Not today at any rate." Claire lifted her feet out of the pool and stood up. Barefoot, dressed in bright pink cropped pants and a scoop-neck T-shirt, she looked more like a college student than a grown-up woman who ran her own event-planning business.

She came over and gave me a hug. "Are you all right? Alice said you'd been talking to the police. We got our news from the neighborhood grapevine, and that was bad enough."

"I'm better now that I'm here," I replied gratefully. I kicked off my shoes and dragged over a nearby chair. Berkley opened one eye as it slid past his nose. Then he rolled over and went back to snoring. "Let me soak for a minute and then I'll tell you all about it."

I dipped my toes in the water, testing the temperature. It was shockingly cold. Perfect. I plunged my feet below the surface. When my toes touched bottom, the water came halfway up to my knees. I closed my eyes and sighed. This was bliss.

"Feels great, doesn't it?" said Alice. "Joe and I bought this pool when the kids were small enough to think they could actually swim in it. We ended up keeping it because Berkley gets hot in the summer and sometimes he likes to take a dip. But this morning I thought, why should the dog have all the fun? So I emptied it out and refilled it."

I opened one eye. "How'd you get the water so cold?"

"Ice." Claire grinned. "We added some right before you got here. We thought you might need a little cooling off."

"You thought right," I agreed. "Let's compare notes. What have you heard?"

It only took a few minutes to ascertain that we'd all heard the same basic story. I didn't know whether to be alarmed or reassured that the local grapevine was just as well informed as the Stamford police. Or at least what Detective Sturgill had chosen to tell me.

"Detective Sturgill," Alice said thoughtfully. "I don't know him."

I slanted my head her way. "Do you know any policemen?"

"Well . . . no," she admitted. "But let me fantasize for a moment without jumping in and wrecking the illusion, okay? I'm just trying to pretend that my life is as exciting as yours."

"Oh please. You know perfectly well you wouldn't trade lives with anybody."

"Try me," she said with a laugh.

Alice was bluffing. I ignored that and changed the subject. "Listen," I said. "You guys haven't heard the most interesting thing that happened this morning."

Claire cocked a brow. "More interesting than a murder right around the corner?"

"Maybe. And it's related."

Both women sat up and gave me their full attention.

"It turns out that Evan wasn't what he appeared to be."

"He appeared to be a mild-mannered nerd who could barely figure out how to shop for food, much less manage his own social life," Alice said. "So . . . what? Did he turn into Batman after dark or something?"

"Unfortunately, it was nothing as exciting as that. But he did have a past."

Alice waved a hand in the air indolently. "Don't we all?"

Claire and I both stared. That was news.

Alice looked at the expressions on our faces and laughed. "Sorry. Just fantasizing again. Go on."

"Do either of you remember hearing a news story about a company named Northeast Wealth Management? They went bankrupt last year, and most of their clients lost all their money."

The two women glanced at each other. Both shook their heads.

"No, but I can look it up if you want," Claire volunteered.

"I already did that after Detective Sturgill left. He's the one who told me about it. Apparently Evan had been implicated in a major financial scandal before he moved to Connecticut."

I spent the next five minutes outlining everything I'd learned. As they listened, Claire and Alice began to look increasingly incredulous. I couldn't blame them. I'd felt much the same way.

"You mean he nearly went to jail?" Alice said at the end.

"We were living around the corner from a felon?" Claire asked.

"Sort of," I replied. "Although I don't think Evan was ever charged with a felony. Because in the end, his lawyers were able to get him off with a suspended sentence and community service. After his legal problems were finally settled in New Jersey, he must have moved to Connecticut to make a fresh start."

"I thought Evan moved here after a messy divorce," Alice said. "Not that he ever said that exactly. It was just the impression I got."

"I wonder if the prosecution and the scandal is what led to his divorce," I mused.

"Who cares about that?" Claire asked. "The divorce is nothing. It's the rest of this business that's so alarming. How did we not know any of this before today? We befriended Evan. We invited him to join the book club . . . and now it turns out that all along he was a criminal."

"At least he didn't go to jail," I mentioned.

Claire grimaced. "Is that supposed to make me feel better?"

"I guess white collar crime isn't the *worst* thing," Alice decided. "I mean, it's not like he was a member of the Mafia." She glanced at me for confirmation. "Right?"

"I hope not. But at this point, who knows?" I winked at Claire. "Maybe Evan had another secret life that we haven't discovered yet. Maybe he was a Russian spy in his spare time."

"Okay, now you guys are just making fun of me." Claire dipped her foot in the pool and kicked a spray of water in my direction.

I dodged to one side but I wasn't fast enough. Most of the water landed in my lap anyway. I'd probably deserved that.

"Detective Sturgill told me something else," I said. "The reason he showed up at my house this morning is because

Bella Barrundy told him that she'd seen me sneaking around Evan's place at around the time he was killed."

"You're kidding." Claire frowned.

"I wish I was," I replied.

"Umm . . ." Alice raised her hand. "Can I say something?"

"We're not in school," I told her. "Speak up."

She refolded her hand in her lap. "Two things. First, I figured the reason the detective came to talk to you is because they just naturally think of you whenever a problem arises."

"Gee, thanks."

"And second—not that I don't love you dearly and would swear under oath that this isn't true—but *weren't* you sneaking around Evan's house yesterday afternoon?"

"Sneaking makes me sound bad," I said. "I might have called it strolling around. And besides, I had a totally legitimate reason for being there. Evan and I had an appointment to work on Bully's training."

"Yes, but Bella wouldn't have known that," Claire pointed out. "She was probably just trying to be helpful."

"Helpful?" I yelped. "She turned me into a suspect. Not only that, but how did she even notice me? I wasn't there long. Does Bella sit inside her house and stare out at the street all day?"

"Could be," Alice muttered.

"Could be what?" I asked.

"Didn't you ever notice the way Bella acted around Evan? She'd get all giggly and calf-eyed. Like she was a teenage girl rather than a woman in her forties. I think she had a crush on him."

"On dweebie Evan Major?" The notion was difficult to contemplate. And even more difficult to believe. "Seriously?"

"Think about it," Alice replied. "Single men are pretty thin on the ground around here. Maybe at her age, she figured beggars couldn't be choosers. Or maybe she actually thought Evan was hot."

We all pondered that for a moment. Then we all shook our heads.

"Nope," I said. "That's not it."

"I do know that when Evan first moved in, she invited him to her house for dinner," Alice told us. "Evan thought that was pretty pushy of her since they'd only known each other for, like, five minutes."

"Did he go?" I asked.

"No, he made up an excuse and declined."

"Now that you mention it," said Claire, "I remember Evan looking surprised when Bella showed up at our second Bite Club meeting. And he looked even more surprised when she said she'd come because he'd invited her."

"Really?" said Alice. "I missed that."

"You were probably too busy sniffing the mac and cheese dish Bella'd brought with her to wonder what she was doing there," I said with a laugh.

"You're probably right," Alice agreed. She leaned back in her chair and tipped her face up toward the sun. "The police don't really suspect you, do they?"

"Right now, I think they suspect everyone." I tried not to sound too concerned.

"Then you'll have to look into what happened, won't you?" said Claire. "If the police think you might be guilty, you don't have a choice."

"I'd imagine that Detective Sturgill wouldn't agree with you about that."

"We don't care what he thinks," Alice replied stoutly. "He's on the other side."

The other side. I liked the sound of that. It made me feel like Claire and Alice were my posse.

"Sturgill made me go to the police station and get fingerprinted," I mentioned. "I stopped and had it done on the way here."

"For real?" Claire said with interest. "What was it like?"

"Kind of weird," I said. "Not something I'd like to repeat."

Alice looked up. "That was because you were inside Evan's house?"

I nodded. "How about you?"

"Just once. Right after he moved in. I took him a plant." She paused and thought back. "I only stepped a few feet inside the door. I don't think I touched anything. Not that there was much to touch."

"Talk about weird . . ." Claire muttered.

Alice looked startled. I just laughed.

"Get your mind out of the gutter," I told Claire. "Alice was referring to Evan's lack of furniture."

"Oh." Her face went red. "That makes sense."

"That reminds me," Alice said. "Where's Evan's puppy? What's going to happen to him now?"

"Bully's still at my house," I told her. "He's fine there for now, but with six dogs already, I can't keep him indefinitely."

Alice glanced in Berkley's direction. The Golden Retriever was beginning to stir. "Don't look at me. One dog is plenty for us. Joe would kill me if I brought home another."

"I can't take him either," said Claire. She had two rescue dogs she'd inherited from her late brother. "You know Thor and Jojo. Neither one of them plays well with others."

"What about Peg?" asked Alice.

Obviously we should have started there. There was nothing Aunt Peg liked more than championing the cause of a dog in need. Over the winter, she'd taken in a homeless Maltese. And now Bully had suffered the same fate. Until the authorities figured out who the puppy belonged to, he could serve as her next project.

"I'll check with her when I get a chance," I said. "I'm sure she'll be willing to help out."

The water in the wading pool was growing warm in the sun. I lifted out my feet and put them in the grass to dry. Sam and Kevin would be home by now. It was probably time for me to move along.

I'd just reached for my shoes when I heard Alice sigh. Loudly.

"What?" I asked.

"I can't help but feel guilty about what happened to Evan," she said in a small voice.

"Why?"

"Because I was the one who dragged him out of his shell, introduced him around, and made him do stuff. I got him to join Bite Club. I was even bugging him to sign up for a gym membership. How stupid is that?"

"It wasn't stupid at all," said Claire. "You were trying to be helpful."

"And look how *that* ended up," Alice replied unhappily.

"That's silly," I said. "None of the things you did with Evan had anything to do with his death."

"You don't know that. What if they did? What if he moved to Connecticut to live a quiet life where he could be anonymous and everybody would leave him alone—and then I came along and ruined everything? It just feels like I must be responsible somehow."

I shook my head at her logic. "You only think that because you're a mother. We feel responsible for everything. Like the fate of the world rests on our shoulders. Which it probably does in most cases. But this time you're being ridiculous."

Alice didn't believe me. She sighed again. "I know you're trying to make me feel better. But you know what would really do that? If this crime could be solved so I don't have to put my kids to bed at night knowing that we live in a neighborhood where a murderer is running loose. I wish the police would hurry up and fix that for me. Or you would. Either way is fine. As long as somebody gets to the bottom of things. And quickly."

With our shared history, I'd do almost anything for Alice. Just as she'd do the same for me.

And I had to admit that I *was* curious. Surely a little poking around wouldn't hurt anything. At least not much.

Chapter 12

There was a dog show on Saturday near Hartford. Aunt Peg had been hired to judge more than a dozen Toy and Non-Sporting breeds. Sam was taking the boys to the beach for the day. I was going to the show with Aunt Peg. She and I had a lot to talk about.

It would also give me the opportunity to meet Crawford's new friend, Gabe, and see what I thought of him. I understood that Terry was worried. But I couldn't bring myself to believe that his concerns had merit. At least not until I'd seen some evidence of that for myself.

Aunt Peg's judging duties meant that she needed to be at the dog show early. It wasn't much past dawn when she arrived at my house. Even though I'd already had my first cup of coffee, I probably still looked a little bleary-eyed when I climbed into her minivan.

"Buckle up," she said.

The advice wasn't a courtesy. Aunt Peg piloted her minivan like a race car driver. She also possessed the uncanny ability to talk her way out of speeding tickets, which meant there was no official deterrent to her behavior. When I'm wide awake, riding shotgun with Aunt Peg can be an alarming prospect. I didn't think that would be a problem today.

Apparently I was wrong.

"Wake up!" Aunt Peg reached over and slapped me on the knee. "What's the matter with you? I didn't offer to drive so you could sit there in silence like a lump of clay."

I opened one eye. At this hour on a Saturday, the roads were mostly empty. We'd made it from my house to the Merritt Parkway in record time. I grabbed the armrest beside me as we went careening up the on-ramp.

"Sorry." I straightened in my seat and checked the clasp on my seat belt. It was holding firm. "I didn't get much sleep last night."

Aunt Peg slanted me a look. "I should hope not, with a member of your book club turning up dead. That would make anyone lose sleep."

Note that now that there was a problem, Bite Club was once again *my* book club.

"If you promise to keep your eyes on the road," I said, "I'll tell you everything I know."

Usually when I was bringing Aunt Peg up to speed on something, she pelted me with questions. Today she said nothing. I hoped that was because she was concentrating on her driving.

Nope. Instead, it turned out that she wasn't impressed by what she was hearing.

"That's it?" she said at the end.

"What do you mean?"

"I read a more complete account than that in this morning's newspaper."

Once the authorities had released Evan Major's name to the media, news outlets had picked up the story and run with it. Now I doubted there was anyone in lower Fairfield County who wasn't aware of both the murder and Evan's past legal troubles.

"Oh, really?" I said. "Did the paper inform you that I currently have custody of Evan's puppy, Bully? Or that Bella Barrundy told the police that they should consider me a suspect? Or that Alice is afraid she somehow got Evan involved in something that led to his death?"

"It took you long enough to get around to the useful details," Aunt Peg muttered. Then she twisted in her seat to face me. "Alice thinks she's responsible? That's ridiculous."

"That's what I told her."

"It's much more likely that someone from Evan's shady past came back to exact retribution." Her eyes had returned to the road, but now Aunt Peg was frowning. "I wish I'd known about all that before Evan went toes up. I haven't met many criminals. It would have been fascinating to pick his brain."

"That's probably just what he didn't want," I told her. "It wouldn't surprise me if that's why Evan was always so quiet. I imagine he had no desire to talk about his past."

"Oh pish," said Aunt Peg. "It's not like I'd have given him a choice."

There was that. Aunt Peg was like a bulldozer in low gear when she saw something she wanted. And heaven help the person who got in her way. I stared straight ahead through the windshield. The scenery was zooming past at an alarming rate of speed.

"So Bella Barrundy ratted you out?" Aunt Peg mused aloud. She did love her gangster lingo. "That's interesting."

"Not to me," I grumbled. "I'm thinking about booting her out of the book club."

"You can't do that."

"Why not?"

"Well, for one thing, I'm not sure you actually *can* do it," Aunt Peg said. "At least not without taking a vote among the other members."

"Who decided that?" I asked. "Are you making up new rules as you go along?"

Aunt Peg ignored the query, as I'd suspected she might.

"And second," she continued blithely, "Bella lives on the same street Evan did—and apparently she likes to keep tabs on what's going on in the neighborhood. Who better to keep us apprised of any new developments?"

Evan's house was empty. Why would anything be happening there now? Then I stopped and thought. On the other hand, if Aunt Peg had Bella as her personal source for inside information, that would keep her off my case. Which could only be a good thing.

"Okay," I agreed. "Bella can stay."

I must have given in too easily, because Aunt Peg looked at me suspiciously. I did my best to look entirely innocent. Apparently I succeeded well enough because Aunt Peg moved on.

"Now tell me about Bully," she said.

I was surprised it had taken her so long to ask. In any conversation, Aunt Peg usually wanted to hear about the dog first.

"He's a Bulldog. He's three months old and totally adorable," I told her. "He's fine at my house for now, but I was hoping you might be willing to foster him for a longer term until things get sorted out."

"What about his breeder? Will he or she take him back?"

"I have no idea. Evan said he got the puppy through an ad on Craigslist."

"Oh." Aunt Peg sighed. "That doesn't sound promising. Yes, of course he can come and stay with me. Poor boy, there's already been a great deal of upheaval in his young life. I'd be happy to offer him some stability for as long as he needs it."

We drove in silence for a while. As we neared the showground, Aunt Peg spoke up again. "According to this morning's paper, Evan's funeral will be held on Monday at the Blackwood Funeral Home in Stamford. I'm planning to attend. I assume you will too?"

The news came as a surprise. "This is the first I've heard of it. Evan told me that he didn't have any family. So I wonder who made the arrangements? And why would they bury him here rather than in New Jersey?"

"Good questions," said Aunt Peg. "Maybe we can get some answers on Monday. In the meantime, I thought I'd call the other Bite Club members and make sure everybody knows about the service. It would be terrible if no one turned out to bid him good-bye."

That ended our trip on a somber note. Aunt Peg ditched the minivan in the judges' parking lot. She took off at a brisk pace toward the officials' tent, leaving me behind to fend for myself. Luckily, I was good at that. Especially when I was at a dog show and there were plenty of interesting things to see and do.

Without even stopping to think, I headed toward the handlers' tent. Although it was early, Crawford and Terry had their setup in place and both were hard at work. None of the three Poodle varieties would be judged until late morning, but several Poodles were already sitting out on tabletops. The handling team's most labor-intensive breed, they always received the first attention. Terry was brushing out a Standard. Crawford was slickering the bracelets on a Mini.

As I made my way toward them, I saw Gabe Summers approaching their setup from the other side. Tall and broad, and carrying a flimsy cardboard tray holding three full cups of coffee, he nevertheless managed to slither between the tightly packed crates and tables with surprising grace.

And yup, he still had the Adonis thing going on. Or maybe it was Thor. Either way, it was hard not to stare.

"Coffee's here," he said, setting the tray down on top of a crate.

Crawford looked up and smiled.

Terry just glowered. Usually he's the happiest person

around—the one who cheers up everyone else. I hated to see that sour expression on his face.

"Good morning, everyone," I said brightly. All three gazes swung my way.

"You're here early," said Crawford. He grabbed a coffee cup, opened the top, and took a sip.

"I came with Aunt Peg. She's judging."

As if they didn't already know. They'd entered under her, after all.

When she'd started her judging career, Aunt Peg had been approved for just one breed: Poodles. Crawford had declined to show under her then, aware that their friendship might give other exhibitors thoughts of impropriety. But now that she judged all the Toy and Non-Sporting breeds—the two groups that made up the majority of Crawford's business—he'd had to put aside his reservations. As for Aunt Peg, she left no doubt about her impartiality in the show ring. She treated Crawford neither better nor worse than anyone else who exhibited under her.

"She is going to *love* Crawford's Mini bitch," Terry said. He gestured toward the other grooming table. "Just wait and see."

"Let's not get ahead of ourselves," Crawford cautioned him. "We still have a long day of judging to get through. Melanie, have you met Gabe?"

"Not yet." I smiled and held out my hand.

Gabe's hand dwarfed mine, but his grip was surprisingly gentle. "Gabe Summers," he said. "It's a pleasure to meet you. Are you a friend of Crawford's?"

"Crawford and Terry both," I told him. "I've known them for a long time."

"Melanie and her family have Standard Poodles," Crawford told him. "Her aunt, Peg Turnbull, is judging today."

"She drew a big entry," said Gabe. "She must be pretty smart."

Chapter 13

It wasn't until I was walking away that I realized that neither Terry nor I had said a word about Evan's precipitous death. Nor the investigation surrounding it, and his upcoming funeral. On any other day—pre–Gabe Summers—the topic would have been at the forefront of our thoughts. Terry and I would have dissected it minutely. Even Crawford would have been drawn reluctantly into the conversation.

And yet today, the subject hadn't even arisen. That fact, more than anything else I'd seen, was a measure of how upset Terry was about Gabe's presence in Crawford's life. I had to do something to help. But unfortunately I had no idea what.

While I waited for the show to settle into stride, I took a tour of the concession stands. I ended up with a show catalog and a snow cone for myself and a new beaded leash for Aunt Peg. When I arrived at her ring a few minutes later, she was judging a decent sized entry of Japanese Chin.

The small, playful dogs were stylish and intelligent. When they moved, their silky hair rippled in the breeze. The Chin in the ring looked like they were having a good time and Aunt Peg did too. I grabbed an open chair and took a seat.

My catalog told me I was watching the Open Dog class.

I laughed. "Aunt Peg would certainly agree with you about that."

Throughout the exchange, Terry had remained silent. And focused on the Standard Poodle in front of him on the table. The third cup of coffee, presumably his, was still sitting, untouched, in the tray. I lifted it out and offered it to him.

Reluctantly, Terry accepted it from me.

"Stop sulking," I said to him under my breath.

"Stop smiling at him," he shot back.

Crawford glanced at the two of us quizzically. He had to be wondering what we were talking about.

"Everything's fine," I told him. "We're discussing the weather."

"What weather?" the handler asked. "It's eighty degrees and sunny. Couldn't be better."

"You do a great job of showing dogs in any weather," Gabe said to Crawford.

Terry muttered something uncomplimentary. So help me I wanted to kick him. And hopefully knock some sense into him. I'd never seen Terry like this before. I wanted my carefree buddy back, not this glum, scowling facsimile.

"You're making things worse," I told him.

"Well, it's not as if you're helping," he snapped.

I turned my back on him. Like that would improve things.

"Where are you from, Gabe?" I asked politely.

"Rochester, New York," he replied. "Snow country."

Surely not in July, I thought, taken aback. Then it occurred to me that maybe while I'd been distracted by Terry the weather conversation had continued. That would be weird. How much was there to say about the weather?

"Have you known Crawford long?"

Gabe's smile was friendly, his expression guileless. He looked like a man who had nothing at all to hide. "We'd met before but we hadn't had a chance to really get to know one another until recently. Crawford and my mother are old friends. When I started thinking about a career in dogs for myself, she told me I should look him up. So I did."

"Crawford's the best," I said. "You could learn a lot from him."

"That's what my Mom said. And she was right. It's an education just watching him handle a dog."

I'd never given any thought to Crawford's youth. The image of him that I had in my mind—always at a dog show with a beautiful Poodle at the end of his leash—was so indelibly imprinted that it was as if he'd never existed anywhere else.

"Does your mother show dogs too?"

"No way." Gabe chuckled. "She's not even slightly interested in this kind of stuff. She likes cats."

"People show cats too," I said. Okay, that was dumb. But it was getting harder and harder to give Gabe the third degree with Crawford standing right there. I tried again. "Have you given any thought to which breeds you might want to specialize in?"

"Not Poodles," Gabe blurted out. Then his face reddened. "No offense or anything. But their grooming is way too intense for me. I want to show athletic dogs. Ones you can run around the ring with."

Another time, Crawford would have stepped in to defend his favorite breed. He'd have said that Poodles *were* athletes, that they made great retrievers and agility dogs. But now he inexplicably remained silent. I hoped it wasn't because he didn't want to contradict Gabe.

Terry didn't say a word either. His silence was easier to explain, however. He'd barely said a word since Gabe had entered the setup.

The loudspeaker crackled with static, putting an end to our labored conversation. An announcer came on and told us that the show was about to begin. Maybe it was my imagination, but it felt like all four of us sighed with relief.

"I'm going to go walk around and see who else is here," I said. "And watch Aunt Peg do some judging. Gabe, I'd be happy to have you join me if you feel like it."

"No, thank you. I think I'd rather hang out here. Crawford doesn't mind. And who knows? Maybe I can make myself useful."

Terry made a noise. It sounded like he was choking on a bone. Or maybe he was considering choking Gabe—who had possibly just implied that Terry's capable assistance wasn't good enough.

"Whatever works." I reached over and thumped Terry on the back. That earned me a sideways glare. "I'll check back later. Good luck today, Crawford."

"Thank you," he replied. "We'll need it."

That was Crawford's standard reply to well wishers. I'd heard him say it dozens of times. Even though we all knew that his success in the show ring owed little to luck, and much to the skills he'd honed so carefully over the years.

But today was different, I thought. Suddenly it seemed as though Crawford did need a stroke of good fortune. He and Terry both did. Because I'd begun to realize that Terry had been right. There was a chance that I was watching something rare and precious unravel right before my eyes.

Crawford didn't seem to be aware of that yet. I could only hope he figured it out before it was too late.

Three black and white dogs were entered. The decision between them must have been a close one because Aunt Peg
took her time determining how she wanted to place them.

After a few seconds, I joined the other people watching
from ringside and began judging along with her. No matter that the official judge was the only one who could in-
spect each dog's bite, or feel the bodies that lay beneath
their coats, we all felt qualified to have an opinion too.
Who says dog shows aren't a spectator sport?

Aunt Peg motioned the third Chin, shown by a blond
woman in a formfitting turquoise suit, to the head of the
line. I'd been looking at the dogs rather than their handlers, but as she turned I realized that the exhibitor in
front was Felicity Barber. The reason she'd turned was to
shoot a triumphant glare at the man now standing behind
her. I remembered Terry mentioning at the book club
meeting that Felicity was a cutthroat competitor. Apparently he'd been right.

Aunt Peg sent the three Chins around the ring and
pinned her class. Felicity accepted her blue ribbon, stuffed
it into her pocket, and quickly moved her dog back into
place for the judging of the Winners class. The red-and-
white Puppy winner reentered the ring.

An entry of four meant that there was a major on the line.
It didn't matter that it wasn't my breed, or that I was barely
acquainted with any of the participants. The thought of a
major still was enough to put me on the edge of my seat. I
leaned forward in anticipation.

Felicity's body language made it clear she thought the
judging was only a formality. She obviously expected to
have her dog quickly named the winner. Instead, Aunt Peg
took her time. She was aware that there was a major to be
had too. She wanted to be sure that the points went to the
most deserving entrant.

The puppy was clearly young, and not as well-behaved
as the Open dog. Aunt Peg had judged him as a single entry

in his class only minutes earlier. Nevertheless, she now crouched down and put her hands on him again. Then she took a long look back and forth between the two Chins.

Felicity's lips pursed in annoyance as the puppy continued to receive the attention she clearly thought was her dog's due. I knew the woman was an experienced and successful exhibitor. Which made it all the more surprising that she hadn't learned to hide her emotions better.

Or maybe, I realized, she was letting her disdain show on purpose. It wasn't unheard of for an influential handler to try and intimidate a judge. Abruptly, I bit back a laugh. If Felicity thought she'd be successful at that, she didn't know my aunt very well. Aunt Peg was the Queen of Intimidation.

Aunt Peg stood up again. Ignoring Felicity, she looked at her Chin one last time. Then she reversed the order of the two dogs.

"I'll have them just the way they are," she said when the red-and-white puppy was in front. "Winners, and Reserve."

Felicity snatched her dog up off the ground. For a few seconds, it looked as though she was going to storm out of the ring without waiting for her striped ribbon. Her losing ribbon. That behavior would have been a severe breach of dog show etiquette—not to mention an insult to Aunt Peg.

Then she obviously thought better of it. Grudgingly she stepped over to the placement markers. She took her position behind the puppy whose handler was bubbling with excitement over the major win. It couldn't have helped Felicity's mood that while she waited for her ribbon, she had to listen to that exhibitor thank Aunt Peg effusively.

"His first points and his first major," he said, pumping Aunt Peg's hand up and down as he accepted his purple ribbon. "You have made my day!"

"He's a nice puppy and a deserving winner," Aunt Peg replied. "I'm sure you'll do very well with him."

The steward called Puppy Bitch class into the ring, but Felicity didn't stay around to watch the rest of her breed's judging. She quickly exited the ring and dropped the Reserve Winners ribbon in the nearest trash can. Dog clutched beneath her arm, she strode angrily down the length of the tent that ran between the two rows of rings.

I followed a few steps behind. Since she was a fellow Bite Club member, I was curious to hear what her take on Evan's death might be. But I didn't see any point in approaching her until she'd had a chance to cool off.

Felicity marched across the narrow strip of open space at the end of the rings. She looked to be heading for the handlers' tent. I continued to hang back, giving her time to regain her composure.

When I approached her setup five minutes later, Felicity glanced up at me with no sign of recognition. The Chin had been stowed inside a small crate. Felicity was rolling up the towel that had covered the top of her matted grooming table. She appeared to be packing up.

"Who are you?" she asked.

"Melanie Travis."

Felicity could hardly have looked less interested.

"We met the other night."

Still nothing.

"At the book club meeting?"

"Oh. I guess so." She opened a small bag and jammed the towel inside.

"It sounded as though you really enjoyed reading *Bootlegger's Daughter*."

"I did." Finally there was a bit of a thaw in her demeanor. "That was a terrific book. And it was by an author who was new to me so that was great." Then she stopped and frowned. "But I'm not sure the book club is going to work out for me."

"No?" I tried to sound surprised. If Felicity didn't know who I was, then she also didn't know that I was related to

Aunt Peg. I had no intention of enlightening her. "I'm sorry to hear that."

"Yeah, well, so am I, I guess."

"Your dog looked great in the ring," I said.

"You were watching the judging?"

I nodded.

"He should have won," Felicity stated firmly.

"I thought so too." Okay, so I had my fingers crossed behind my back. And what did I know about Japanese Chin anyway? My opinion on the breed was pretty much meaningless.

Felicity didn't care about my credentials however. She just liked that my opinion agreed with hers. "I'm glad that everyone *outside the ring* knew a good Chin when they saw one. Today's win would have finished my dog. Not only that, but we would have had a chance in the group."

I was pretty sure I hadn't been speaking for everyone at ringside. Not to mention that to get to the Toy Group, Felicity's dog would have had to beat the Japanese Chin special. And the Winners Bitch. Apparently the woman didn't lack for confidence. Or maybe that was hubris.

"It was terrible what happened to Evan Major, wasn't it?" I said.

"Who?" she asked—then belatedly made the connection. "Oh, you mean the car accident? I wouldn't worry about it. He didn't seem upset. I'm sure he'll be fine."

"Fine?" The word choked in my throat. "No, Evan won't be fine. I guess you haven't heard?"

Felicity had returned to packing her things. She was lining up a row of brushes and combs in her tack box. She glanced back over her shoulder. "Heard what?"

"Evan died a few days ago. He was murdered in his home."

"No." She spun around. "Really?"

"I'm afraid so. I can't believe you didn't know. It's been all over the news."

Felicity shrugged. "I avoid the news as much as possible. Politics, terrorists, people protesting just about everything. Who wants to hear about that stuff?" Then her gaze sharpened. "Who killed him?"

"The police don't know yet. I was wondering if you had any ideas."

"Me? Why would I? I barely knew the guy. I don't think we said three words to each other all night."

"Evan was pretty quiet," I said. "He didn't talk much to anyone."

"I guess that turns out to be a good thing, doesn't it?" Felicity snapped her tack box shut. She was good to go. "It means his loss won't make much of an impression on the group."

I opened my mouth to reply, but no words came out. *Wow*, I thought. That was cold. Cold enough to make me shiver despite the summer warmth.

I backed away. "Good luck next time," I said.

"Thanks." Felicity's face relaxed into a smile. She'd finally gotten over her fit of pique. I hoped Evan's death hadn't cheered her up.

I spent the next few hours spectating at Aunt Peg's ring. Her judging was meticulous and based on a wealth of knowledge. She also had a wonderful hand on a dog and endless patience for the antics of inexperienced puppies. Exhibitors who showed under her knew that while they might not agree with her placements, they could always expect a fair and impartial assessment of their dogs.

And once again, Terry had been right. Aunt Peg did love Crawford's Mini bitch. She awarded her Best of Variety.

Early afternoon, I grabbed lunch at the food concession and headed to the Greyhound ring. The entire entry was just four Greyhounds, so I didn't dare be late. Thanks to the catalog, I knew that Jeff Schwin would be showing both a class dog and a class bitch.

I retained only a vague impression of Jeff from the time we'd spent at the book club meeting. I remembered that he was tall and wore glasses, and that he'd liked Margaret Maron's book. Jeff and I had happened to take seats on opposite sides of the room, which had prevented us from having any kind of personal conversation. Now I was hoping to remedy that.

Salukis were the breed before Greyhounds. Their judging was wrapping up when I arrived at the ring. Jeff was standing near the gate, armband in place, ready to go. Except for one thing. He was currently holding two Greyhounds—one in each hand.

Unlike professional handlers, whose assistants were ever ready to juggle extra dogs at ringside, owner handlers with multiple entries often had to depend on the kindness of other exhibitors for help. Or of friendly book club members, as the case might be.

I walked over and smiled. "You look like you could use a hand."

Jeff's head swiveled my way. Up close, he looked to be around forty. He had friendly brown eyes, lightly pockmarked cheeks, and two slightly crooked front teeth. He also looked relieved.

"Oh boy, could I. A friend was supposed to meet me here, but she must have gotten held up. You're Melanie, right? We met at Bite Club. Sorry, I don't remember your last name. Oh, look, they're already calling dogs. I have to go." He extended the hand that held the bitch's leash. "Do you mind? This won't take long."

That was when I remembered the other thing I knew about him. Jeff talked fast. Words tumbled out of him so quickly that his thoughts all seemed to run together.

Now he didn't even pause to wait for my reply. My fingers had barely closed over the end of the lead before Jeff was hurrying through the gate into the ring. The brindle bitch looked up at me quizzically, as if she was assessing my fitness to be her temporary guardian. I ran a reassuring hand down her muscular back. You had to love a dog with no hair to mess up.

Jeff was right. The judging didn't take long. With just two Open dogs to decide between, the judge had the pair out of his ring within minutes. Jeff's dog lost. He accepted his ribbons philosophically.

The brindle bitch and I were waiting for him right beside the in-gate. We switched Greyhounds, he switched armbands, and then he was gone again, back to the ring. Now I had a blue dog to hold. He accepted me with the same equanimity the bitch had shown. Together we moved to one side, out of the way.

This time the judging went in Jeff's favor. The brindle was awarded Winners Bitch. She then competed against the Winners Dog for Best of Breed. Jeff looked perfectly happy when she ended up with the lesser award of Best of Opposite Sex.

"Another day, another point," he said, when he came to collect his blue dog. "Could be worse. Thanks for helping out."

"It's nice to see someone who's happy even when everything doesn't go their way," I said. We walked out from beneath the tent together.

"What, you mean the dog?" Jeff nodded downward. "I knew he was never going to win. I only brought him along to make sure the point would hold. It'd be a shame to come all this way for nothing. But now Lily's up to twelve. One more major and she'll be done. Thanks again. If you ever need a hand yourself, just let me know."

"Actually there is something you could do for me."

Jeff had started to walk away. He stopped and turned back. "What's that?"

"Tell me what you thought of Evan Major."

Abruptly Jeff's face fell. I hoped I hadn't ruined his happy day.

"Oh." He frowned. "The guy who died. That was terrible, wasn't it? Murder, they said. In Stamford, of all places. I'm from Ridgefield myself. You don't think of things like that happening around here. At least I don't. What do you want to know?"

"Anything you think is useful," I said. "Any thoughts you have about why he might have been killed."

"I'm afraid I can't help you with that. I just met Evan the other night. He and I chatted a bit before the meeting started. I gather he was new to the area. It turned out that we were both divorced. That gave us something to gripe about a little. But beyond that . . ." Jeff shrugged. "The rest of what I know is just the stuff the media's been talking about. I certainly wouldn't have figured Evan to be the kind of guy who almost ended up in jail."

"Me either," I said when he paused to take a breath. "I think that came as a shock to everybody."

"Well, not everybody," Jeff pointed out. "Somebody must have known. Someone was looking for payback, don't you think?"

"Maybe—" I began, but Jeff was still rolling.

"I'll tell you what though. It makes me rethink whether or not I should go to the next meeting. I love to read. Heck, I can blast through three or four books a week. Peg Turnbull's the one who told me about the book club. She's a nice lady and I'm sure she meant well. And combining socializing and reading seemed like a good idea. But I read for relaxation, you know?"

This time I just nodded. It didn't even slow down the stream of words.

"But it's not relaxing to belong to a club where people are getting killed." Jeff finally paused. Like he thought he'd said something profound and he wanted to ponder it for a while. He started to walk away again.

When I didn't follow, he turned back to have the last word. "Maybe the other Bite Club members will feel differently. But as far as I'm concerned, that's not what I signed up for at all."

Chapter 14

Terry waylaid me on my way back to Aunt Peg's ring. I'd stopped to admire a class of Afghan Hounds that were gaiting in unison when he popped up beside me and grabbed my arm.

"*So?*" he said urgently.

I jumped in place. Like any normal woman would under the circumstances. Then I realized who it was.

"What?" I said.

"You know what." He sounded snippy. "What have you found out about Gabe?"

"Nothing yet," I admitted. "Just what you heard us talking about earlier."

"Well, hurry *up!*"

I turned and stared at him. "What do you expect me to do—walk up to Gabe and ask him if he has the hots for Crawford?"

Terry actually paused to consider the idea. "That might work."

"No, it won't. Because I'm not doing it."

I'd have thought that was obvious. But in Terry's current state of mind, apparently not.

I turned back to the ring. The Afghans were now under the tent. Four were relaxing with their handlers. The fifth was being examined by the judge.

I didn't know anything about Afghans aside from the fact that they were incredibly beautiful hounds. But I pretended to be watching the judging anyway. What I really wanted was for this conversation with Terry to be over. I hoped that if I ignored him long enough, he would go away.

"How about this?" he said. "What if you just warn Gabe off?"

"Warn him off?" I repeated incredulously. "*Warn him off?* You must be mad. Why would Gabe pay any attention to that? He doesn't even know me."

"He knows you're a friend of Crawford's."

"So are you," I pointed out.

Terry rolled his eyes. "Well, *obviously* I can't tell him to get lost."

"Why not?"

"Because then I would look bad. I would come off like some sort of catty, jealous, uptight—"

"If the shoe fits," I said.

That earned me a glare.

"Terry," I said gently, "you know Crawford loves you."

"Well, sure," he replied. He didn't sound sure at all. "But maybe that isn't enough."

I turned my back on the dogs in the ring and really looked at him. "What do you mean?"

"When Crawford and I first got together," he said, "I thought he was lucky to have me. I was a cute young guy at the top of my game. I mean, come on, look at me. I look like a Ralph Lauren model. And Crawford was . . . you know . . . older and kind of staid. He needed someone like me to liven up his life."

I nodded. Terry was right. Crawford *had* changed when the two of them became a couple. The handler had become less intense. His dark moods had lightened. He could even occasionally crack a joke now.

Terry frowned before continuing. "But now I realize

that I had it all wrong in the beginning. Crawford is my rock. He's the best man I've ever known. I don't just love him, I admire everything about him. What an idiot I was to ever think that Crawford was lucky to have me—when all along *I* was the one who was incredibly lucky to have him."

"Oh, Terry." I might have been sniffling. "That's beautiful."

"It's the truth," he said softly. "Crawford has enriched my life in more ways than I can count. I don't know what I would do without him."

"Don't say that. Don't even think it. Because you're never going to find out."

"That's not what Gabe thinks."

In the ring, the judge was handing out ribbons. I'd been rooting for the silver Afghan because I thought she was pretty. The judge gave Best of Breed to a black dog. A red bitch was Best Opposite. The silver left the ring without a ribbon. That was why Aunt Peg was a judge and I wasn't.

I looked back at Terry. He'd pled his case. Now he was waiting in silence for me to speak.

"I'll go talk to Gabe," I said.

Terry wrapped his arms around me. "Thank you."

"I'm probably an idiot," I muttered. I stepped back and poked his chest with my finger. "And if I get into trouble with Crawford, *you're* going to fix it."

"Not me," said Terry. "Peg. She'll put in a good word for you."

I wasn't so sure about that. Especially not if she knew what I'd been up to.

"Let's hope it doesn't come to that." I glanced down at my watch. Aunt Peg still had at least another hour's worth of judging to do. "Do you know where Gabe is now?"

"Crawford's at the Tibetan Terrier ring." Terry briefly looked guilty. "He thinks I'm back at the setup working on his Chow. I'm sure you'll find Gabe wherever Crawford is. So probably outside the Tibbie ring."

We headed off in two different directions, Terry looking pleased with himself and me looking like a prisoner on the way to her execution. I felt for Terry, I really did. But I was pretty sure that this task he'd set for me was impossible. Still, I supposed it couldn't hurt for me to have a little chat with Gabe to sound out his intentions.

Terry's guess had been spot on. Dog in hand, Crawford was standing near the in-gate of the Tibetan Terrier ring, awaiting his turn. Gabe had chosen to avoid the crowd of exhibitors beneath the tent. He was standing out in the sun, observing from the other side of the ring. He gave me a friendly wave as I approached.

"Hi, Melanie! Did you come to watch Crawford show Lion too?"

I stepped in beside him. "Lion? That's the dog's name?"

"Yup." Gabe lowered his voice. "Crawford says it's fitting. This Tibetan is a good one. He thinks he has a shot in today's group."

"Good for him," I said. "But first he has to get out of the breed."

"Oh, that's a given," Gabe replied with the easy confidence of the uninitiated. "You'll see."

Nothing in the world of dog shows was ever a given. No matter how good a dog was, or how many times it had won in the past, it still had to deliver the winning performance *on the day*. And as dogs were often apt to remind their handlers, they were living beings with their own notions and whims. Even an experienced show dog with a sterling reputation could throw in a clunker if it was so inclined.

While we'd been talking, the steward had called the first Tibetan Terrier class into the ring. Two Puppy dogs were being put through their paces. According to the catalog, we had five more classes to wait through before Best of Breed. Even so, Gabe's attention was already riveted on the activity in front of us—as if he hoped his total concentration might influence the outcome of the judging in Crawford's favor.

Good luck with that, I thought.

"So," I said brightly. "You're from Rochester."

He darted a surprised glance my way. "You know Rochester?"

"Well, sure. Doesn't everybody?"

Doesn't everybody? What was I thinking? I'd never been to Rochester. I'd only been trying to get a conversation started.

I threw out a line and hoped it wasn't entirely off base. "You know, they have dog shows there and stuff."

To my relief, Gabe nodded. Then I realized that the gesture wasn't meant as agreement. It was just an acknowledgment that I was talking. Gabe wasn't actually paying any attention to me at all.

The puppies got their ribbons. A single Bred-by-Exhibitor entry came and went. With four in it, the Open Dog class took some time.

Gabe studied the dogs in the ring intently. I wondered if he really knew what he was looking at. It took most people a long time to develop the discerning eye needed to accurately sort out a class of dogs that were similar in type and quality.

"None of those are as good as Crawford's dog," Gabe said dismissively.

Oh good. We were talking again.

"Lion is a champion," I pointed out. "He's older and more mature than those dogs. Plus he has more hair, and it's been styled by one of the best."

"Crawford is the best," Gabe agreed. "That's why he's going to win."

"Probably." I would never bet against Crawford's chances.

I let him watch for another minute, then asked, "How

long will you be staying in Connecticut? Is this an extended visit? Or do you have a job you need to get back to?"

"No, I can stay as long as I like. In fact"—he smiled—"if things turn out the way I'm hoping, I might even move here."

It felt like a lump had lodged in my throat. "That sounds like a big change to make."

"Yeah, but it'll be worth it. When you really want something, it only makes sense to do whatever you have to do to get it."

I swallowed heavily. I hoped he didn't mean what I thought he meant.

"You must want a handling career pretty badly then," I said, hoping against hope that he would agree with me.

Gabe ducked his head. I couldn't see his expression. "Yeah, something like that."

The dog classes had finished. The Tibbie bitches were being judged. Looking across to the other side of the ring, Gabe caught Crawford's eye and waved. To my surprise, the handler lifted a hand and waved back.

Terry wasn't imagining it, I thought. There was definitely a connection, a growing closeness, between these two men. The realization left me feeling slightly sick.

"It looks like you and Crawford are getting to be good friends," I said.

"I hope so," Gabe replied. "He's a great guy. I'm really enjoying getting to know him."

"Crawford is terrific," I agreed. "And he and Terry have a wonderful relationship. They've been together for a long time."

"Almost eight years." Gabe nodded. "That's what Crawford told me. It seems crazy to me. I'm surprised anyone can have a relationship that lasts that long."

"Really? Why?"

"I guess it just isn't my experience, that's all. Growing

up, I didn't have the most stable family life. My mother's been divorced twice. So long-term commitments aren't something I know a lot about. But who knows? Maybe I'll get lucky." Gabe smiled suddenly. "Someday I'd love to have a relationship like Crawford's."

He'd said *like Crawford's*, I told myself firmly. That didn't mean *with Crawford*.

"Look." Gabe gestured toward the ring. "There he is. Finally."

Once their turn came, Crawford and his Tibetan Terrier made short work of the competition. There was one other special entered, but the judge only had eyes for Lion. We'd spent more time waiting for Crawford to compete than we did actually watching him do so.

It would have been nice to think that I'd used that time wisely. But as Gabe strode around the ring to congratulate Crawford after the judging was over, and I saw the two men clasp hands and smile at each other happily, I wasn't sure I'd accomplished much of anything.

The next person I ran into was Vic Landry.

"Hey," she said when we crossed paths near the rings. "You're Melanie, right?"

"Yes. And you're Vic." We both stopped. "We met at Bite Club."

"Bite Club." Vic laughed. "Great name."

She was probably around my age—late thirties—but I could see at a glance that Vic was in much better shape than me. Both her tank top and pants were made of some stretchy material that clung to her enviable body like a second skin. She had very pale skin, white-blond hair that was cut short and spikey, and numerous piercings in her ears. When we shook hands, the muscle in Vic's upper arm flexed.

"Peg ran through a whole bunch of introductions at once when Rush and I arrived at the meeting," she said. "I wasn't sure if I got everybody's name right. Except for

Evan Major. When he came in all dinged up like that, it got everybody's attention."

"I guess you heard about what happened to him," I said.

Vic nodded. "I saw it on the news. What a shock that was—having the story turn out to be about someone I knew. Wild, right? Especially since the idea of joining a book club seemed pretty lame to me. That's really not my kind of thing at all."

"So why did you join?" I asked.

"Rush wanted to. He even got all excited about it. And when Rush wants something he always figures out a way to get it. So when he decided we were both going to the meeting, I knew there was no point in arguing with him."

Her words matched my first impression of Vic's husband. Rush had struck me as the kind of man who liked to be in charge.

She shook her head. "I mean, me in *a book club*? Come on. I thought the best thing about it would be the name. I certainly wasn't expecting any excitement."

"Me either," I said.

Vic sounded a whole lot more pleased by the way things had turned out than I did.

"Rush got really upset when he heard about what had happened to Evan. Man, it was almost like he was pissed or something."

"That's odd," I said. "Did you ask him why?"

"I asked all right, but he didn't answer. That's Rush for you. He likes to have his secrets. I think it makes him feel important when he knows stuff that other people don't."

I'd have to sic Aunt Peg on him at the next book club meeting. Whatever Rush's secret was, I was pretty sure she could weasel it out of him.

"Bite Club is getting together again on Tuesday," I said. "Will you and Rush be there?"

"Are you kidding?" Vic laughed. "Now that I know

what really goes on, I wouldn't miss it. I even have a copy of the book."

I should hope so, I thought. That was the whole point.

"Have you read it?" I asked.

"Not yet. But I still have what"—she held up her fingers and counted—"four, five days to get it done?"

"Three," I corrected. "*The Scent of Rain and Lightning* is a great book. You'll love it."

"It could happen." Vic didn't sound convinced. "See you then!"

By late afternoon, Aunt Peg and I were in the minivan on our way home. She spent the first half hour talking about the dogs she'd judged. When that topic began to wind down, she turned to me and said, "Your nose is sunburned."

I could well imagine. It felt as warm as it probably looked. "I should have brought some sunblock with me. I spent most of the day running around near the rings."

"Perfect," said Aunt Peg. "Tell me something interesting. What else happened while I was busy judging all day?"

Usually I wouldn't have hesitated to tell her everything. But I didn't want to talk about Terry's problems. And nobody else I'd spoken to had had anything useful to say. All of which was pretty demoralizing.

I leaned my head back against the seat and closed my eyes.

"It was just another dog show," I said.

Chapter 15

Monday afternoon, Aunt Peg and I went to Evan Major's funeral. Blackwood Funeral Home was a modest mortuary on a side street in downtown Stamford. I'd probably driven past the place dozens of times, but I'd never previously noticed its presence.

The somber brick building had a small parking lot behind it. I wasn't expecting Evan's service to draw much of a crowd, but when Aunt Peg and I arrived the lot was already full. We parked on the street and made our way inside.

There was a guest book on a table just inside the front door. Aunt Peg signed both our names, then spent the next several minutes attempting to decipher the remaining signatures in the book. The third time the funeral director tried to wave us through to the chapel, I finally turned around and gave her a sharp poke.

"Come on," I whispered. "We have to go."

"But this is interesting," she hissed back. "There's quite a list here. Don't you want to know who the other mourners are?"

"Presumably I'll see them inside. Maybe some of them will speak."

A bottleneck had begun to form in the doorway behind

us. The funeral director had stopped motioning politely. Now he was giving us the stare of death.

Aunt Peg didn't notice. She was still rifling through his book. Which meant that I bore the brunt of the man's displeasure.

I gave Aunt Peg thirty more seconds to snoop. Then I looped a hand through her arm and started walking down the hall. Luckily it only took a step or two before she began to cooperate because I wouldn't have succeeded in dragging her very far.

"That was rude," Aunt Peg snapped under her breath.

"Yes, it was," I snapped back.

I suspected we weren't talking about the same thing.

Inside the chapel, a small crowd had begun to gather. People were standing in groups of two or three, chatting quietly among themselves. I saw only a few familiar faces. Claire and Alice had come. They were talking to a couple of other neighbors from Flower Estates.

Several men who looked like they were trying to be inconspicuous were observing the activity from the back of the room. I assumed they were police. Detective Sturgill must have sent them there to keep an eye on things.

The chapel had two rows of pews divided by a center aisle. The front of the room featured a slightly raised dais with a podium in the middle. Behind the podium was a rather meager display of flowers. Sadly it looked as though whoever had made the arrangements for Evan's service had opted to purchase the bargain package.

"There's Marge Brennan," Aunt Peg said. "And she's talking to Toby Cane. I'm glad to see some other Bite Club members made the effort to appear. Let's go say hello, shall we?"

Marge and I didn't know each other well, but we'd crossed paths at numerous dog shows. Like Evan, her chosen breed was Bulldogs and she'd bred some very good ones. It occurred to me that if he'd waited a little longer to purchase a puppy, he'd have met Marge at the book club meeting and might have gotten one from her.

Dressed in a somber black suit with her gray hair swept back off her forehead and held in place by a black headband, Marge looked every bit the proper mourner. I remembered now that she and Evan had been sitting next to one another at Aunt Peg's house that night. Maybe they'd been better friends than I realized.

As for Toby Cane, aside from our communal book discussion, I hadn't had a chance to speak with him at the meeting. I knew that he'd been the only participant to complain about our choice of reading material.

Perhaps he was complaining again now, I thought, as I watched him frown over a point he was making. Toby was in his fifties, old enough for disgruntlement to have etched permanent lines in his face. He had come to the funeral wearing blue jeans. That seemed like an inappropriate choice to me, but at least he'd topped them with a rumpled sports coat.

"Hello, Peg, Melanie." Marge stepped away from Toby and made us part of their group. "I'm glad to see you both here. Whatever his faults, Evan deserved a proper send-off."

"Evan's faults?" I asked.

"As we all know, no one with an ounce of discernment would respond to an online ad and purchase a puppy from a probable puppy mill."

Toby snorted under his breath. "Apparently that was the least of Evan's sins. I'm sure we've all heard the things that have been reported about him by the media. Just look around the room. Half the people here are members of the press looking for a scoop they can use to enhance their stories."

Surprised, I followed the direction of his gaze. "That's why there's such a crowd?"

"Sure, what did you think? It's not like Evan would have had a lot of friends."

Aunt Peg cleared her throat in annoyance. "Perhaps not. But I would like to think that he knew at least a few people who thought well of him and came to lend their support. Melanie and myself included."

The pastor stepped up to the podium. He tapped the microphone with his fingertip and it screeched in protest. The man winced in apology, then said, "Ladies and gentlemen, if you would please find your seats. We're ready to get started."

The short eulogy that followed sounded as though it might have come straight out of a primer on the subject. The pastor told us that Evan was a good man. He assured us that Evan would be missed. He advised that we should look to God to heal our hearts. After that he ran out of things to say.

"That was a lot of blather," Aunt Peg huffed at the end. "You'd think he could have managed to find at least one personal thing to mention about Evan."

As I leaned over to shush her, the pastor looked around the room. "Would anyone like to step up and say something about the dearly departed?"

I felt Aunt Peg shift in her seat. I hoped she didn't intend to go up there and chastise the other mourners as she'd done with Toby.

The pastor's gaze went to a pew toward the back of the chapel. "Perhaps Evan's brother would like to speak?"

Evan's brother?

I wasn't the only one who was taken by surprise. There was a general rustling of bodies as nearly everyone turned to have a look. The man who'd suddenly become the cynosure of all eyes sat slumped in his seat. He looked as though the last thing he wanted to do was walk up to the podium and speak.

Not only that, I realized with a start, but I recognized him. Evan's brother was the man Evan had tried to avoid at the dog show. The one he'd ended up arguing with.

"Please come up, Mr. Major," the pastor called to him again. "I'm sure these fine people would like to hear what you have to say."

Reluctantly Major levered himself to his feet. Gaze lowered, he avoided making eye contact with anyone on the short trip to the dais. He stepped behind the podium and lifted his head.

Shaggy brown hair had fallen forward over his eyes. Major brushed it back impatiently. His hands gripped the sides of the lectern as though he was holding on to a lifeline. The microphone, adjusted to the pastor's height, was too low for him. He didn't seem to care.

"I'm Mark Major," he said. "Evan was my brother. We knew each other for a long time."

Someone tittered. The sound was quickly hushed.

"Maybe most of you didn't really know Evan," Mark continued. "But he had some good qualities. He had some bad ones too. I guess I'm sorry he's gone."

He stepped away from podium and quickly left the dais. I thought he would return to his seat. Instead, Mark Major kept walking. There was a door in the back corner of the chapel. He exited through it.

"Oh my," said Aunt Peg. "That was painful."

The pastor asked everyone to stand up and sing a hymn.

"I'll be right back," I whispered to Aunt Peg.

As the assembly began to warble the first words of "Amazing Grace," I was already hurrying to the same exit Mark had just used. It turned out I needn't have worried about catching up with him. The door led only to a small porch that overlooked the parking lot ten feet below us. Having presumably made a hasty departure from the service to avoid the other mourners, Mark was now stuck in place until the chapel emptied.

Leaning back against the waist-high wrought iron railing behind him, Mark had just placed a cigarette in his mouth. He lit a match and held it to the tip. The cigarette flared and he inhaled deeply.

As the door closed behind me, Mark gazed over without interest. "If you're from the press, I'll tell you the same thing I've told everyone else. No comment."

"I'm not." The porch was so small there was no way to escape his smoke. I walked over to stand beside him at the railing. "I'm sorry for your loss."

Mark grimaced. He didn't bother to acknowledge my condolences. "Were you a friend of Evan's?" he asked.

"Yes. I live here in Stamford. We'd known each other for about a month."

"I didn't know Evan had any friends."

"He told me he didn't have any family," I replied.

Mark turned away. He looked out over the parking lot. "What he probably meant was that he didn't have any family that was still speaking to him."

"And yet here you are," I pointed out.

"The police notified me about what happened," he said shortly. "Somebody had to make the arrangements." He sounded annoyed that the duty had fallen to him.

"Why bury your brother here rather than back home in New Jersey?"

"New Jersey isn't Evan's home anymore. After everything that happened, Evan couldn't get away fast enough. He wanted nothing more to do with the place. I figured he might as well go in the ground here as anywhere."

No wonder Evan had felt like he didn't have any family.

I could hear sounds from inside the chapel. The service was over. The mourners were beginning to leave. Nobody came through the door behind us. I was pleased about that, except for one thing. Aunt Peg was my ride. I hoped she didn't go home without me.

"How did you and Evan meet?" Mark asked suddenly.

"I started a book club," I told him. "Evan became a member."

"Really?" His brow lifted. "I never thought of him as a reader. Computers were his thing."

"A neighbor brought him along to one of the meetings. She knew he was new to the area and she thought it would help him meet people."

Mark gazed at me as though he still wasn't sure what to make of me. And whether or not he ought to believe the things I was telling him. I had seen Mark at the dog show but clearly he hadn't noticed me—even when I'd been standing right next to his brother.

"Plus, Evan had just gotten a new Bulldog puppy," I said. "He asked me to help train it."

"A Bulldog?" For the first time Mark looked interested in what I had to say. "Like the UGA mascot?"

I nodded.

"Is it worth money?"

"Probably not a lot," I told him. "But Bully's very cute."

And just that quickly, I lost him again. Mark's eyes shuttered. He took a deep drag of his cigarette.

"I saw you at the dog show in Mount Kisco," I told him. Mark swiveled my way. "What are you talking about?"

"I was there with Evan that afternoon. I saw him try to avoid you, but then you caught up with him anyway. What were the two of you arguing about?"

"Just old business."

"It looked pretty serious."

Mark brushed a hand through the air, dismissing my comment. "We've always been like that. If you think that was a fight, you should have seen us when we were eight."

"Evan told me that was his first dog show," I mentioned.

"So?"

"So how did you know to look for him there?"

Mark frowned. "Not that it's any of your business, but I'd stopped by his house looking for him. One of his neighbors came over and asked who I was. When she heard that Evan and I were related, she told me where he'd gone. If all his neighbors were like that lady, I can't imagine why he was having trouble meeting people."

Bella, I thought. It had to be.

"What will happen to Bully now?" I asked.

Mark flicked a section of ash over the railing. "What do you mean?"

"He belonged to Evan and now Evan's gone. Who will inherit his possessions? And his money?"

Mark laughed. It wasn't a happy sound. "What money? Evan doesn't have any money. It all went to pay the lawyers."

"What about his things?" I hated to refer to Bully that way, but I needed an answer.

"Who knows?" Mark shrugged. "Who cares? Evan didn't have a will."

"No will?" I stared at him. "But he was married. He owned stuff. How is that possible?"

"Don't ask me," Mark replied. "In case you haven't noticed, Evan and I weren't exactly close. I'd guess that after the divorce, his company's bankruptcy, his partners' court cases, not to mention his own legal troubles, Evan had had enough of lawyers to last him a lifetime. A will was probably the last thing on his mind."

"Is there other family?" I asked. "Or was it just the two of you?"

Mark started to nod. Then he narrowed his gaze instead. "What did you say your name was again?"

Actually, I hadn't mentioned it earlier. "Melanie Travis."

"Well, Melanie Travis, for someone who isn't a member of the press, you sure ask a lot of questions." He straightened and tossed his cigarette butt over the railing. The parking lot was nearly empty now, but it bounced off the hood of a parked car below us. "It's time for me to go."

Mark brushed past me. He opened the door, went through, then slammed it shut behind him.

I gave him a half minute, then followed. Mark was nowhere in sight. Aunt Peg was waiting for me in the foyer.

"That took long enough," she said. "I hope you managed to learn something useful."

"Evan had a brother who didn't like him."

Aunt Peg grimaced. "I think we *all* learned that. Hopefully you were able to elicit something more?"

I walked outside and down the steps. Aunt Peg followed. She fished in her purse for her car keys as we strode along the sidewalk.

"Mark Major is the man I saw fighting with Evan at the dog show," I said. "He wouldn't say what their argument was about. He did tell me that Evan didn't have a will. Nor much money. Apparently it all went for legal fees. Mark has no idea who Bully belongs to now."

"Evan's brother looked like a very unhappy man," Aunt Peg mused. "I do wish you'd been able to find out why he and Evan were at odds."

"Mark just said that things had always been that way between them."

"Aha," she said with satisfaction. "A long-standing grudge. And now one brother is dead. It's the story of Cain and Abel all over again."

I stopped and stared at her.

"What?" she asked. "I've been sitting in a chapel for

half the afternoon. Is it any wonder that I'm pondering Bible tales?"

I supposed not.

"That leads us to the important questions," Aunt Peg said as she unlocked the minivan. She waited until we'd taken our seats and fastened our seat belts before continuing. "What kind of man is Mark Major really? And could he have been angry enough at his brother to want to kill him?"

Chapter 16

"Your puppy made a mess in the kitchen," Davey told me when I got home from the funeral.

"How did that happen? You know the rules. Whoever opens the crate has to immediately pick Bully up and take him outside."

"I know the rules," Davey said. "Sam knows the rules. Even Kev knows the rules. But he got distracted."

I tossed my purse on a table near the door and went to see what needed to be cleaned up. "Distracted by what?"

"I dunno." Davey shrugged. "I think it was Oreos."

"Wait a minute." I stopped and looked back at him. "*My* puppy?"

"Who else's would he be?"

"Not mine," I assured him. "We have enough dogs in this house already."

As if to punctuate that point, Sam and Kevin came in the back door. Five Standard Poodles bounded into the kitchen with them. Bud and Bully scrambled along behind.

Seeing me, the whole canine crew raced across the room to say hello—and to see if I might be handing out biscuits. I was accustomed to their rambunctious greetings. Even so, as they jostled for preferred position in the enclosed space, the Poodle posse just about knocked me over.

"I'm glad I'm not the only one who realizes we already

have enough dogs," Sam said. "I thought you told me Bully's stay was going to be temporary."

"It is."

"Okay." Sam processed that. "But just so you know, it's been nearly a week."

A change of subject was definitely in order. I strode over to the counter, grabbed the roll of paper towels, and looked at Davey. "I'm supposed to be mopping something up. Where is it?"

Kev pointed. And giggled. "Bully pee'd on the floor."

I didn't see anything. Nor did I smell anything. I was an old hand at puppy messes. *I must be losing my touch*, I thought.

"What are you looking for?" asked Sam. "I cleaned that up an hour ago."

I turned to Davey. "Then why am I hearing about it now?"

"I just thought you might want to know what goes on in your house when you're not here."

Was that a dig? I wondered. I was pretty sure it was.

"Hey," I said in my defense, "I'm here almost all the time."

"Nearly every day," Sam replied.

I shot him a look. *You're not helping.*

"You didn't go to the beach with us on Saturday," Kev pointed out.

"Or to the supermarket today," said Davey.

Even the Poodles were beginning to look at me accusingly. That wasn't fair. With Faith as their leader, the dogs were supposed to take *my* side when the going got tough.

Then I realized what Davey had said and brightened. "Wait a minute. You guys have already been food shopping? That's great. What's for dinner?"

Sam and Davey shared a look. "I think she's trying to change the subject again," Sam whispered—loudly enough so that I'd be sure to hear.

"Would you rather talk about funerals?" I asked. "Because that's where I've been all afternoon."

"Not particularly," Sam admitted.

"That's depressing," said Davey. "I guess you have a good excuse." He looped an arm around Kevin's shoulder and steered him out the back door. "Come on, squirt. Let's go up to the tree house."

After they left, I sank down in a chair. "Did somebody mention Oreos?" I asked. "I think I could use a few."

After dinner, Alice called.

I thought she might want to talk about Evan's funeral, so I sat down and got comfortable. Faith came over and rested her head in my lap. Her dark brown eyes gazed up at me adoringly. Too adoringly. She was apologizing for taking part in the uprising earlier.

"It's all right," I told her as I tangled my fingers in her topknot and scratched beneath her ears. "You're forgiven."

"What?" asked Alice. "Who's forgiven?"

"Sorry about that," I said. "I was talking to Faith."

"Oh. Did she answer?"

"She wagged her tail. Does that count?"

Hearing her name, the big Poodle wagged her tail again. We were once again a team. All was right in her world. And mine.

"Sure, why not?" Alice was easy. "You're lucky you have dogs you can have a conversation with. Berkley only ever has one thing to say. *Food! Food! Food!*"

"Maybe you should try feeding him." I laughed. Berkley weighed a ton.

"That's not funny. Now listen. I just remembered something I should have told you the other day. Remember when we were talking about Evan and things that might have contributed to his death?"

"Of course."

"Back when you lived down the road, did you ever meet a man named Jim Bolden?"

I paused to consider. The name sounded familiar. "Maybe. I'm not sure."

"He's an older guy, probably in his eighties. White hair, wears his pants pulled up to his armpits? He's lived here in Flower Estates longer than any of us. That makes him think he's entitled to act like some self-appointed block monitor. He complains that people's yards aren't neat enough. He yells at kids when they're playing outside and making noise. Last year he told me my Christmas wreath was too gaudy."

"You're kidding," I said.

"Nope." Alice sounded peeved. "And I *liked* all those flashing lights. I thought it made my house look festive."

"It did," I assured her. "And now that you're describing him, it's all coming back to me. Whenever Mr. Bolden saw me outside with Faith, he used to make an ugly face and tell me that Poodles belonged in the circus."

Faith's tail thumped up and down. She didn't care what we were saying as long as we were talking about her.

"Yeah, that's the guy. He doesn't like dogs."

"Actually, I don't remember him liking much of anything."

"You're right about that," Alice agreed. "And included among the things he didn't like was his new next-door neighbor, Evan Major."

"Oh?" That was interesting. "Poor Evan. I didn't realize he had the bad luck to move in beside Mr. Bolden. Were they squabbling about something in particular or was it just general animosity?"

With Jim Bolden, either way was possible. Evan had only been living in his new house for a month. Welcome to the neighborhood indeed.

"Evan was going to put up a fence," Alice said.

"I know. He said something to me about it. I told him a fence would be a much better way to contain Bully than an ex pen."

"I figured you had," Alice replied. I'd told her the same thing with respect to Berkley. "But Evan was talking about fencing in his yard even before he got the puppy. He wanted one of those six-foot, cedar panel, privacy fences so no one could see into his house."

My backyard had been similarly enclosed when I'd lived in Flower Estates. It had taken some negotiating with my neighbors before I'd been able to put in a fence that tall. The fact that I owned big, black dogs that nobody wanted running loose had probably tipped the scales in my favor.

"I'm not surprised Jim Bolden objected," I said.

"Me either. You know how small the plots of land are here. Our houses are virtually right next to each other. Mr. Bolden told Evan that a fence that size was out of the question. That it would block the light in his living room. And when he looked out his windows, the fence was all he'd be able to see."

"Then what happened?" I asked.

"Evan redrew his proposed plans twice. But it didn't help. You know what Mr. Bolden is like."

"He still didn't approve," I said.

"Of course not." Alice sounded annoyed. "So then Evan went to the Homeowners' Association. He pointed out that there was precedence for letting him proceed."

"I wonder where he got that idea," I said with a laugh.

"Okay." She laughed with me. "I might have shown him the fence around your old backyard and steered him in that direction. But if you ever tell Mr. Bolden that, I will never ever speak to you again."

"Consider my lips sealed. Did the HOA approve Evan's request?"

"They didn't have time to reach a conclusion. When Evan died, they were still considering it. But I'm betting they would have let him go ahead in the end."

"You're probably right," I said.

"Think about it, Melanie. Everybody knows Mr. Bolden has a temper. What if this situation with Evan made him angry enough to take matters into his own hands?"

I pondered that for a minute. The notion seemed pretty far-fetched.

"Do you really think Evan could have been killed in a dispute over a *fence*?" I asked.

"I don't know what to think," she said. "But here's what I *know*. All these things that have come out about Evan's past—the Ponzi scheme and the bankruptcy, and all those people who lost a lot of money? That's all terrible stuff—but none of it is new. Evan's been living with, and dealing with, the fallout from those issues for nearly two years."

That was true, I realized.

Alice pressed on. "And even while the worst of that was hitting the media, and the courts, and the financial markets in New Jersey, Evan didn't get murdered then. No, it happened *here*, after he'd moved. Somebody stabbed Evan with a knife from his own kitchen. Like maybe someone who lost his temper and grabbed the nearest weapon he could find."

"Jim Bolden is in his eighties," I said.

"You know that wouldn't matter if he took Evan by surprise."

I thought about that for a few seconds. "You should tell Detective Sturgill everything you've told me."

"That is *so* not happening," Alice replied. "Joe would divorce me if I got myself involved in a murder investigation. And I'd probably lose my job too."

She was exaggerating, but I still took her point.

"Besides," she said, "I've been following the developments in the media. The police are mostly investigating people Evan was involved with before he came here. Ones who found their lives turned upside down by the whole NEWealth mess. The authorities are looking at the big picture."

"That's because they have access to resources that I don't," I pointed out.

"Yes, but the reverse is also true. You know this neighborhood. You *knew* Evan. Your resources may be different but they're equally valuable."

Her praise made me smile. I hardly got any time to bask however.

When Alice wanted something, she could be relentless. Now she drove her message home. "What if the police are looking in the wrong place? What if Evan's murderer lives a whole lot closer than they think?"

"Alice, you are a very persuasive woman," I said.

She blew out a breath. "Of course I am. I have to be. Things come up all the time. Who persuaded Mrs. Dingle to give Carly a role in *The Nutcracker* after we missed the auditions because of a doctor's appointment?"

I chuckled at the memory. "And who neglected to mention that the appointment wasn't for Carly?"

"Hey, it's not my fault if Mrs. Dingle didn't ask the right questions. And Carly made a lovely Sugar Plum Fairy."

Indeed she had. We'd all enjoyed the recital.

"I'll talk to Mr. Bolden," I said. "Will that make you happy?"

"Yes. But don't forget, I still live around the corner from him. So whatever you do, don't tell him I sent you."

Never a dull moment around here.

The next morning I had errands to run. Kev was coming with me. Davey had three lawns to mow and Sam was meeting with a client. So I figured Kevin and I would get an early start and be home in time for lunch.

Until the doorbell rang just after nine a.m.

"Somebody's heeere!" Kevin squealed. He loved visitors just as much as the Poodles did.

There was an immediate mass scramble in the direction of the front hall. I was the only one who hung back and comported myself with dignity.

Kevin knew better than to open the front door by himself. And while the Poodles could jump up and look out the front windows, they weren't good at turning knobs. Luckily Bud and Bully were out in the backyard. That cut down on some of the confusion.

Even so, when I opened the door, the woman who was standing there looked like she wanted to beat a hasty retreat. Few people dropped by unannounced at my house. Aunt Peg was usually the worst offender. At a glance, I pegged this woman as a multilevel marketing salesperson. Whatever she was selling, I wasn't interested.

Her eyes went wildly from one Poodle to the next. "Is this place a kennel?" she asked.

"No." I smiled complacently. "Why would you say that?"

The query apparently left her speechless. I was about to close the door when she held up a hand and said, "I'm looking for Melanie Travis."

Oh damn, I thought. She'd come to the right place.

"And you are?" I inquired.

"Annette Major. I'm Evan's ex-wife."

Now I was the one who was speechless. First because I had no idea how she'd found me or why she was there. And second, because I hadn't expected Evan's ex-wife to resemble a supermodel.

Annette Major's height topped mine by at least six inches. Our weights were probably about the same. She had a radiant complexion, glossy blond hair, and the whitest teeth I'd ever seen on a live person. Everything she was wearing was made of white linen, and the outfit was perfectly tailored to fit her twig-like figure. Even her expertly manicured fingernails glistened.

"Yes, well." I tucked my grubby hands into the back pockets of my jeans. "That's me."

"Good," said Annette. "We need to talk."

Okay, that was different. Usually I'm the one trying to get people to talk to me. This made for a pleasant change.

"Give me a minute," I said. The last thing I saw was the surprised expression on her face as I shut the door between us.

"Kev, how would you like to go out back and play in your sandbox?"

"Nope." He shook his head. "I want to talk to the nice lady."

"It's business," I told him. I figured that sounded suitably important.

"I like business." Kev folded his arms over his small chest.

Most days I liked my children to express their opinions. Right that minute, not so much.

"Let's make a deal," I said. "If you go outside and play in your sandbox for fifteen minutes, after we're finished running errands you and I will stop for ice cream."

"Before lunch?" His eyes widened.

"We might even have ice cream *for* lunch."

That sealed the deal. Kev spun on his heels and started down the hall.

"Take the Poodles with you," I called after him. Four of the five were already on their way. That left just Faith, who was holding her ground by my side.

"You too," I told her. When she still hesitated, I added, "Somebody's got to keep an eye on him."

That she understood. Faith went padding away toward the kitchen. I waited until I heard the back door slam. Then I opened the front one again.

Annette was still there. She was looking down at her phone, thumbs moving busily. I waited thirty seconds, then cleared my throat. The woman didn't look up.

"I'm tweeting," she told me.

As if I cared. Kevin had me on the clock. I'd be lucky if he gave me ten minutes, much less fifteen.

"And I'm running out of time," I said.

Annette tried to grimace, but her face remained largely immobile. Upon closer inspection, I realized she was older than I'd initially thought. Botox and filler were probably holding the lines at bay.

Annette shoved the phone in her purse and stepped inside the house. "This had better be worth my while," she muttered.

Chapter 17

I showed Annette into the living room.

She cast an assessing gaze around as if she was mentally totaling up the value of the furniture. And the electronics. And the artwork. And maybe the dog toys too, for all I knew.

She didn't look impressed. Too bad Sam wasn't there. His presence would have elevated my stature in her eyes. He was worth more than all the material stuff in the world.

Annette chose the best chair in the room and sat down. That chair was also Tar's favorite seat. I opted not to mention that and sat down opposite her.

"I want the dog," she said.

I hadn't been expecting that. "What dog?"

"Evan had a dog. Now that he's gone, it belongs to me."

I fixed a surprised expression on my face and said, "Evan had a dog?"

No way in hell was I letting Bully leave my house with this woman.

"Don't play dumb with me," said Annette. "You think I don't know what my ex-husband was up to?"

"To tell the truth, I don't know what you think," I said. "You're the one who came to me. And by the way, how did you get my name?"

"That's not important. The only thing that matters now is that you have something that belongs to me."

"No, I don't," I replied. "Evan's brother told me that Evan didn't have a will. I'm guessing that means that his possessions will go to his next of kin. And since you're his *ex*-wife, I'm pretty sure that isn't you."

Annette gazed at me through narrowed eyes. Then she tried out a small smile. "Let's talk, woman to woman," she said.

Oh sure, I thought. *Like that would help.* Aside from our common gender, Annette and I might have been two entirely different species.

Which didn't mean I wasn't curious to hear what she had to say.

"Go on," I said.

"Evan and I are divorced, that's true." Her lower lip gave a little quiver. "But I never stopped loving him."

"So the divorce was his idea?"

She nodded. "Evan was a good man. Terrible things were happening in his life, and he wanted to shield me from them. That was why we separated."

That was definitely not the impression I'd gotten from Evan. Nevertheless, I was happy to play along.

"It seemed like most of Evan's troubles were behind him when he moved here," I mentioned. "So how come the two of you hadn't gotten back together?"

"We were working on it." Annette glanced up at me through lowered lashes. She was checking to see whether or not I was buying her story. "Evan was just ironing out the last of his legal issues."

"Like what?"

"Relocating his probation, arranging his community service . . ." Annette straightened in her chair. "Look, I didn't come here to tell you my life story."

"No, you came to pick up a dog. Do you like dogs?"

"Well, sure. I guess. Anyway, what does that matter?"

I stared at her across the room. "It matters a great deal if you're planning to adopt a puppy."

"Who said anything about adopting a puppy? I'm collecting Evan's assets."

"Assets?" The word felt bitter on my tongue. "Bully isn't an asset."

"Sure, he is. Evan paid money for him. Probably a lot of money. I'm not an idiot. I see those dog shows on TV. Maybe you aren't aware of this, but a dog with a pedigree is a valuable commodity."

A pedigree was nothing more than a piece of paper with a dog's ancestors written on it. The fact that one existed was no guarantee of value. A pedigree's worth was determined by the quality of the dogs it contained.

"What would you do with Bully if you had him?" I asked.

"I'd sell him," Annette replied without hesitation. "I'd use the money to pay off my debts."

"Bully's just a puppy. He isn't worth much."

"Of course he is." She looked at me like I was the stupid one. "He has to be."

"What makes you think that?"

"Because despite his shortcomings, Evan was a clever man. Anybody can see that. The guys he worked with all went to jail—or they're on their way there. Meanwhile Evan got off with probation."

This time, Annette's smile looked real. And gloating. "Plus the authorities are busy trying to claw back that boatload of money his partners raked in. But Evan pled poor. He said he'd never received any financial compensation other than his salary. I'm not that gullible. I'm sure he must have had money tucked away somewhere. And now I'm entitled to my share."

"Didn't you receive your share during the divorce proceedings?"

"You'd *think* the wife would be the first one to get paid,"

Annette snapped. "But Evan's money grubbing lawyers were billing him by the hour—and there were hundreds of hours of work devoted to his case. Sure, eventually they got him off, but at what cost?"

I'd imagine Evan must have thought the cost was worth it. Annette, on the other hand, sounded as though she would rather have had a rich ex-husband in jail, than a poor one who'd earned his freedom through the legal system.

"Evan was nearly broke when our divorce was finalized. At least that's what his lawyers managed to convince the judge. The alimony I was awarded is a pittance— barely enough to cover my shoe budget."

Bear in mind that the shoes she was wearing cost enough to feed my family for a week.

"I'm sorry," I said. I wasn't really, but I thought it sounded good.

"Thank you. So now you understand why I need your help."

"*Excuse me?*" At no point in our conversation had I understood anything of the sort.

"I. Want. The. Dog." Annette spoke slowly and with emphasis, as if she'd begun to fear she was dealing with a moron.

Unfortunately that feeling was mutual.

"Evan's dog wasn't an investment," I told her. "And if you really believe he had a secret stash of money somewhere, you should be looking in the Cayman Islands. Or maybe Switzerland."

Annette shook her head. "No, Evan didn't have that much imagination. Plus, he hated to fly."

She stood up. Our conversation had apparently come to an end. "I've already wasted too much time here. Go get my dog for me."

"I don't have him." The lie slipped out easily.

"Of course you do."

"What makes you think that?"

"My attorney made inquiries. Some policeman gave him your name."

"I was going to take him," I said with a shrug. "But as you might have noticed, I already have too many dogs of my own."

Sorry guys, I thought. *It's for a good cause.*

"Then where is he now?"

I shrugged again.

"You'll be sorry you ever tried to play games with me." Annette sneered. "That dog belongs to me, and if you don't hand him over, I'll sue. If anybody's going to profit from that dog it will be me."

"I guess you'll have to find him first," I said mildly.

"I doubt that's going to be too difficult." She looked around the living room as though she thought Bully might be hiding under a couch. "I know he's here somewhere. The next time you see me, I'll be back to retrieve my property with a police escort."

"That sounds impressive," I said. It also sounded nonsensical. I was pretty sure the police had better things to do than squire Annette around town in search of a missing dog.

"Bet on it!" she snapped.

Annette strode to the front door and yanked it open. Her silver Lexus was sitting in the driveway. The woman obviously wasn't too badly strapped for cash.

"You don't seem to be very broken up about your husband's death," I said.

Annette had started down the walk. She spun back around. "My ex-husband," she corrected.

"I thought the two of you were getting back together."

"Well, that won't happen now, will it?"

While I still had her attention, I threw out one last question. "Did your ex-husband have any enemies?"

She snorted out a brief laugh. "What do you think?

Evan's company took people's savings. It destroyed their dreams. It drove some of them into the poorhouse. Of course he had enemies. The only question is, how many?"

Once the Lexus had disappeared from view, I went out back to retrieve Kevin.

"Time for ice cream?" he asked happily.

"Soon," I told him. "We just have to make one stop first."

I scooped up Bully and led the way to the garage.

"You guys mind the house," I told the Poodle posse. "Don't let anyone in. Even if they have a police escort."

"Yay, police!" Kev grinned as I got him settled in the backseat of the Volvo. "They wear uniforms. They have guns! Are we going to talk to the police?"

"Not today, sweetie. We're going to go see Aunt Peg."

I called ahead once we were underway. Aunt Peg was waiting for us when we arrived. She snatched Bully out of my arms and hurried the puppy inside the house as if she was afraid someone might pop up out of her bushes and attempt to forcibly abduct him.

"Evan's wife sounds like a real piece of work," she said when Bully had been introduced to her Poodles and we'd all found seats in her kitchen.

"She is," Kev replied seriously.

"Oh? Did you meet her?"

"I did."

"Only briefly," I interjected.

Neither one of them was listening to me.

"What was she like?" Aunt Peg asked Kevin.

"Pretty. She looked like an angel."

"Annette has blond hair," I explained. "She was so skinny you could almost see through her. And she was dressed in white."

"Just like an angel," Kev confirmed. He slid down off his chair. The dogs were lying on the floor around us. He began to play with Zeke.

"She doesn't sound like an angel to me," Aunt Peg muttered. "Thinking she could sell that poor puppy for real money. The woman must be delusional."

"Or grossly misinformed," I said. "Annette said Evan was a man with many enemies."

Aunt Peg cast a glance downward. Happily absorbed in the dogs, Kevin wasn't paying any attention to our conversation. "Of course the man had enemies," she said. "He's dead, isn't he?"

"Alice thinks I should talk to Evan's next-door neighbor. Apparently he and Evan were engaged in a dispute over a fence, and Mr. Bolden was about to lose. He's known to be a man with a temper."

"It can't hurt." Aunt Peg nodded. "And of course you'll be at the Bite Club meeting tonight?"

"Of course." I was surprised she'd even felt the need to ask.

"I had an interesting idea about that. Who better to have useful thoughts about potential murder suspects than a group of people who enjoy reading murder mysteries? I thought I might pose the question and then open the floor for discussion. What do you think?"

"I think Claire is supposed to be in charge of tonight's meeting," I said. "Isn't it being held at her house?"

"That was the original plan," Aunt Peg informed me. "But Claire was happy to abdicate responsibility, so the location has been changed."

Happy to abdicate my foot, I thought. Aunt Peg had probably hatched her plan and then run roughshod over Claire until she got her way.

"I sent out an e-mail this morning informing everyone of the change. Didn't you see it?"

"I'm sure it's waiting for me," I said. "I've been a little busy."

Aunt Peg pursed her lips in annoyance. She hated to be

overlooked. "Did you at least have a chance to read the book?"

"Of course I read the book." That was a given. "Not that it sounds like we'll be spending much time talking about it."

"That won't be a problem," Aunt Peg said blithely. "If things get too lively tonight, we can always hold the book discussion over for next time."

"Speaking of the meeting, Vic Landry told me that Rush was quite anxious to become a member of the book club. And that he was very upset when he heard that Evan had been killed. I thought you might like to find out why."

Aunt Peg slanted me a look. "We were *all* upset when we heard about Evan's untimely demise. Or are you insinuating there's more to his reaction than that?"

"Apparently Rush likes keeping secrets," I mentioned. "Maybe almost as much as you like ferreting them out."

Aunt Peg pondered that for a minute, then nodded. Rush was on her radar now. That was good enough for me.

She reached down, picked up Bully, and settled him across her knees. The puppy lifted a front paw and batted at her chin. Aunt Peg smiled down at him fondly. "Bully is a dear. Maybe when all this is behind us, Marge can find us a good spot for him."

"Marge Brennan?"

"Of course, Marge Brennan. She breeds Bulldogs. She probably knows all about their local rescue group."

"At the funeral she seemed rather put out about Bully's origins."

"Perhaps, but that's hardly *his* fault." Aunt Peg ran her fingers down the length of the puppy's back. "Don't worry, I'll speak to her. I'm sure she'll be willing to help."

Kevin stood up. "You told me there was going to be ice cream. It's been *hours*. Are we ready to go *yet*?"

"We're leaving right now," I said.

Bully was in the best possible hands. My mission had been accomplished.

Aunt Peg walked us to the door. She still had the puppy in her arms.

"I hope you'll keep him out of sight during tonight's meeting," I said. "Now that Annette is on his trail, I'd hate for her to discover where he is."

Aunt Peg frowned. "That woman is from Evan's old life. In New Jersey. What would make you think that she might be acquainted with any of our Bite Club members?"

"I don't know that she is. But I'd still rather be careful."

"I suspect you're overreacting," Aunt Peg said, but she nodded anyway. She loved a good subterfuge. "Mum's the word."

"No," Kevin said firmly. He took my hand and tried to tug me out the door. "You're wrong. The word is ice cream."

"I can't argue with that," I told him.

He and I stopped at Häagen Dazs before wrapping up the rest of the errands. I had a small butterscotch sundae. Kev had an enormous banana split. I figured that helped with his dairy and fruit requirements for the day, and even added a little protein to his diet.

Best of all, it really improved my son's mood. That's how motherhood works. Sometimes you take a win any way you can get it.

Chapter 18

Even with the last minute change of venue, every remaining Bite Club member showed up for the meeting that night. Most even arrived early. The mystery novel we were meant to focus on was wonderful. But I knew perfectly well that it wasn't the main attraction.

Alice and Claire walked in together. Bella brought a homemade pie. Toby looked glum, as usual. Vic headed straight for the sideboard and poured herself a generous glass of wine. Her husband, Rush, looked impatient for the meeting to start.

Marge and Felicity entered the house chatting about the previous weekend's dog shows and quickly found seats side by side. Despite the reservations he'd expressed earlier, Jeff Schwin arrived right on time. Terry came rolling in last.

Aunt Peg had arranged her living room with care. All the seats had been placed close to one another. Each one faced the rest of the group. Anyone who thought they might get away with muttering a quiet aside to a neighbor would be clearly visible to all.

Aunt Peg's troupe of Standard Poodles acted as a welcoming committee for each new arrival. But then the dogs had the good sense to make themselves scarce. By the time we'd helped ourselves to refreshments and found our seats, there wasn't a single big, black Poodle to be seen. I was almost a little envious of their license to disappear.

Terry sat down next to me. He had a glass of white wine in one hand and a scone slathered in clotted cream in the other. I hoped those two things would keep his mouth occupied, but no such luck.

"Tick, tock," Terry said under his breath.

"What now?" I asked him.

"Do you really have to ask?"

No, I supposed not.

I had no desire to tell him about the conversation I'd had with Gabe at the dog show. That wouldn't make either one of us happy. So instead I said, "Keep your shirt on, Terry. I'm working on it."

"If taking my shirt off would help, I'm all over that."

"You most certainly are not," Aunt Peg said, from her seat at the head of the group. That woman can hear a whisper at forty paces. She stood up to address the room. "If everybody's ready, it's time to call the meeting to order."

Before Aunt Peg's intervention, we'd just been a group of people who enjoyed talking about books. Now apparently we needed *order*. Next she'd be introducing Robert's Rules.

"As you're all aware there has been a tragedy in our midst since the previous meeting," she began. "One of our members, Evan Major, has passed away. He was killed in his home last Wednesday."

Surreptitiously I glanced around the room, gauging people's reactions. The announcement wasn't news to anyone, and nobody looked unduly shocked. Nor did anyone have the grace to look guilty. Everyone simply sat and listened, waiting to hear what Aunt Peg would say next.

"Before we start our book discussion, I'd like to devote a few minutes to this subject—"

"Good idea," Rush broke in. He was seated between his

wife and Felicity Barber. "I'll start. Here's an interesting fact. Apparently one of our Bite Club members was the last person to see Evan alive."

Rush had barely finished speaking before most of the heads in the room swiveled my way. Some people gazed at me with suspicion. Others appeared merely curious. Terry, damn him, looked as though he wanted to laugh.

"Clearly that's not true," I said firmly. "Because I didn't kill him."

"But you were there," Rush prodded.

"I was outside Evan's house, yes, but I didn't go in. He and I were supposed to meet there that afternoon."

Jeff had a plate holding a scone balanced across his knees. His fingers were tearing at the pastry, crumbling it into little pieces. "Rush has a point though. Obviously you must feel remorse about what happened, because you've been going around asking questions about why Evan was killed." Jeff looked up at the gathering. "Unless I'm the only one she cornered?"

A chorus of voices rose in reply. None of them sounded happy.

Felicity's rose above the rest. "No, you most certainly are not. I must say that I was quite surprised to find myself being interrogated like a common suspect."

Interrogated? I thought. Hardly. Our conversation had only lasted a few minutes and she'd barely even known who Evan was.

"Now, Felicity," Aunt Peg said soothingly. "I'm sure Melanie wasn't trying to hurt your feelings. Indeed, if she hadn't spoken to you, you might have felt left out, isn't that right?"

"I doubt it," Felicity snarled.

Claire sent me a sympathetic look from the other side of the room. This wasn't going well at all.

"Is that why you went to Evan's funeral?" Toby asked

me. "So you could snoop around and gather dirt on the rest of us?"

"I went to pay my respects," I told him. The fact that I'd run into Evan's brother there had simply been a fortuitous bonus. Considering the current tenor of the conversation, it was one I had no intention of mentioning.

"You've done this before," said Vic. It sounded like something she and Rush might have discussed. "Some billionaire died in Greenwich. You were mentioned in the stories that were written about it." She turned to face Claire. "You were too."

Claire held up her hands in a gesture of innocence. "I worked for Leo Brady, that's all."

"But you did more than that, Melanie," Vic insisted. "You might have even solved his murder. Dog shows thrive on gossip, you know. And your name comes up more often than you might think."

Somehow she didn't make that sound like a compliment.

"That's because we love Melanie," Terry interjected quickly. He reached over and put an arm around my shoulders in a gesture of support. "And because she leads such an *interesting* life."

"You say interesting, I say nosy," Bella muttered.

She was a fine one to talk. If she didn't spend so much time staring out her front window, the police wouldn't have been on my case to begin with.

"You were the one who told the police that I was at Evan's house that afternoon," I said to Bella. "How did you know that?"

The woman sank down in her chair. Her shoulders hunched defensively. "I see things. It's my neighborhood. I like to keep an eye out."

"I understand that. So what else did you see?"

"What do you mean?" Bella asked plaintively.

"Well, obviously you were aware that I came to visit Evan. So now I'm wondering who else you might have observed in the area—when you were watching Evan's house."

"Nothing. I saw nobody. It was a quiet day."

"A *quiet* day?" I repeated.

"Yes." Bella nodded. "That was why I noticed you. Over there hanging around where you didn't belong. And probably up to no good."

"This is exactly what I mean," Toby said in a loud voice. "Just because Melanie has found herself under suspicion doesn't mean that Bella should be made to feel like a suspect too. This is beginning to border on harassment."

Once again, several voices chimed in to agree.

"That's quite enough," said Aunt Peg sternly. "There's no reason to stray off topic. We're supposed to be discussing Evan's murder—not any involvement that Melanie may or may not have had in the investigation."

"The police are the ones doing the real investigating," Marge spoke up for the first time. "Anything we talk about here is pure speculation."

"But interesting nevertheless," Aunt Peg insisted. "Especially with the addition of new information that has come to light. As we now know, Evan was involved in events in his former life that were quite disturbing."

"And they probably led to his death," Jeff said. He gazed around the group. "Wouldn't we all agree?"

"Not necessarily," Alice replied. "If those things that took place in New Jersey are what placed Evan in danger, why did he come through them unscathed? And yet, as soon as he moved here and joined our little club—"

"Surely you don't mean to point the finger at one of us," Rush said sharply. "That would be absurd."

"I'm not pointing fingers. I'm simply airing my thoughts on the matter." Alice paused to take a sip of wine. "And I'm not at all sure that the timing of Evan's demise was a coincidence."

"But what motive could one of us have had?" Jeff demanded. "We were barely acquainted with Evan. We knew nothing about those other things he'd gotten up to."

Marge cleared her throat. "Strictly speaking, that isn't entirely true."

Well. That got everyone's attention in a hurry.

"I'm only speaking for myself," she said. "But I recognized Evan's name as soon as I heard it. In my younger days, I worked in a bank. The things people do with money—and the things they will do to get money—have always been fascinating to me. So naturally I followed the whole NEWealth debacle. That story was right up my alley. Of course, I never expected to find myself sitting across the room from one of the chief perpetrators."

"But he wasn't one of the main culprits, was he?" Toby pointed out. "Otherwise he'd have ended up in a jail cell too. According to what I read, Evan was just the computer guy. He didn't have anything to do with the financial end of the business. He was an underling who got duped by the company partners."

Terry was shaking his head. "If you actually believe *that*, I have a bridge to sell you. It's no wonder that Evan moved away from northern New Jersey—aka the scene of the crime—as soon as he could. I think he was lucky to escape being charged with the others."

"Either that or he had a better lawyer," Claire chimed in.

"I knew there was something wrong with that man right from the start," Felicity sniffed. "What kind of person would buy a puppy from a random ad on the Internet? Not anyone I would want to be associated with."

Alice looked increasingly unhappy with what she was hearing. "I disagree. I thought Evan was a nice man. Sure, he was shy and he didn't say much. But he seemed like he meant well. Maybe the rest of you weren't surprised by what we found out about him, but I certainly was. I had no idea."

"Well, in the interest of full disclosure," Rush spoke up. "I did."

The room quieted. We waited for him to continue.

"It's not a coincidence that Vic and I joined Bite Club. I decided to take part because of Evan. When Peg mentioned the names of the other members, I knew immediately who he had to be. NEWealth was based in Fort Lee, but the company had investors from all over the tristate area. Vic and I were among them."

I glanced at Vic. She looked as surprised to hear that as I was.

"We didn't have a lot of money invested, so luckily our exposure was limited," Rush continued. "But finding myself associated with a criminal case like that—even peripherally—came as quite a shock. As I'm sure you can imagine."

We all nodded.

"I'll confess that I didn't come to last week's meeting to talk about books. I came because I wanted to look Evan Major in the eye and see for myself what kind of man it took to swindle innocent people out of their life savings. Then he came walking in the door with his face all busted up. . . ." Rush's sudden grin had a feral quality. "Man, that just about made my night."

"You might have mentioned that you had a previous connection," Aunt Peg said drily.

"Why? It wasn't anyone's business. Besides, what kind of idiot would I look like if people knew I'd been taken in by a Ponzi scheme? I'm only saying something now because you and Melanie seem to have the mistaken impression that you are sitting in a room full of potential suspects. I figured you both ought to know that nothing could be farther from the truth."

Rush's firm pronouncement brought our discussion of Evan's murder to an abrupt end. Even Aunt Peg had been silenced for once. It was Vic, of all people, who held up her copy of that week's mystery novel and deftly steered the conversation back to more conventional matters.

We'd devoted so much time to talking about Evan that Nancy Pickard's novel ended up getting short shrift. Indeed, the only good thing about the brief book chat that followed was that it finally took the focus off me.

While the others spoke, I observed the rest of the people in the room. After a few minutes I realized that I wasn't the only person doing so. Many of the people gathered in the circle seemed to be reassessing their initial impressions of their fellow Bite Club members.

Aunt Peg wrapped things up at nine o'clock. People might have been inclined to hang around to chat afterward, but Aunt Peg was ready to be done. She shooed everyone out the door.

Except for me. As Aunt Peg had previously pointed out, I wasn't a guest. I stayed behind to help her clean up.

"That went well," she said as we gathered up cups and plates and piled them on a tray.

"You think? *Really?* Because I felt like I was standing in front of a firing squad."

"Don't be so dramatic. It was all in aid of a good cause. Now we know that Rush and Marge both had a previous connection to our victim."

I picked up the tray and headed toward the kitchen. "I would hardly call what Marge said about him a connection. She only admitted that she knew who Evan was."

"And if she was willing to admit that much, then surely she knew more." Aunt Peg grabbed the platter that had held the scones and fell in behind me. "A woman who used to work in a bank and is fascinated by how far people will go to make money sounds just like the sort of person who might have gotten herself involved in NEWealth's scheme. I wouldn't be surprised if she was an investor too."

"Speaking of investing," I said, "did you catch the look

on Vic's face when Rush told the group that the two of them had lost money with NEWealth? She looked as surprised as anyone in the room."

"No, but if that was the case, you may consider me officially appalled. Vic is old enough to know better. What kind of ninny would blindly allow a spouse to manage money that belongs to both of them?"

I set the heavy tray down on the kitchen counter. "Maybe one who's become so accustomed to following her husband's lead that she doesn't think to question him?"

Now that everyone was gone, Standard Poodles reappeared from all corners of the house. I crouched down and opened my arms wide. Within seconds, I was engulfed by warm, wiggly bodies. That felt like coming home.

Eve's littermate, Zeke, jostled me from behind. I fell sideways onto my butt and began to laugh. That made the Poodles jump up and down. Five big, black, bouncing dogs was a sight. Sprawled on the floor among them, I laughed even harder.

"Good Lord, what have you done to my well-behaved Poodles?" Aunt Peg glared down at me. "Somehow you've started a riot in here."

She held out a hand and I grabbed it. Aunt Peg pulled me to my feet. We returned to the living room to rearrange the furniture.

"How did you happen to ask Rush and Vic to join the book club?" I asked as I separated a trio of chairs.

"I didn't actually." Aunt Peg nibbled on a leftover scone. "Rush approached me. The only thing I thought about it at the time was, the more the merrier."

That wasn't surprising. Aunt Peg always enjoyed having additional people to boss around. Then I was struck by another thought.

"Wait a minute," I said. "That doesn't make sense. Think about what Rush said earlier. Why would he have asked to join Bite Club if he wasn't aware that Evan was a member until you told him?"

"Good question." Aunt Peg frowned. "That hadn't occurred to me."

It seemed we hadn't succeeded in flushing out all of Rush's secrets.

"Maybe it should have," I said grimly.

Chapter 19

Thursday morning after breakfast, Sam went to his home office to work. I wanted to drive down to the Stamford Police Department and talk to Detective Sturgill. I also wanted to be able to concentrate fully on our conversation. Which meant I needed to make the trip by myself.

Faith and I found the boys in the living room. Davey was teaching Kevin how to play a new video game. Davey wasn't booked for any jobs today, so I was hoping he'd be willing to watch Kevin while I was gone.

"Sure, I'd be happy to babysit." He paused the game and looked up. "But it's going to cost you."

"Cost me?"

Davey nodded. "I'm a working man now. I have real jobs. My time is worth money."

"I already pay you," I pointed out. "What about your allowance?"

"That's for doing chores."

"Looking after your little brother is a chore," I said without thinking.

From the depths of the couch Kev immediately piped up in outrage. "I am *not* a chore!"

"Of course you're not, sweetie. I didn't mean that the way it sounded."

Davey grinned. "Is there a good way to mean that?"

Probably not, I thought. Even Faith was amused.

"I'm not saying I'm *going* to pay you," I told Davey. "But just as a matter of interest, what do you make per hour?"

He named a sum and my eyes widened.

"Seriously? You're thirteen years old. People actually give you that much money?"

Davey shrugged. "It's minimum wage. Plus, I do a good job. If the neighbors didn't hire me, they would have to pay an adult just as much. Or maybe more. And they *know* me. I'm local and I'm totally dependable."

My mother's heart swelled with pride.

Then I got real. There was no way my own son was going to charge me minimum wage for babysitting.

"I want the family rate," I said.

"This is one crazy family," Davey replied with a chuckle. "That'll cost you even more."

"One crazy family," Kev repeated, giggling.

"Hey, don't sound so proud of yourself," I told him. "You're included in the family too." I turned back to my older son. "This is extortion."

Davey wasn't fazed. "I think of it more like free enterprise. I'm offering a service. If you think the price is fair, you can take me up on it. If not, you can hire someone else."

When I was a single mom, I'd had a babysitter on speed dial. But Joanie had long since left for college. Davey had me over a barrel and he knew it.

"I won't be gone long," I mused. "And Sam is here in the house. Maybe Faith could keep an eye on him."

The Standard Poodle looked up at me and wagged her tail. She was on board with that plan.

"Sure, Faith could do that," Davey replied easily. "Just like she keeps an eye on Bud. Did you know that he brought a baby bunny into the house the other day?"

"No, he didn't," I said firmly. Not because I didn't believe him, but because I really, really, hoped it wasn't true.

"Did too!" Kevin informed me gleefully. "Dad had to rescue it and take it back outside."

"So who knows what might happen if you leave Faith in charge?" Davey asked. "You could end up with baby bunnies all over the place."

"That would be cool." Kevin grinned.

"*So not* cool," I muttered under my breath.

Davey turned the video game back on. Music began to play. Something small went hopping around the TV screen. I hoped it wasn't a bunny.

"That's a new game," I mentioned. "It might take you an hour to teach Kevin how to play it."

"It might," Davey agreed. Feet up on the coffee table, he settled into the couch.

"Perfect." I reached down and gave Faith's head a pat. Then I walked out to the hall and swept my purse off the table. "Keep up the good work. I'll be back in an hour."

The Stamford Department of Police Services was housed in an imposing brick and concrete building on Bedford Street. The three-story structure looked as though it had been designed for the express purpose of intimidating law-breakers. Though I liked to think of myself as a responsible, law abiding citizen, it still had that effect on me.

I walked inside, gave my name to the officer behind the reception counter, and asked to speak with Detective Sturgill. I rambled a bit when asked to state the nature of my business, but I must have been convincing enough because I was shown to a seat and told the detective would be with me shortly.

Sturgill's idea of shortly and mine turned out to be two entirely different things. When he finally arrived, I had to make an effort to smile as I stood up to face him.

"We met last week," I said. "I'm Melanie Travis."

"I know who you are."

So we weren't off to the best start.

The man still reminded me of a scrappy Scottish Terrier. Scotties do best with a smart owner, one who treats them with respect but doesn't back down. I decided to handle Sturgill the same way.

"I was told you wanted to see me," he said.

"You gave me your card. You told me I should get in touch if I had any additional information about Evan Major's murder. Here I am."

He frowned. "I expected you to call."

"And yet, here I am," I repeated. "Is there someplace we could go and talk?"

"We're talking now, Ms. Travis. If you have something to tell me, let's hear it."

"All right." I sat back down in the plastic chair. Sturgill didn't move. After a moment, I reached over and patted the seat next to mine.

He stared down at me. "Are we going to be here a while?"

"Probably." I gave him another smile. The detective still didn't look impressed.

"Come on," he said. "We'll talk in here."

In here turned out to be a small room off the lobby. It wasn't an interrogation room. It didn't even have a two-way mirror. It did have a couple of chairs and a small table. This time we both sat down.

"Now," said Detective Sturgill. "What's this about?"

"I told you that I had seen Evan arguing with someone at a dog show a few days before he died. It turns out that the man was his brother."

"Mark Major." Sturgill nodded. "We spoke to him."

"Did he tell you what he and Evan were fighting about?"

"Money. He said he'd lent Evan some money to help with his legal bills. He wanted to be repaid."

"A family argument over money just a few days before he died. That's interesting," I said. "Does Mark have an alibi?"

"I'm not going to discuss that with you, Ms. Travis."

"Why not?" I asked. "Am I still a suspect?"

"Let's just say, you're not at the top of the list."

"There's a list?" I asked with interest.

Sturgill frowned. "Don't press your luck, Ms. Travis. Just be happy that we looked into your background and your association with Evan Major, and decided that you didn't appear to have anything to gain by his death." He hesitated, then added, "And Detective Young from the Greenwich PD might have put in a good word. He said you were nosier than you ought to be but basically harmless."

Harmless? I wasn't sure I liked that.

"Detective Young also implied that you have a penchant for finding trouble."

"I think trouble finds me," I said.

"I don't care which way it works," Sturgill replied. "As long as you take care to stay out of trouble on my watch."

"I always take care," I told him. It just didn't always help.

"Is that all you had to tell me?" The detective started to rise.

"Evan's ex-wife," I said.

He sat back down. "What about her?"

"She was also after Evan's money."

"How would you know that?"

"She came to see me. She wanted Evan's dog."

"Which you said you didn't have."

I looked at him, surprised. I asked him the same question he'd just asked me. "How do you know that?"

"Annette Major showed up here to complain about you. She wanted us to force you to hand over the animal."

"Which I don't have," I stated. Just in case there was any doubt.

"I don't care who has the dog," Sturgill said. "Or who it belongs to. That's up to the court to decide. It's not police business. And it isn't relevant to Evan Major's murder."

"Except that—like his brother—Evan's ex-wife was also arguing with him about money."

"Apparently that was nothing new. Major and his ex had been arguing over money for a while. And about other things. It was a pretty acrimonious divorce."

I'd doubted that what Annette had told me was true. But it was still nice to have my suspicions confirmed. Now that the detective was finally loosening up, I couldn't resist fishing for a little more information.

"Annette told me that she and Evan had separated because he wanted to shield her when the scandal broke."

"Not likely." Sturgill shook his head. "And that's not what he told his lawyer either. The matter of domestic abuse was raised as well."

"You're kidding," I blurted out. "*Evan?*"

My shocked reaction must have jolted him back to an awareness of whom he was talking to, because Detective Sturgill didn't bother to reply. Instead, he stood up again. The move was clearly meant to be my cue to do the same.

"Are we done here?" he asked.

The detective was already striding toward the door. Maybe I had time to squeeze in one last question.

"Do you think Evan's death was related to those issues with his company, or to family problems, or maybe to something else entirely that happened after he moved to Connecticut?"

Sturgill sighed. "We're looking into all those things, Ms. Travis."

"But why was he attacked now? And why here—"

"That's enough," he said sternly. "It's time for you to go."

The detective had left the door partially open when we'd entered the room. Now he drew it open wide and walked out to the lobby. Three quick strides took him to the outer door. I had to hurry to catch up.

"Thank you for taking the time to talk to me," I said.

"My pleasure," Detective Sturgill replied.

Thank goodness for good manners. Otherwise we'd have been left with nothing to say to each other.

I had hoped that would go better, I thought as I walked across the parking lot to my car. Apparently my idea of useful information was not the same as the detective's. But at least I'd learned one good thing. *My name wasn't at the top of his list.*

Well two things, actually. I was glad to know that he had a list.

I hadn't spent much time at the police station. That gave me the opportunity to do something else before my allotted hour elapsed. The trip home would take me right past Flower Estates. This seemed like the perfect time to drop in on Evan's neighbor, Jim Bolden.

Since the houses in the subdivision had all been constructed from the same basic blueprint, most residents individualized their homes with distinctive paint jobs or landscaping. Not Jim Bolden. His house was white with black shutters. The grass in his small yard was clipped short. The area was uncluttered by such frivolities as colorful flowers or ornate borders.

The look was simple. Classic. It probably hadn't changed since the house was built in the 1940s.

I coasted slowly past Evan's house. Everything appeared to be locked up tight. I had no desire to stop and take a look. The last time I'd been there—when I'd stood and pressed my nose against Evan's windows—he'd been lying dead inside. The thought made me shudder.

I parked the Volvo farther down the street and walked back to Jim Bolden's driveway. A curtain flicked open, then shut, in the front window of his house. The small movement reminded me that Bella lived on the other side of the road. No doubt she could see Mr. Bolden's home just as easily as she'd seen Evan's. I wondered if she was watching me now.

Clearly someone in the house was aware of my arrival. Even so, I had to ring the doorbell twice before the front door opened. Mr. Bolden was small and wizened and his sparse white hair needed to be combed. The ornery expression on his face sharpened to a glare when he saw me. He left the screen door in place and talked to me through it.

"Go away. Whatever you're selling, I don't want any."

"I'm not selling anything, Mr. Bolden. I'm Melanie Travis, remember? I used to live around the corner?"

"Melanie Travis." He sucked on his tongue as he repeated the name thoughtfully. "You had a kid."

"Yes, I did. I do." No sense confusing things by telling him that I now had two.

"And a big dog. A black one. You said it was a Poodle, but I'm not stupid. Poodles aren't that big."

"Yes, I'm the one with the big, black dog," I confirmed.

"You moved away." Mr. Bolden's tone changed. Now he sounded accusing. "So what are you doing back here?"

"I'd like to talk to you for a few minutes if that's all right. Can I come in?"

"In my house?"

"Or somewhere else, if you'd prefer. But maybe just not out here on your front step?"

He considered that. I thought time was supposed to move more quickly when people got older, but apparently Mr. Bolden hadn't gotten the memo. After a minute had passed and we were both still standing there, I was tempted to give up and go home. That was probably what he was hoping for.

"I guess you might as well come in," he said finally, unlatching the screen door. "But you can't stay long."

"No, of course not." I stepped inside. "I'm sure your time is valuable."

"You know it."

I hadn't been sure what to expect, but the house was just as neat inside as it was on the outside. Tables gleamed with polish. A display of Hummel figurines had recently been dusted. The cushions on the couch were freshly plumped.

"We'll go in here," he said, heading toward the small living room. "What's this all about?"

I sat down in a straight-backed chair and said, "It's about your neighbor, Evan Major."

"Who?"

I was sure he'd heard me the first time, but I repeated myself anyway. "Evan Major. He lived next door to you."

"Yup, he did." Mr. Bolden nodded with satisfaction. "He's dead now."

"Do you know anything about that?"

"About what?"

I bit my tongue and said, "His death."

"What's to know? The newspapers covered everything. If you have questions, you ought to call them."

There was no sense in beating around the bush. At this point, I wasn't sure Mr. Bolden would give me a straight answer about anything. If indeed he had one to give.

"I heard that you and Evan Major were in the middle of a dispute when he died," I said.

"Yes, we were. It's over and done now though. Man thought he could put up a big fence right outside my window. Thing that size would have destroyed property values on the whole damn block."

"That must have made you angry," I said.

"Damn right, it did. I guess I showed him."

I gulped. "You *showed* him? How did you do that, Mr. Bolden?"

The old man cackled happily. "I outlasted him, that's how. Nobody's going to be building a fence over there now."

"No, indeed," I agreed. "It must have been difficult for you to hear about the changes Evan wanted to make. I imagine you might have been tempted to strike out at him."

"Tempted? Sure." Mr. Bolden grinned. "At my age, how much time do I have left? I'll use any shortcut I can get my hands on."

"Like perhaps a knife?" I asked quietly.

Abruptly his smile died. "What are you talking about now? I didn't stab the guy, if that's what you're saying. And anyway, if I did do something like that, I wouldn't brag about it."

He sprang up out of his seat with a surprising burst of agility. It occurred to me that when Mr. Bolden was angry, he suddenly moved like a much younger man.

"It's time for you to go," he snapped.

I was already standing up. When we reached the door, I flicked a glance down the street. "I know you've always been involved with your neighbors. You must enjoy living across from Bella Barrundy."

"What do you mean by that?" Now Mr. Bolden was suspicious of everything I said.

"Only that she seems like a nice lady. Someone who's concerned about what goes on in the neighborhood, just like you are."

"Used to enjoy it just fine," he grumbled.

"Why do you say that?"

He nodded toward a house a few doors down. "Until a few months ago, Bella lived there on her own. Seemed perfectly happy that way. Then her mother moved in with her. Now nobody's happy. Those two women fight like cats and dogs."

"That's a shame," I said.

"Tell me about it." Mr. Bolden yanked open the screen door and ushered me outside. "This used to be a quiet place to live. A man could enjoy a little peace in his own home. But between the fracas next door and the one across the street, sometimes I think the whole damn neighborhood has gone to hell."

Chapter 20

That afternoon I sat out on the deck, reading a book. Davey and Kevin were kicking a soccer ball between a pair of net goals that were set up at either end of the backyard. Tar, Augie, and Bud were trying to take part in the game—so there was a lot of barking and yelling going on.

The three bitches, Faith, Eve, and Raven, were ignoring all that activity. They were relaxing in the shade of the oak tree. Considering that it was eighty-five degrees and sunny, it wasn't hard to decide which of those two canine groups looked more intelligent.

I'd just turned a page when I heard the side gate open. Eve and Raven went speeding around the side of the house to check things out. Faith got up and came to me. All the males in the vicinity were making too much noise to realize that we had a visitor.

A moment later, Terry appeared with a Standard Poodle dancing happily on either side of him. Raven and Eve looked inordinately pleased with themselves. As if they thought they'd conjured our guest out of thin air.

I stood up and waved him over. Usually Terry was perfectly groomed; today he looked almost scruffy. He hadn't shaved and his shirt was rumpled. There were dark circles under his eyes. I took that to mean that he hadn't come with good news.

Terry glanced at the game in progress, then stepped up onto the deck. He crouched down and gave Faith a smooch on the nose. Then he stood up and waggled his fingers at me. Note who received the better greeting.

"What are you doing here?" I asked. "It's Thursday. Shouldn't you be clipping Poodles, or bathing them, or doing something useful?"

"I told Crawford I needed a personal day." Terry pulled up a chair and sat down.

"A personal day?" I put down my book and stared at him. "How does that work? Isn't everything between the two of you personal?"

"One would hope. But Crawford wasn't even curious. He didn't ask what I needed to do, he just said okay. It's not like he needed me—he had Gabe helping him. When I left, the two of them were working together like best friends." He looked at me pointedly. "Or more."

Oh. That wasn't good.

Terry gazed out over the yard. For want of something better to do, I followed suit.

Davey and Kevin were nearly ten years apart in age. Davey could have run rings around his little brother. Instead, he was making sure that Kev had plenty of opportunities to dribble the ball and shoot.

The same couldn't be said for the dogs. They were a huge impediment to the action. Especially Bud, who was more coordinated than Kevin and had no compunction about stealing the ball away from him.

"That looks like fun," Terry said after a minute.

"Feel free to join them," I suggested.

I wasn't dumb. I knew what Terry wanted to talk about. I also knew that I had nothing encouraging to tell him. Frankly, I would rather have watched him play soccer with my kids than have that conversation.

"Moi?" He sniffed. "I don't think so. I'm not the sporty type."

"Of course you are. You run around the dog show ring all the time. And very gracefully I might add."

Usually Terry's a sucker for flattery. Today he didn't even notice.

"That's different." His gaze returned to me. "Don't think I don't realize you're stalling. You were *supposed* to be helping me."

"I'm trying."

"Apparently not hard enough. Because my life is going from bad to worse."

"That's not my fault," I told him.

Terry shrugged. "I have to blame somebody."

I was already feeling guilty about my lack of success. This pile-on didn't help. I snapped back at him. "Quit feeling sorry for yourself. And quit bugging me. Most people I try to help step back and let me do my thing in peace."

"Most people you try to help are dead," Terry pointed out. "And what is your *thing* exactly, anyway? Because now that I'm involved, I don't see much of any*thing* happening at all. Just so you know how serious this has become—last night Crawford cooked Gabe dinner."

I stared at him in surprise. Crawford didn't cook. Crawford *never* cooked. His idea of cooking was heating up a frozen pizza. If he remembered to take it out of the box first.

"That's not right," I said.

"Tell me about it." Terry sounded morose. "In all the years we've been together, Crawford's never cooked anything for me. It's always been my job to keep us fed. But Gabe shows up and suddenly Crawford's getting busy in the kitchen."

That was an unexpected development. I couldn't even figure out how to address it. Finally I asked, "Is he a good cook?"

"No." Terry managed a small smile. "The meal was terrible. I think Crawford opened up the spice cabinet and threw in a dash of everything he saw without thinking about how the flavors were supposed to go together."

I smiled too. It was nice to know there was one thing Crawford wasn't good at. Then I realized what Terry had said.

"Wait a minute . . . you were there too?"

He nodded. "It was the three of us sitting at the dining room table. The old boyfriend and the new boyfriend, seated side by side. Talk about awkward."

"Crawford wouldn't do that to you," I said firmly. "I know he wouldn't."

"Trust me. He did it. I was there. Crawford said he wanted us all to get along. One big happy family. Like *that's* ever going to happen. I keep hoping this is just some kind of midlife crisis—that one morning Crawford will wake up and come to his senses. But it's been almost a month and Gabe's still here."

Kev's shriek of outrage drew our attention back to the yard. It looked as though Tar had knocked the soccer ball away just as Kevin had been about to score a goal.

"Goal tending!" Davey cried quickly.

Kev propped his hands on his hips. "What does that mean?"

"It means you get a free shot."

Davey retrieved the ball and set it in front of the goal. Then he herded the Poodles and Bud away while Kevin lined up and kicked. The ball went flying into the net. Celebratory high fives ensued. Davey realized we were watching. He turned and gave us a thumbs-up too.

"You have no idea how lucky you are," Terry said softly.

"I do," I replied. "I think about it every day. But you and Crawford have something equally wonderful."

"We did—until Gabe showed up. I know you talked to him at the show. What did he have to say?"

"Not much."

Terry tipped his head my way and waited for me to continue. He knew I was stalling again.

"Gabe told me he might be staying here for a while," I admitted.

Terry looked pained. I knew that wasn't what he'd wanted to hear.

Quickly I changed the subject. "What did you think of last night's Bite Club meeting?"

The new topic was a good idea. Mention of that debacle made Terry start to relax. He almost smiled when he said, "I found it highly entertaining."

"You would." I laughed. "Who knew that people would get so crabby about answering a few questions?"

"Maybe that's because they have guilty consciences," he considered.

"*All* of them?"

"How would I know? You're the one who's supposed to be sorting things out. But if I had to point a finger at someone it would be Rush Landry."

I nodded. I could see that. "Rush thinks a great deal of himself. He really hated admitting that he'd been duped."

"He probably hated losing his money even more. What he said about joining the book club and coming all this way just to get a look at Evan? You'd have to be pretty angry to do something like that."

"All what way?" I said, surprised. "Where do he and Vic live?"

"Some town in northern New Jersey. Even without traffic, it must take them an hour to get here."

"An hour's drive is nothing for people who show dogs, you know that."

"Well, sure." Terry grinned. "Anyone would travel that far for *points*. But for a book club?"

"We're a very fine book club," I protested.

"We certainly are," he agreed. "If you think about it, we're probably the most exciting book club in the whole tristate area."

"Hey Mom, we're thirsty. What do we have to drink?"

Davey and Kevin had come racing across the yard. They bypassed the steps, opting instead to jump up onto the deck from the grass. It was lucky no one got hurt—especially since they were surrounded by a pack of galloping Poodles. And of course Bud. All the dogs were panting. The boys looked as though they wished they could do the same.

"You know what we have," I replied. "Lemonade, green tea, apple juice, and water. It's all in the refrigerator. Would you please say hello to our guest?"

"Hey, Terry," Davey said. His little brother sketched a wave. "What's new? We're hot. You want something to drink?"

"No, thanks." Terry rose to his feet. "It's time for me to be on my way."

"On your way where?" asked Kev.

"Good question." Terry crouched down in front of him. My son had a smear of bright red raspberry jelly across the front of his T-shirt. Terry didn't notice. He and Kev were eye to eye. Man to man. "Do you have any ideas?"

"It's too hot here," Kevin said brightly. "How about the North Pole?"

Terry laughed ruefully. "Right now, that sounds pretty good to me."

Mark Major called the next morning. He wanted to get together. That came as a surprise. When we'd parted at the funeral, I'd been left with the impression that he wanted nothing further to do with me. But I wasn't about to turn down the opportunity.

I had no idea where Mark lived, or where he might be

coming from. I figured that was his problem. I proposed that we meet at The Bean Counter, a café in North Stamford that was jointly owned and run by my brother, Frank, and my ex-husband. If Mark Major proved to be as surly as he had at our previous meeting, it occurred to me that I might be happy to find myself on friendly turf.

Sam agreed it was his turn for kid duty and said something about the Nature and Science Museum. That alleviated any guilty feelings I might otherwise have felt. Now I was free to kiss the Poodles good-bye and head out for an early lunch.

I called ahead and Frank had saved me a booth near the front window. Even though it was only eleven thirty, there was already a line of customers waiting to order food. I bypassed the crowd and slid into my seat. I knew that sooner or later a meal—not necessarily one I would have chosen for myself—would be set down in front of me.

My brother liked to use me as a taste tester for potential additions to the menu. Sometimes his new creations were wildly successful. On other occasions, they were barely edible. This morning's selection resembled a quesadilla.

Frank was too busy to deliver the plate himself, but he did give me an encouraging wave from behind the counter. That was enough to make me wary. Where my brother's culinary experiments are involved, proceeding with caution is never a bad thing.

I was poking at the plate when Mark Major entered the café. He paused just inside the door to get the lay of the land. Ignoring the long food line, he headed straight to the gourmet coffee counter. A couple minutes later, he sat down across from me.

"If you're hungry, we can split this." I slid the plate into the middle of the table between us.

Mark stared at it dubiously. "What is it?"

"I'm guessing it's a quesadilla."

He looked up. "Don't you know?"

"Not really. See that guy over there behind the counter? That's my brother. He lets me try out new menu items."

"He lets you? Like you want to do that?"

"Well, actually, he makes me."

"That sounds more likely." Mark leaned back in his seat. As if he wanted to put some space between himself and the mystery plate. "Why does it have zucchini in it? And what's that stuff that looks like relish?"

"I have no idea." I cut off a small piece with my fork, put it in my mouth and chewed slowly. The dish tasted mostly of cheese and salt. It wasn't the worst thing I'd ever had—but I wouldn't have paid money to eat it.

Mark watched me through narrowed eyes. After a minute, he dumped a packet of sugar in his coffee. He probably figured that was safe enough to drink.

"I want to apologize for my behavior the last time we met," he said. "I acted like a jerk."

"You did," I agreed. "But it was your brother's funeral. That earns you a bye."

"It shouldn't." He lifted the cup to his lips and took a sip. "As you heard, Evan and I weren't the best of friends."

I nodded. "So why did you want to see me now?"

"Now I know who you are. I mean, you're not a reporter who's trying to land a scoop. You and Evan were actually close."

Close seemed like an exaggeration when it came to describing our relationship. Then again, I had ended up with Evan's puppy. Maybe that made us closer than most.

"Go on," I said.

"I want to hear about Evan's last days. He and I weren't in touch after he moved. You know how it is with families. Things happen, little fights blow up into big feuds. You always think you'll have time to repair the damage." Mark shook his head. "It never crossed my mind that I wouldn't see my brother again."

The dog show had happened after Evan's move, I thought. Mark and Evan had been together then. Call me a cynic, but something about Mark's supposedly heartfelt confession wasn't ringing true.

"You're looking for Evan's money too, aren't you?" I asked.

Mark choked on a swallow of coffee. He recovered, then quickly schooled his features into an expression of innocence. "Why would you say that?"

"Because it's the only thing that makes sense. Last time we met, you wanted nothing to do with me. What's changed since then? Who told you that Evan and I were close?"

Mark didn't reply.

After a moment, I realized he didn't have to. I already knew the answer. "It was Evan's ex-wife, wasn't it?"

"Annette?"

"Does he have more than one?"

"No . . . no. Just Annette." He stumbled over the name.

"She came to me looking for Evan's puppy," I said. "I wondered how she knew about Bully. You told her, didn't you?"

"Maybe." Mark scowled. "You told me that dog wasn't worth anything."

"He isn't. But Annette was convinced that Evan had assets that he'd stashed away somewhere. I'm guessing you are too."

"Here's the thing." Mark shoved the plate to one side. He leaned toward me across the table. "My brother wasn't stupid. Sure, he got himself caught up in a giant mess that spiraled out of control. But Evan was the kind of guy who always had a backup plan. When things got bad, he made a run for it. And I know for a fact that he wouldn't have left empty handed."

"For a fact?" I said skeptically. "Did Annette tell you that too?"

"Why do you keep bringing that woman up?" Mark demanded. "Annette is nobody. She's just his ex-wife."

"Annette told me that she and Evan were getting back together."

"That's ridiculous," Mark snapped. "Once Evan was finally rid of her, he would never have taken her back. Not in a million years."

"You sound very sure of yourself."

"If there's one thing I know about my brother, it's that. Evan was too young to know better when he married Annette. He fell for her little girl voice and glossy exterior. But once they were married, he saw her for who she really was—a fraud and a bully. Annette had to have everything her own way. And if she didn't get it, she lashed out. Hard."

I gulped. When Detective Sturgill had mentioned domestic abuse, I had imagined something totally different.

"But . . ." My voice trailed away uncertainly.

"What? Evan didn't tell you? No, I don't suppose he would have. He was embarrassed. He wouldn't even admit to himself what was happening, much less talk about it to someone else."

Mark almost smiled. He caught himself just in time. "I'd have been embarrassed too, if I couldn't stand up for myself like a man. That was the real reason he and Annette got divorced. The scandal had nothing to do with it. Evan finally manned up and cut her loose."

"When was their divorce finalized?" I asked.

"In the spring. After that Evan pulled up stakes and moved away. There was nothing left for him in New Jersey. The idea that he and Annette were getting back together is a joke. Maybe Evan said something like that to placate her, but that's all it could have been."

I shook my head. "But if they were already divorced, why would he care about placating her?"

"I can tell you haven't seen Annette in action." Mark smirked. "She can be one crazy lady. Nobody wants to get on the wrong side of her temper."

Chapter 21

"**I** have an idea," I said to Sam that evening after dinner. Thanks to summer's long days, it was still light out. The boys were outside shooting hoops. Sam and I were working in the small grooming room off the kitchen. Sam was clipping Tar's face and feet. I was running a pin brush through Eve's thick coat.

The remainder of the Standard Poodles, plus Bud, were lying on the kitchen floor. They watched us through the open doorway, supervising the activity. Anyone who thinks that show dogs don't enjoy the extra attention that premium coat care requires has never owned a Poodle.

"Is that so?" Sam waited to hear more before commenting further. Over the years, he has heard plenty of ideas from me. He hasn't liked all of them.

I already knew he wasn't going to like this one.

Aunt Peg, however, would think it was splendid.

"It's about the dog show," I said.

The next day we were meeting Aunt Peg and Coral at a show near Paramus, New Jersey. Davey would once again be handling Coral in the Puppy Class. The Standard Poodle entry was small and Aunt Peg had high hopes for the outcome.

Sam looked up. "Don't tell me you're not coming with us."

"Of course I'm coming." That wasn't even in question. "But I was thinking I might drop you and the boys off at the show in the morning, then go run an errand while you get Coral ready. I'll be back in plenty of time to watch Davey take her in the ring."

"An errand," Sam said drily. He'd already heard about my meeting with Mark Major. "Evan was from New Jersey. I'm guessing this is related?"

"I want to drop in on his ex-wife."

"Drop in? As in, uninvited and unexpected?"

I nodded. Taking people by surprise often led to unguarded answers. My favorite kind.

"Where does she live?"

"Englewood," I said brightly. I'd looked up her address online. "Annette showed up here without any warning. It's my turn to reciprocate."

Sam considered that as he lifted Tar's ear out of the way, then ran the clipper up the curve of the Poodle's throat. "If you think she had something to do with Evan's death, you should give your information to the police and let them handle it."

"I just tried that, and it didn't go particularly well."

Sam was using a forty blade and the naked skin on Tar's back skull had a pale cast. The hair would grow back quickly, however. In two days, the Poodle's face would look like black velvet.

"If you suspect this woman might have committed a murder, are you sure you want to go see her by yourself?"

"I'll be fine," I told him.

Sam cocked a brow. "Will you?"

His skepticism was warranted. Things didn't always turn out the way I planned. I'd gotten myself hurt before and we both knew it.

I put down my brush and began to untangle a snarl with

my fingers. "Annette is tall and skinny, and looks like she'd hate to do anything that might break a nail. Plus, she has about as much muscle mass as a swizzle stick."

"And yet you think she was capable of overpowering her ex-husband," Sam pointed out. He put down the clippers for a minute so he could reposition Tar on his grooming table.

"That's different. She and Evan had a weird dynamic."

Sam glanced my way. "The domestic abuse?"

I nodded. "I'm guessing she was the one responsible for the bruise we saw on Evan's jaw at the book club meeting. I know he was stronger than she is. He could have held her off—or he could have fought back. But he didn't."

"Maybe she took him by surprise," Sam said.

He flipped the switch and the clipper began to buzz. He lifted one of Tar's front feet and deftly zipped off the hair between the toes. Tar had been clipped dozens of times before. He was half asleep.

"I'll be careful," I told him. "I'm not going to allow that to happen to me."

Sam set the shaved foot back down and paused before picking up another. "How long do you expect to be gone?"

"I can be there and back in an hour."

"You'd better be," Sam replied. "Or I'm coming after you."

"You can't," I said with a laugh. "You have to help Davey get Coral ready for the show ring."

"Peg would be happy to take over. Probably more than happy. That would make her day. Especially if she thought I was riding to your rescue."

"Like my knight in shining armor?" I smiled.

"Something like that. Only light on the armor."

I was finished brushing Eve. I let her stand up, then

lifted her down off the table and set her on the floor. Eve had a long, luxurious shake.

"I'll take you any way I can get you," I said to Sam.

Alice called while Sam was finishing up with Tar. The noise from the clippers made it hard to hear. I grabbed my phone off the kitchen counter and took it outside. The sun was low in the sky, dropping behind the trees. In another few minutes it would be dark.

"What's up?" I asked.

"I did something," she said. "Maybe something stupid. But it's too late to rethink that now."

"Okay." I sat down on the chaise and pulled my feet up underneath me. Faith hopped up and lay down beside me. She was feeling left out. She probably wished I'd brushed her too. I would have except that Faith was already perfect, just the way she was.

"What did you do and why are we worried about it?" I asked.

"You know I love you dearly."

"Of course." I laughed. "And that is *so* not an answer."

Alice didn't laugh with me. That was a bad sign. I sat back to listen.

"It pissed me off the way everyone treated you at Bite Club the other night," she said. "Like you were some kind of nut who goes around poking your nose into everybody's private lives for no reason."

"They might have had a point—" I began.

"No, they didn't," Alice replied stoutly. "So I decided that someone needed to step up and defend you. That's why I went and yelled at Bella Barrundy."

I hadn't been expecting that. Neither the Bella part, nor the yelling part. In fact I wasn't even sure I'd ever heard Alice raise her voice. Except maybe when the kids *really* deserved it.

"You yelled at her about me?" I asked.

"Of course about you. What other reason would I have? First she told the police about you. Then she had the nerve to air her accusations again at the meeting. She's trying to make it sound like Evan's death was your fault. I told her to cut it out."

Alice Brickman, *my champion*. Right that moment, her armor was even shinier than Sam's.

"What did she say to that?"

"Bella wasn't happy. She told me to mind my own business. So I said she was a fine one to talk. Flower Estates used to be a nice place to live. Now everything is in an uproar and she isn't helping."

"Alice, I could kiss you," I said gratefully.

"Yes, well . . . that wasn't how things ended."

"Oh?"

The single syllable dangled between us for several seconds before Alice spoke again.

"Bella's mother moved in with her recently," she said finally. "Did you know that?"

"Actually I did. Mr. Bolden mentioned it when I spoke to him the other day."

"Well, I had no idea. Not that it matters. But there I was giving Bella what-for and the next thing I knew, this older woman appeared in the doorway behind her. And yes, I said doorway—because I was still standing outside. Bella hadn't even had the good manners to invite me in."

"Under the circumstances, can you blame her?"

"I guess not," Alice admitted. "But that's beside the point. So Mrs. Barrundy pushed Bella aside and glared at me like she couldn't believe I had the nerve to talk to her daughter like that. Her adult daughter, I might add. So I can talk to Bella any way I want."

"Yes, you can," I agreed.

"Especially when I think her actions are out of line," Alice added. "Which I do."

"Me too," I agreed. Listening seemed to be my chief contribution to the conversation. I was happy to keep doing so as long as Alice wanted to talk.

"Then Mrs. Barrundy started yelling at me. She said Bella was right to be worried about a murder in her own neighborhood. And that anyone with an ounce of sense would do everything she could to see the killer brought to justice. She paused to take a breath and I tried to get a word in—but Mrs. Barrundy just started up again and talked right over me. So who knows, maybe she doesn't even need to breathe?"

"I'm pretty sure she does," I said.

"The longer that woman kept yelling, the more upset Bella looked. Her own mother wouldn't let her say a thing either. Eventually Bella and I weren't even listening anymore. We were just standing there exchanging empathetic glances. Or maybe horrified ones. Because if I had to live with my mother and she was anything like Mrs. Barrundy, that's how I would feel. Absolutely horrified."

"You must have escaped at some point," I said. "Because you seem to have survived the encounter and here we are talking on the phone."

"Oh, I survived all right. But I didn't accomplish what I set out to do. Rather than making Bella feel bad, now *I* feel rotten instead. I was so mad when I knocked on her door. But after meeting Bella's mother, I see the problem. If I had to live with Mrs. Barrundy, I'd be crabby all the time too. So now I feel sorry for Bella, and that's the last thing I wanted."

"I appreciate your coming to my defense, even if things didn't turn out the way you wanted." It was a good thing Alice couldn't see me. I was biting my lip to hold back a grin. "I know you meant well."

"You're welcome," she said in a small voice. "Despite how many scrapes you get yourself into, I know you always mean well too. That's all I was trying to say to Bella. That you're trying to help. And that she was wrong to try and blame you for something that clearly isn't your fault. But, Mel?"

"Hmm?"

"Please hurry up and get this figured out so we can all go back to enjoying our normal problems. I want my quiet neighborhood back. I want my peaceful life back."

"Don't we all," I said.

Annette Major lived in a brick, four-story apartment complex on the outskirts of Englewood. There was a wide, tree-shaded lawn in front of her building, and plenty of available parking in the lot that adjoined it.

I was afraid I might need to be buzzed in to the building, but a resident who was exiting the lobby as I arrived held the door open for me. Annette's apartment was on the third floor. I took the elevator up.

It was nine thirty on a Saturday morning. I hoped Annette was the kind of person who liked to sleep in on weekends. She didn't answer the first time I rang the doorbell, but I remained optimistic.

Maybe she was inside the apartment tweeting, I thought. That activity seemed to require her undivided attention.

After two minutes passed and a knock on the door also went unanswered, I began to reevaluate the wisdom of my plan. At this rate, I would be back at the dog show before anyone had even had a chance to miss me.

A ding sounded behind me. The elevator door slid open. Annette stepped out. Her blond hair was gathered back in a ponytail and there was a light sheen of sweat on her brow. She was dressed in fashionable jogging gear and carrying a bag from Starbucks.

Fishing for her keys in a small pouch at her waist, Annette had almost reached her apartment before she saw me standing there. Then she stopped short. She was probably surprised to see me, but with the Botox it was hard to tell.

"Oh! Hello," she said. "Can I help you?"

"I'm Melanie," I told her. "We met at the beginning of the week."

"I know that. What are you doing here?" Annette glanced around behind me as though she thought I might be hiding something. "Did you bring me the dog?"

Yes, I thought. *He's in my pocket.*

"No," I said aloud. "I came to talk."

Annette slid past me. She fit her key into the lock, then glanced back at me over her shoulder. "About what?"

"Is that a serious question?"

She pushed the door open and walked inside. "No, I guess not."

"Can I come in?"

"If you must. But not for long. I have a busy morning."

The door opened directly into a medium-sized living room that was crammed full of furniture. Two couches, a trio of chairs, and half a dozen tables all vied for space. *No wonder Evan's house was nearly empty*, I thought. Everything he and Annette had owned jointly must have ended up here.

Annette went straight to a kitchen area that was separated from the living room by a low counter. She pulled a large cup out of the Starbucks bag and popped off the plastic top. The aroma of freshly brewed coffee filled the room. I felt my stomach rumble in response.

Annette took a long swallow of coffee. Then she dumped the bag in the trash and said, "Sit."

It wasn't lost on me that Annette had placed herself in proximity to the knives. But with the counter still between us, I figured I was safe enough. I chose a chair on the other side of the room.

Annette took another gulp of coffee. I waited for her to finish.

She set the cup down on the counter and glared at me. "You'd better start talking. I don't have all day."

I didn't either, so I led with my best shot.

"I understand you liked to beat up your husband," I said.

Chapter 22

I'd hoped to shock her, but Annette's expression barely wavered. Maybe that was the Botox again. Or maybe she didn't really care that people knew how she'd treated Evan.

"Ex-husband," she corrected. "What's it to you?"

"Your ex-husband is dead," I said.

"I know that. Everybody knows that. It's a huge inconvenience. Are you here because you think I killed him?"

"The thought has crossed my mind. I've heard you have a temper."

Annette laughed gently. "Don't tell me. You've been talking to Mark."

My silence was probably answer enough.

"He never liked me." She paused for another swallow of coffee. "I never liked him either."

"Was he wrong in what he said about you?" I asked.

"No, not really." She lobbed the empty cup into the trash. If I'd drunk that much coffee that quickly I'd have been so buzzed I could barely stand. Annette seemed oblivious to its effects. "Evan and I had what you might call a tumultuous relationship."

"Funny thing about that," I said. "Evan wasn't a tumultuous kind of guy when I knew him. Just the opposite, in fact."

She walked around the end of the counter and perched on the arm of an upholstered chair. "That was part of the problem. Evan was a smart man who never understood his own worth. He had talents. He could have risen far in business—but he didn't know how to put himself forward, to make himself indispensable to the people he worked with. Evan should have been a partner in Northeast Wealth Management. Instead, he was content to toil away in his little office . . . doing his little computer things."

"The men who were partners in NEWealth were indicted," I pointed out.

Annette waved a hand in the air, dismissing the comment as though it wasn't important. "I married Evan for his potential. It was my job to see that he realized it."

"By hitting him," I said quietly.

"You don't understand anything," Annette snapped.

"Feel free to enlighten me."

"Why should I bother? You've already formed an opinion of me. All you really want is for me to confirm what you think you already know."

"Did you kill your ex-husband?"

"No, of course not."

"Evan showed up at a book club meeting two weeks ago with a fresh bruise on his jaw. He said he'd been in a car accident but his car didn't have a scratch on it. Was that your doing?"

Annette shrugged. "It might have been."

"What potential were you hoping he would realize that night?" I asked.

"If you must know, I'd come to tell Evan that I needed more money."

"And he wouldn't give it to you."

"He said there wasn't any more money. That everything had gone to pay the lawyers. That I should be happy he'd been able to use it to keep himself out of jail. As if I cared about that," Annette sniffed. "After the news hit the media—after the scandal became all anyone could talk about—Evan was unemployable. So what did it matter where he was?"

Holy crap. With this bitch for an ex-wife, it was no wonder Evan didn't have much to say for himself.

"You didn't like your ex-husband very much, did you?"

"So what?" She turned an accusing gaze my way. "That doesn't mean that I killed him. Why would I have bothered?"

"Mark said you had a terrible temper. Maybe you lost it."

"Now we're back to Mark again." Annette looked annoyed. "That man's a liar. And an opportunist. I'll bet he came to you looking for money too, didn't he?"

I nodded.

"Believe anything he says at your own peril. I may not have been a perfect wife, but Mark's no saint either. After Evan moved away, it meant that Mark couldn't keep an eye on him in person anymore. So he had someone spying on Evan."

Spying on him?

I frowned. "What are you talking about?"

"Oh, for Pete's sake," Annette snapped. "Try to keep up."

"I guess we're still talking about the money."

"You think?" She rolled her eyes. "Mark was sure that Evan would slip up eventually. That he would start spending money. Or at least talk about it. And when that happened, he planned to swoop in and demand his share."

Detective Sturgill had mentioned there was friction between the two brothers due to money owed. "Mark had lent Evan money to help with his legal bills," I said. "Right?"

Annette stared at me like I was stupid. "Where did you get that idea?"

"Just a bad guess," I quickly backpedaled. "Go on."

"It was old business, from when they were younger. Mark gave Evan money for a start-up company. Some dumb dot-com thing. Evan said he would make them both rich, but instead the company went bust. Mark wanted to be paid back. Evan told him tough luck—he'd understood the risks when he'd invested."

Annette smiled with satisfaction. "That was my doing. Evan never would have stood up for himself on his own. We'd just gotten together and I convinced him that our future was much more important than any obligation he felt to his brother."

"I can see why you and Mark don't get along," I said.

"Nobody gets along with him. That's not my fault. Mark even had the nerve to show up here when Evan and I were getting divorced. He wanted to look through Evan's business files. As if I would have been willing to let him do that."

That was interesting.

"Why do you have Evan's files?" I asked.

"Because he didn't think to safeguard them when he moved out of our house," Annette said with a crafty smirk. "And as everyone knows, when you're in the middle of a divorce you grab everything you can get your hands on. Especially stuff your spouse might pay to get back."

Annette pushed herself up off the edge of the chair. "Evan had his faults, but his record-keeping was meticulous. He backed up *everything*. Both when he was trying to get his own company off the ground, and then later at NEWealth. He made personal copies of anything that crossed his desk."

I stood up as well. "I'd imagine that the authorities might have wanted to see those files."

"They might have. If they'd known they existed. But Evan didn't volunteer to tell them. So I didn't see a need to either." She spun around and headed toward the door. "Are we done here?"

Instead of answering, I simply followed her. Annette opened the door and waited for me to walk out.

"Next time you see Mark, you tell him to stay the hell out of my business," Annette snapped.

I was barely through the doorway before she slammed the door shut. I was lucky it didn't hit me.

Back at the showground, things were proceeding smoothly. Or as smoothly as they could when two people with strong personalities each thought that they were in charge of preparing one Standard Poodle to walk into a show ring.

"Finally! She arrives." Terry sent me a smooch from Crawford's neighboring setup when I entered the handlers' tent. He added in a loud, carnival barker's voice, "And welcome to *Family Feud*! Peg is ahead on points but Davey may yet eke out the win. Kevin has locked himself inside a crate, while Sam appears to be acting as referee for this edition of our game."

"Wonderful." I stared at my squabbling relatives. "I wouldn't have left you alone if I didn't think I could trust you to play nicely."

"Aunt Peg has too many rules," Davey grumbled under his breath.

"And you, young man"—she poked his side with the tip of a knitting needle—"try to take too many shortcuts. Doing a job right is all about the details."

"The judge doesn't see the details," Davey retorted. "He looks at the big picture. Mostly from the other side of the ring."

"That's enough." I inserted myself between them. Coral was sitting up on her table. She looked relieved by my intervention. "Davey, I'd like to have a word with you. Let's step outside the tent."

"I can't leave. The minute I'm gone, she'll redo everything I've done."

I raised a brow in Aunt Peg's direction. She frowned in reply. That was *not* a promise of good behavior. More like an indication of why they'd been having problems.

"Go," Sam said to Davey. "I'll keep an eye on things here."

"Coral isn't a thing," Aunt Peg said huffily. "She's a Poodle. *My* Poodle."

"Unless you want to take *your* Poodle in the show ring yourself," I told her, "you'd better figure out a way to keep your hands to yourself for a few minutes."

Davey and I walked outside the tent. Before I could even open my mouth, he was already starting his defense. I gave him two full minutes to air a litany of complaints. Aunt Peg didn't think his line brushing was thorough enough. She wanted Coral's ears wrapped while he thought they should be brushed out and banded. She was sure the puppy's show ring topknot was too loose.

Eventually Davey began to wind down.

"Are you finished?" I asked.

"I guess."

"Do you feel better?"

"Not really," he replied. "No matter how hard I try, Aunt Peg makes me feel like I can't do anything right."

Welcome to the club, I thought.

"You know what she's like," I said. "When it comes to her Standard Poodles—and her relatives—Aunt Peg has exceedingly high standards. So through no fault of your own, you've got the double whammy."

"She's the one who asked me to handle Coral," Davey protested. "She must have thought I was good enough then. But now she won't leave me alone and let me do my job."

"Of course you're *good enough*," I told him. "But you don't know everything. Wouldn't you like to be better?"

Davey frowned, then slowly nodded.

"You still have a lot to learn and Aunt Peg is the best teacher you could possibly have. That is, if the two of you could figure out how to work together."

"She doesn't want to work together. All she wants to do is boss me around."

"That's because Aunt Peg is naturally bossy," I said.

The two of us shared a complicit grin.

"And also because Coral is her puppy—descended from a long line of illustrious Cedar Crest Standard Poodles. Every time one of Aunt Peg's Poodles walks into a ring, people pay attention. What that Poodle looks like, and how it behaves, reflects back on her even if she isn't the one showing it."

My son nodded. He was listening.

"That's why Aunt Peg is so determined to make sure that everything is just right—and why you have to be too. Even if that means biting your tongue sometimes."

"More than sometimes," Davey grumbled, but he smiled to let me know that he didn't mean it.

"Showing Coral is a privilege," I told him. "But that doesn't mean it's something you have to do if you'd rather not."

"No!" Davey looked up quickly. "I want to handle her."

I slung an arm around his shoulder. "Then let's go do it. And try not to take everything Aunt Peg says to heart. This is supposed to be fun, you know."

"You know what would really be fun?" Davey asked as we headed back toward the tent.

"No, what?"

"If you dragged Aunt Peg out here and gave her a lecture too."

I snorted out a laugh. "You must think I have a death wish. That is not happening."

Back at the setup, Sam and Coral were waiting for us. In our absence, Aunt Peg had disappeared. If only she'd done that before I'd arrived, the whole mother-son talk wouldn't have been necessary. But no, that would have made my life too easy.

While Sam and Davey went back to work on Coral, I got Kev out of the dog crate and set him up in a chair with a coloring book. Crawford and Gabe returned from the ring with two Finnish Spitz. The ribbons Gabe was carrying indicated that Crawford had won, and the two men were chatting with animation. Terry pointedly ignored them both.

I shot him a look of sympathy. Terry ignored me too.

The Finkies went back in their crates. Crawford checked the schedule taped to the open lid of his tack box, then he and Gabe each took out a Miniature Poodle. Minis wouldn't be judged until an hour after Standards were finished. These dogs hadn't even been brushed out yet.

At the previous show, Gabe had merely watched as Crawford and Terry groomed their entries. Now it looked as though Gabe had since been promoted—because Crawford was trusting him with the most basic show ring prep, brushing out a Poodle. Both men laid their Minis down on grooming tables in the narrow aisle. Both began to line brush through the dogs' hair.

Crawford's and Gabe's hands were moving in sync. The rhythm of their movements was steady enough to be almost hypnotic. Watching the two men work side by side, I was struck by how similar their mannerisms were.

That made sense, I thought. Crawford had taught Gabe everything the younger man knew about performing this process. It was only natural that their movements and body language would look the same.

My brow furrowed. I continued watching for another minute. Something was niggling at me. Then all at once I knew what it was.

It wasn't just their deft stroke-work that looked similar. It was also the set of the two men's shoulders as they leaned over their dogs. And that Crawford and Gabe both possessed the same graceful hands and long, agile fingers—perfect for flying nimbly through dense Poodle hair.

Why hadn't I noticed that sooner?

I sidled over to the edge of their setup and took a closer look. Small things I'd never previously observed now seemed glaringly obvious. Gabe and Crawford shared the same square jawline. And although Crawford's hair was gray, and Gabe's brown, the texture was similar: smooth and thick, with just a hint of curl. Now that I stopped and thought about it, even their smiles looked alike.

Well damn, I thought. Having finally noticed what had been right in front of me all along, I wondered how I could ever have missed it. How we *all* could have missed it.

My gaze fastened on Crawford, willing him to turn around. He and I needed to talk. The sooner, the better. Because I didn't dare say anything to Terry until I was sure that what I suspected was true. If I was correct, this was good news. No, it was *great* news.

I sensed Sam's presence beside me before he spoke. I glanced up to find him staring at me quizzically.

"Are you all right?" he asked.

"Sure, I'm fine. Totally fine. Absolutely fine."

I looked over at Terry and grinned like an idiot. He didn't see me making a fool of myself. He was still ignoring me.

"You don't look fine." Sam sounded concerned.

"Really." I leaned up and kissed his cheek. "I'm good."

Sam didn't look convinced, but he knew better than to

argue. "In that case, would you mind running up to the ring and getting Coral's number? Davey and I will be right behind you."

"Sure." I grinned. "I can do that."

I didn't run to the ring. Instead, I was pretty sure I danced. I was feeling that good.

Today was turning out to be a terrific day.

Chapter 23

When I reached the Poodle ring, Aunt Peg was already there. She was watching the end of the Boston Terrier judging—and probably weighing her own opinions against those of the official judge. She glanced over at me when I came to stand beside her.

"I've already picked up Davey's armband," she said tartly. "I assume you trust me to do that much?"

"Self-pity does not become you," I replied. "Nor sarcasm."

"On the contrary, I'm quite good with sarcasm. Though I must admit I don't have much experience with self-pity."

"Well, don't start now on my account."

The entrants in the Boston Terrier Best of Breed class were gaiting around the ring. One of the small dogs hopped in the air over a tuft of grass. Aunt Peg and I smiled together as the Boston threw in a little buck for good measure upon landing.

"I hope you told Davey he was wrong," she commented. Her head faced forward, her eyes still on the ring.

"I told him you were both wrong," I said. "And that you're too bossy."

"Too bossy." Aunt Peg sniffed. "As if there is such a thing. How will he learn if I don't show him what to do?"

We'd been in this position before. On the previous occasion, Davey had been showing one of our Standard Poodles. That had been bad enough. Now he was handling one that belonged to Aunt Peg. That made things worse.

"Davey's almost fourteen," I pointed out. "He'll be starting high school in the fall. You can't continue to treat him like he's still a child. If you keep pushing, he's going to push back. You've already seen that."

"Oh pish," said Aunt Peg. "I push you." She paused, then added, "Come to think of it, I push everyone."

Nobody I knew would argue with that assertion.

"Well, it doesn't work with Davey. You have to sprinkle some praise in among your complaints. And sometimes you have to let him do something wrong and learn from it."

"I suppose I might be able to do that," Aunt Peg mused. "As long as any mistakes he makes are corrected *before* Coral enters the ring."

Aunt Peg was a fierce competitor, especially when it came to her Poodles. If she was asked to pick between keeping peace in the family and winning, I was pretty sure she wouldn't hesitate to choose the latter.

In the ring, the judge was awarding the ribbons to his Boston Terriers. Standard Poodles were next. The entry was small. Two class dogs would be followed by two class bitches, and then Crawford's special. Poodles and their handlers were beginning to gather.

Sam appeared with Kevin. Behind them were Davey and Coral. The Poodle puppy looked superb. At nine months of age, she finally had enough hair to make a proper topknot and fill out her trim. The finish on her scissoring was so good I was sure Sam must have helped. Even Aunt Peg wouldn't be able to find fault with the way the puppy looked.

She beckoned Davey over. When he saw she had his number, he held out his arm. Aunt Peg ran two rubber bands up his sleeve, then slipped the armband underneath them and snapped it into place.

"It seems I must apologize," she said to my son.

Sam looked at me and raised a brow. He hadn't expected that. Neither had I. I shook my head slightly.

"Apparently I came on too strong earlier," she added.

"I need to apologize too," Davey replied. "I know you know a lot more than me. I should have listened better."

Sam and I shared another look. I don't know which one of us was more astonished. We were also both pleased. Detente was a rare commodity in my family.

The two Standard Open dogs entered the ring. Aunt Peg and Davey stood with Coral between them. In a low voice that didn't carry beyond their small circle, Aunt Peg critiqued the performances they were watching. I saw Davey nod, then ask a question.

Sam sidled over next to me. I took Kevin's hand in mine so he wouldn't disappear while we were watching Davey. My younger son was apt to follow any dog with spots.

"You must be a miracle worker," Sam said, nodding toward Davey and Aunt Peg. "Those two were at each other's throats all morning."

"I'm a mother." I grinned. "It's kind of the same thing."

The two dogs exited the ring with their class and Winners ribbons. The Puppy Bitch class was next. Coral was a single entry. Aunt Peg patted Davey on the back and wished him luck.

Of course it didn't take much luck to win a class in which you were the only participant. But the judge wouldn't just be deciding whether or not Coral was worthy of the blue ribbon. He would also be thinking ahead and evaluating her chances against the Open bitch to come.

Coral was on her toes in the ring and Davey managed her exuberance well. He skillfully navigated the fine line between keeping the puppy under control and letting her show off her natural flair. When the judge smiled to himself as Davey and Coral gaited around the ring for the final time, I was sure they'd made a great first impression.

The Open bitch was big, and white, and had a lot of hair. She was shown by the same professional handler who'd just gone Reserve Winners in dogs. I knew he had to be thinking that now it was his turn to take the points.

As the class progressed, I looked at the white Poodle critically. She had a lovely face and a melting expression. And she was certainly more mature than Coral. But beyond that, there was no comparison in the quality of the two bitches. I could only hope that the judge agreed with me.

Kevin's fingers slipped out of mine. He sidled over to give Coral a pat. I grabbed him back just in time.

"Not yet," I told him. "Coral still has to go back in the ring. She needs to be judged again."

"But Davey already won."

Kev proudly showed me the blue ribbon he had tucked in the waistband of his shorts. Davey had given him the scrap of fabric when he'd come out of the ring. Aunt Peg didn't care a whit for blue ribbons. She only wanted purple or better.

"I know," I said. "But there's more."

It all happened quickly after that. The white bitch got her own blue ribbon, then Coral was called back to the ring. Davey placed her in line behind the Open bitch.

The judge stepped back so that he was standing in the middle of the ring. Shading his eyes with his hand, he stared at the two Standard Poodles in front of him. Then, without any fanfare at all, he simply pointed.

"The puppy is my Winners Bitch," he said. "The Open bitch is Reserve."

"Oh, well done!" Aunt Peg cried. She gave a little leap in the air.

Davey heard her. He looked over and the two of them shared a delighted smile. My own contribution to the win had been minute, but my heart swelled with pride anyway.

Beside me, Kevin clapped his hands with excitement. "Go, Davey!" he yelled.

I quickly shushed him but Davey didn't care. He was still grinning when he accepted the purple Winners ribbon. Crawford led his champion bitch into the ring. The Winners Dog came in behind him. Davey shoved the ribbon into his pocket, then hustled Coral into place at the end of the line.

Coral had already won the single point that was available today. So anything that happened now was gravy. Still, it was gratifying to have Coral named Best of Winners over the dog, who was Best of Opposite Sex to Crawford's champion.

We all waited at ringside until the judge took a break for pictures. Davey invited Aunt Peg to stand with him in Coral's win photo. Aunt Peg politely declined.

"This is your triumph," she told him. "Yours and Coral's. You should take the credit."

It wasn't hard to get everyone to smile when the show photographer snapped the picture. Even though it was a small win, it felt as though we'd surmounted a few hurdles along the way. I could only hope that Coral's career would proceed more smoothly in the future.

We were about to head back to the grooming tent when I heard someone call my name. I turned and saw Vic Landry heading in my direction.

"Go on ahead," I told Sam. "I'll catch up with you guys in a minute."

I skirted around the ring and met Vic halfway. Today she was dressed in neatly pressed slacks and shoes she could run in. I took that to mean that she was probably showing one of her Belgian Tervurens.

"I'm glad I caught you," she said. "I figured you'd be hanging out at the Poodle ring."

"My son just put a point on a Standard Poodle puppy," I said happily.

"Congratulations! That's tough to do in your breed."

Most dog show exhibitors celebrated each other's successes. We all knew how much dedication and hard work went in to every single win.

"Thank you. He's thrilled. What's going on with you?"

"Tervs don't go in the ring for another hour. In the meantime, I was hoping we could talk?" Vic put a hand on my arm and guided me away from the crowded area near the rings.

"Sure. Is something wrong?"

"I wanted to apologize for the way Rush treated you the other night at the meeting. Actually, I guess for the way everyone treated you."

"I appreciate that," I replied. "But it wasn't your fault."

"Not entirely—but I know what Rush can be like. He wants to take charge of things. He's always sure that he's the smartest man in the room. I probably should have warned you that he might come gunning for you."

Rush hadn't been the only one, I thought. In fact, his reaction had been more restrained than that of some of the other members. Nevertheless it was interesting to me that Vic had apparently gone to the meeting expecting there might be trouble.

"What made you think that?" I asked.

Vic looked quickly from side to side. As if she was afraid that someone might be listening to our conversation. Even though nobody was near enough to hear what we were saying, she still lowered her voice. "That stuff Rush said at the meeting about joining the club so he could see what kind of man Evan was? That was a load of crap."

I nodded. "I thought you looked surprised when Rush said that the two of you had had money invested with NEWealth."

She frowned angrily. "I found out about our financial losses at the meeting, along with everybody else. Talk about feeling like an idiot. On the drive home I asked Rush if there was anything else I ought to know about *our* involvement in the situation. He hates it when I ask questions—he'd rather just tell me what to do. He said no."

Vic lifted her chin. "But this time I wasn't buying it. I kept asking, pushing until he finally admitted that he'd been in the same fraternity in college with a guy named Mark Major."

I stared at her. That was unexpected. "Evan's brother?"

"Apparently so. Although Rush had never met Evan. Or even knew he existed. Rush had lost touch with Mark over the years, so he was surprised to hear from him recently."

"What did Mark want?"

"He asked Rush to do him a favor." Vic frowned. "One that had to do with Evan."

"Mark told Rush he was looking for Evan's money, didn't he?" I guessed.

Vic looked at me curiously. "How did you know that?"

"He contacted me too."

"Then I guess you know that Mark was convinced Evan had gotten away with a bundle of cash when his company went belly up."

For Pete's sake, I thought. Evan drove an economy car. He'd lived in a barely furnished house. I was pretty sure that Mark and Annette were barking up the wrong tree. But it wasn't the first time I'd seen a family dispute over money get totally out of hand.

"Mark was keeping tabs on his brother," Vic said. "You probably know about that too?"

"So I'd heard," I replied. Just that morning in fact. This was all beginning to sound familiar. "Is that where Rush came in?"

Color rose in Vic's cheeks. She was clearly embarrassed. I didn't blame her. I'd have been embarrassed too if I'd found out that my husband had taken part in a scheme like that. For all his blustering, Rush hadn't struck me as a foolish man. I wondered why he'd agreed to the plan. There had to be something I was missing.

"Mark knew that Evan had joined Bite Club," Vic said. "And he checked into Peg Turnbull's background and found out she was a dog show judge. That reminded him of his old buddy, Rush."

She shook her head. "So now you had two guys talking to each other—both of whom had lost money with Evan, and both of them wanting it back. It wasn't hard for Mark to convince Rush to use his dog show connection to get himself invited to join the club. Hunhh." Vic looked disgusted. "I should have known Rush was up to something when he said he wanted to join a *book club*."

I was half tempted to defend my book club, but then it occurred to me that I had more important things to worry about. "So you didn't know a thing about Evan, or Mark, or NEWealth before you came to that book club meeting?"

"Zero," Vic admitted. "Zilch. Which is why I'm here talking to you. Payback for Rush keeping me in the dark. It would piss the crap out of him if he knew I was telling you about how he got himself mixed up in this mess."

"How much money did you and Rush lose when NEWealth went bankrupt?" I asked.

Vic thought for a few moments, then shrugged.

"Didn't you *ask*?"

"Why would I? What's the difference? The money's gone now."

I sent up a brief prayer for patience, then said, "It makes a difference because I'm wondering how angry your husband might have been about being defrauded out of his investment."

"No way," Vic said. "If you're thinking Rush had something to do with Evan's death, you're wrong."

"I wouldn't be so sure of that if I were you," I said. "You know your husband was keeping other secrets from you. Maybe this was one more."

It turned out that Davey wasn't the only one who had a successful day at the show. Crawford put points on a Toy Poodle, and won the variety in both Minis and Standards. Crawford's Mini was a previous Best in Show winner. He would be handling that dog in the Non-Sporting Group, while Terry would be showing the Standard.

In the lull before the group judging started, the mood at the setup was relaxed and happy. The two variety winning Poodles were lying on their tabletops, waiting to compete again. Aunt Peg and Davey were debating the merits of the Mini Poodle entrants they'd watched earlier. Gabe was cleaning out ex pens. Sam and Kevin went to the parking lot to retrieve our car.

When Terry left in search of a bathroom, I took the opportunity to pull Crawford aside. "I need to talk to you about something important."

Crawford lifted a brow. "Go ahead."

"Something private," I said. "Can I stop by your place this week?"

Crawford and Terry lived in Bedford. In dog show distance—a measurement that ran counter to dog years—that was right around the corner.

"If you want, sure. Pick a day."

"What are you doing Monday?"

"Probably sleeping." Crawford chuckled. "These hectic weekends are hard on an old man."

Yeah, right. Crawford would still be running around the show ring with champion Poodles when the rest of us were in nursing homes.

"In the afternoon then," I said. "Just you and me. Is that all right?"

The handler's expression turned somber. "Whatever you need, Melanie. You know that." He reached out and laid a hand on my arm. "Is everything okay?"

"I hope so," I said.

Chapter 24

Saturday had been interesting in more ways than one. I spent the evening mulling over everything I'd learned. When I woke up Sunday morning, I knew I needed to talk to Aunt Peg.

Consulting with Aunt Peg can be a doubled-edged sword. She has the sharpest mind of anyone I know. And her devious streak serves me well when I am trying to puzzle out people's motives for wrongdoing. On the downside, she loves to meddle. And she's inclined to magnify even the smallest complication into something much bigger. Which means that Aunt Peg is just as likely to multiply my problems as she is to solve them.

On the whole, I decided to chance it.

The sun was up but the rest of my household was still asleep when I got out of bed. Faith opened her eyes and cocked her head ten minutes later when I was ready to go. I beckoned my fingers, inviting her to come along. My husband didn't even stir. I left him a note.

Faith and I stopped on the way to pick up fresh bagels. I knew that Aunt Peg was an early riser. She'd certainly been known to pop in on me at the crack of dawn. But even if we caught her in her pajamas, I figured she'd have to forgive us. One whiff of that big, white bag of onion bagels would be enough to ensure that.

When I arrived at Aunt Peg's house, however, she was not only up and dressed, she was expecting me. Faith and I were barely out of the car before Aunt Peg's pack of Standard Poodles came spilling down the front steps in a wave of scrambling feet and wagging tails.

A joyous welcoming ensued. Six black Standard Poodles raced around the front yard together. They bounded in the air and skidded around the corners of their exuberant circles. Aunt Peg's Poodles were Faith's family too. She was having the time of her life.

Aunt Peg waited on the porch until the commotion had died down. As I approached, she eyed the bag in my hand and sniffed the air delicately.

"You brought me food?" she said with delight. "Sam said you were on your way. He didn't tell me you were bringing goodies. Not to mention the lovely Faith."

Hearing her name, the big Poodle looked up at Aunt Peg adoringly. Her tail whipped back and forth—the classic canine greeting.

"Sam called?" I said, surprised.

"He'd said you'd snuck out of bed like a thief in the night."

"More like a wife with work to do." I shook the big bag enticingly as I climbed the steps. "The early bird gets the onion bagels."

"That sounds perfect. Cream cheese?"

"Vegetable chive," I told her. "Extra creamy."

Aunt Peg snatched the bag out of my hands and waved to the Poodles. "You lot, hurry up. It's time to come inside."

Just like everyone else, the dogs leapt to do her bidding.

Bully hadn't been part of the canine crew that ran outside to greet us. I surmised that due to his age and lack of training, the puppy hadn't been granted run of the house, and it turned out I was right. When we reached the kitchen, Bully was waiting for us.

A baby gate blocked the doorway between that room and the hallway. The chubby puppy was standing on his hind legs with his front feet braced against the gate's upper edge. When he saw us coming, Bully *woofed* softly under his breath.

I stepped over the gate and scooped him up in my arms to say hello. Bully responded by reaching up and licking my chin. His warm body wriggled happily. Our previous acquaintance had been pretty brief. I wasn't sure whether he recognized me or whether the friendly puppy treated everyone to the same exuberant greeting.

When Aunt Peg unlatched the baby gate and set it aside, the other dogs came swarming into the kitchen with us. I returned Bully to the floor. He immediately disappeared into the Poodle group.

The dogs drank two full bowls of water. As I refilled their supply, Aunt Peg got out knives, and napkins, and plates. She'd already brewed a cup of Earl Grey tea for herself. A jar of instant coffee was sitting on the counter for me. I put the kettle on the stove to boil.

Five minutes later, we were both seated at the table. The dogs were arrayed on the floor around us. The Poodles liked bagels too. They weren't allowed to beg but they knew they'd get their share eventually.

Aunt Peg cut open a bagel. She spread a liberal amount of cream cheese on one half and sighed with satisfaction. "I assume you've come because you need advice," she said. "Are you going to tell me why or shall I guess?"

I would have answered but my mouth was full of food. I'd just taken a big, delicious bite and I wanted a moment to savor it. As usual, Aunt Peg moved on without me. She liked nothing more than to get the conversational ball rolling with a provocative statement. It was no surprise, then, that she chose one that made me swallow in a hurry.

"I saw you canoodling with Crawford yesterday," she said.

"*Canoodling?*" I yelped, then coughed. I'd swallowed the wrong way. "We were *not*."

"So you say. But you looked pretty cozy to me. What was going on?"

"It was a private matter."

I wasn't about to reveal what Terry had told me in confidence until after everything was settled. And maybe not even then. My reticence only heightened Aunt Peg's curiosity, however.

"Private?" Her eyes narrowed. "How very interesting. Does it have anything to do with that Gabe character who always seems to be hanging around?"

I should have known. There wasn't much that escaped Aunt Peg's notice. I grabbed another piece of onion bagel and stuffed it in my mouth.

"I wonder what that's about," she mused aloud. "Do you suppose Crawford is auditioning for a new assistant?"

"Why would he want to do that?" I asked when I could speak again. "Terry does a great job."

Aunt Peg nodded. "Maybe Crawford needs more help. Maybe he's thinking of expanding his business."

"At his age?"

As soon as the words were out of my mouth, I wished I could call them back. Aunt Peg stared pointedly down her nose at me. She was older than Crawford and still going strong. And woe to anyone who even implied that Aunt Peg might be ready to hang up her judging shoes.

"That's not what I meant to say," I said quickly.

"Yes, I'm quite sure it wasn't."

I'd expected her to snap my head off. Thank goodness for the bagels. They must have mellowed her response. I lifted another one out of the bag and placed it on her plate.

"Has Crawford said anything to you about Gabe?" I asked.

"Not a blessed thing. Which of course makes me all the

more curious. Where did he come from? Why is he here? One day he simply showed up and then he never left. He reminds me of a lost puppy looking for a new home."

If there was one thing I really didn't want to do right now, it was get into a discussion of what—or who—Gabe reminded me of. Instead, I steered the conversation in another direction.

"Rush Landry," I said.

Aunt Peg looked up with interest. "What about him?"

"He was spying on Evan Major."

"No! To what end?"

"It turns out that Rush and Evan's brother, Mark, were once fraternity brothers."

"Mark Major sounded like an idiot at the funeral," Aunt Peg groused. "His eulogy—if one could call it that—was thoroughly distasteful. Evan deserved better."

"He certainly did. And as for Mark being an idiot, you won't hear an argument from me. He's convinced that Evan stashed away a significant sum of money before his company went bankrupt."

Aunt Peg picked up a knife and smeared another layer of cream cheese on her bagel while she considered that. "Mark thought that Evan was somehow going to lead Rush to the money?" she asked dubiously.

"I was skeptical too," I said. "But yes."

"And that's why Rush asked to join the book club?"

"Yes."

She scowled ferociously. "He *used* me to further his own ends."

"Yes, again," I said.

"That scoundrel," she snapped. "That reprobate! He pretended to be a book lover."

As if that was his biggest sin.

"Rush wasn't just keeping an eye on Evan on Mark's behalf," I told her. "Don't forget, he'd also lost money with Northeast Wealth Management."

"How much money?"

"I don't know. I asked Vic, but she didn't know either."

Aunt Peg sighed. "Leaving the man in charge of the money. Vic will learn to regret that. If she hasn't already."

She took another bite of her bagel. The layer of cream cheese that topped it was so thick that it looked like frosting on a cake.

"Rush and Mark made some kind of deal," I said. "I don't know the details but I'm guessing that if either one of them succeeded in turning up the money, they would split the proceeds."

"Turning up." Aunt Peg snorted. "What a polite euphemism. As if one of them might have found it lying around underfoot. You've seen Rush in action. He seems to think of himself as a tough guy. I wonder if he decided to go to Evan and force the issue."

"You mean with a knife?" I asked.

Aunt Peg nodded.

I wasn't surprised. I'd been wondering the same thing.

"And perhaps his fists," Aunt Peg mused. "Considering what Evan looked like when he arrived at my house for the meeting."

"Rush didn't do that," I told her.

"Was it Mark, then?"

"No. Annette."

Aunt Peg's eyes widened. I'd managed to shock her. "The ex-wife?"

"That's right."

"I thought you said she was a spindly thing."

"A spindly thing with a temper," I said. "And apparently a husband who didn't fight back."

"Some family," she muttered.

Like we should talk.

"That settles it," Aunt Peg decided. "We are never letting that woman have Bully. If she sends the authorities after me, I'll tell them that he ran away."

"You have a fenced yard," I pointed out.

"He could have jumped out."

Aunt Peg's fence was four feet high and totally secure. And Bully was . . . well, a Bulldog. A breed definitely not known for its leaping ability. For Aunt Peg's sake, I hoped she never had to attempt to sell that excuse.

She and I each helped ourselves to another bagel. That was two for me and three for her. Not that anyone was counting. The Poodles continued to watch us hopefully. Their turn would come.

"So Rush had several possible motives for murder," Aunt Peg said after a few minutes. "Number one, he'd lost an unspecified amount of money with Evan's company. Two—and perhaps even more important for a man with an ego the size of his—he'd been made to look like a fool in the process. And three, when the furor over the financial scandal had finally begun to die down, Mark appeared and pushed him to get reinvolved."

Once again Aunt Peg's thoughts mirrored my own. That didn't prevent me from playing devil's advocate however.

"*If* Evan had money hidden away—and I still think that's a big if—Rush wouldn't have had anything to gain by killing him," I pointed out.

"Unless he'd located the money and wanted to be able to access it without Evan standing in his way."

I shook my head. "But Mark and Annette wouldn't still be looking for the stash if it had already been found."

"Unless Rush didn't tell them."

That was a possibility, I realized. According to the woman who knew him best, Rush was a man who liked to be in charge. *And to keep secrets.*

"That brings me back to my earlier question." Aunt Peg stood up, walked over to the counter, then returned to the table with her laptop.

"What's that?"

"How much money did Rush lose?" She raised the computer's screen and placed her fingers on the keyboard. "When Bernie Madoff created his financial disaster, a number of news sources—Bloomberg, the *Wall Street Journal*, and Reuters among them—disclosed names of the investors and how much they'd lost. I wonder if Northeast Wealth Management's collapse was large enough to merit the same sort of attention."

Aunt Peg opened a search engine and typed in a question. I got up and walked around the table to look over her shoulder. There were several older stories about the company's early promise, and many more about its subsequent fall from grace. There were also newer stories about Evan's partners' legal woes. But the only specific information about NEWealth's investors named only the very largest clients—private trusts and public institutions.

Fifteen minutes later, Aunt Peg closed the laptop with a disappointed sigh. "That's too bad. I was hoping we'd find that Rush and Vic had lost a significant sum of money—something large enough to bolster my belief that Rush ought to be in trouble up to his ears."

"I have an idea." I pulled out a chair and sat down next to her.

Aunt Peg perked up. "What's that?"

"When I was talking to Annette, she mentioned that she still had Evan's old work files."

"Why on earth would she have possession of those?"

I waved away the query. "It's a long story. But the important thing is that both she and Mark told me that Evan was incredibly organized, and obsessive about backing things up. I'm betting that a list of investors was exactly the kind of information Evan would have held on to."

"Goodness gracious, that sounds interesting." She looked at me accusingly. "You might have started by telling me that."

"Sorry," I said. "I just thought of it."

"Now, how do we find out if Annette has what we need?"

I considered for a minute, then said, "Annette's an acquisitive woman. We offer her something she wants in return."

As one, we turned and looked at Bully. The tan-and-white puppy was snoozing happily on the floor, surrounded by a passel of Poodles. Bully's lips fluttered up and down as he snored. His feet were paddling in the air. I wondered if he was dreaming of rabbits.

"Not happening," Aunt Peg said firmly. "What else?"

"She wants money," I mentioned.

"Also not happening," she told me.

I was fast running out of options. "Maybe we don't have to give her anything. After all, by itself, a list like that doesn't have any value."

"Yes, but as soon as we ask for it, Annette's antennae will go up. She'll know it means something to us."

"Maybe I can appeal to Annette's better instincts."

"Does she have any?" Aunt Peg asked drily.

Good question.

"What if the police got a search warrant?" I proposed.

"The police wouldn't need a search warrant to find out that information," Aunt Peg pointed out. "All they'd have to do is arrest Rush and ask him."

Which obviously had yet to happen.

I pushed back my chair and stood up. "I'll call Annette tonight. In the meantime, I'll think of a way to convince her."

"You don't sound very sure of that," Aunt Peg commented.

There was nothing I could say to that. I make it a habit to never argue with the truth.

Chapter 25

Sam, the boys, and I spent the afternoon at the beach at Tod's Point. The early evening was devoted to unpacking the picnic hamper, rinsing sand out of crevices, and apologizing to the Poodles for leaving them behind. Dinner was hamburgers and corn on the cob cooked on the grill. After that, I finally had a chance to call Annette.

I'd spent the afternoon thinking about what I was going to say. I thought I had a plan. Or at least the beginning of an idea. But when she answered the phone, I blurted out, "Hi, Annette, it's Melanie. Please don't hang up!"

There was a long silence while we both waited to see what she would decide to do.

Finally, Annette said, "Go on."

"When we were talking the other day, you mentioned that you still have Evan's files from NEWealth."

"You mean when you barged in on me?"

I bit my tongue and merely said, "Yes, then."

"I might have told you that," Annette replied. "What of it?"

"I'm hoping you might be willing to do me a favor."

"That's rich." She snorted. "I was hoping you might be able to find my money. Have you done that yet?"

Well, no, I thought. And with good reason. I hadn't been looking.

"That's what I thought," Annette said when I didn't answer. "Why should I do anything for you?"

"Because you're a good person?"

"Says who?" Annette inquired.

I'm pretty sure neither of us expected me to come up with an answer for that. Instead, I said, "You should do it because it might help bring Evan's murderer to justice."

"The police are working on that. I don't see why it has anything to do with you."

"Right. The police," I said. "If you don't want to cooperate, I guess I could go and tell them what I've learned. Then they could get a search warrant to look at Evan's things." I was bluffing—Detective Sturgill hadn't been interested in anything I'd had to say—but Annette wouldn't know that.

"I'm done talking to the authorities." She sounded annoyed. "I've already done it more times than I care to. Probably more times than anyone would care to."

"I can totally see that," I agreed. "That's why I was trying to spare you another interview."

She sighed loudly. "What is it precisely that you need?"

"A list of the individuals who had money invested with Northeast Wealth Management. The size of their investments and how much they ended up losing. Do you think Evan had that information?"

"I'm sure he did. He had everything." She sighed again. Like talking to me on the phone was the most tedious thing ever. "If I help you with this, will you leave me alone forever?"

That depended on what I found on the list. "Probably," I answered honestly.

"Not good enough," Annette snapped. "I'm hanging up now."

"No, wait!" I could tell she hadn't disconnected. "Yes, I promise."

"Are you sure?"

It was hardly flattering. Apparently the only bargaining tool I possessed that would convince her to help us was the assurance that she would never have to see or hear from me again. Aunt Peg would probably get a laugh out of that. I might too—later.

"I give you my word," I said solemnly. I hoped I wouldn't have cause to regret it. "Evan's files—are they paper or digital?"

"Both," Annette told me. "It might take me a little time to find your list."

"Sooner is better," I said.

"Let's be clear. You are in no position to make demands. Give me your e-mail address. If I find something, that's how you'll hear from me. After that, I expect we will have no further communication of any sort. Is that correct?"

"That's correct," I said.

I gave her the information she needed. As soon as I was finished, Annette ended the connection. I hoped she would keep her word. There was nothing more I could do to convince her. For now, I could only wait and see.

Crawford's Bedford Kennels was located just on the other side of the New York–Connecticut state line in Bedford. The trip from North Stamford was a quick jaunt mostly through beautiful countryside. I knew the way by heart since I drove it often. Terry had been cutting my hair for years.

The small road that led to Crawford's driveway was bordered by a crumbling stone wall at least a century old. His house was a classic white colonial, centrally positioned on a spacious plot of land. Visible behind the house was the matching kennel building where Crawford conducted business.

Chain-link dog runs extended outward from either side of the kennel. Covered runs were to the left, uncovered ones on the right. Most of the enclosures were filled with dogs. As I parked the Volvo at the top of the driveway, I counted at least a dozen different breeds. Some were sleeping in the shade on raised beds. Others were playing or fence-running with their neighbors. All of them looked content and well cared for. I wouldn't have expected anything less.

Crawford answered the door himself. Even on his day off, his shirt was ironed, his pants creased, and his shoes freshly shined. I wondered if he'd told Terry about our meeting. It seemed odd to walk inside this house and not immediately be accosted by him.

When I glanced around, Crawford answered my unspoken question. "I got the impression you wanted to talk to me alone. A new client sent in two Standards this morning. Their coats needed work. I told Terry to bathe them both this afternoon. That should keep him busy—and give us some time to ourselves."

"Thank you," I said. "I appreciate that."

Terry always worked on my hair in the kitchen. That was the room I automatically gravitated toward. But Crawford headed the other way. He led me to a room at the end of a short hallway. His office, I saw when we walked inside. The inner sanctum.

Over the years, Aunt Peg had amassed a voluminous collection of ribbons, trophies, and win pictures. They'd been on display in her kennel building. Sadly, all had been lost the previous summer when the building burned to the ground. Gazing around Crawford's office now, I saw that his collection of memorabilia was even more impressive than hers had been.

Most interesting to me were four decades of photographs from the Westminster Dog Show. The progression from oldest to newest revealed how much both the event, and the way Poodles were presented in the show ring, had changed over those years. Crawford gave me a few minutes to look around in awe. Then he motioned me to one of two wing-back chairs placed on either side of a brick fireplace.

"I know how much you value your privacy," I began when we were both seated.

Crawford nodded.

"What I came to talk to you about goes way beyond boundaries I probably shouldn't cross. But I feel like I have to say something because Terry is worried about you."

"Me?" Crawford looked surprised.

"Both of you, actually. He's concerned about your relationship."

A fleeting look of displeasure crossed his face. I had known this wasn't going to be easy. I could only hope that Crawford would still think of me as a friend when we were finished.

"Our relationship is none of your business," Crawford said flatly.

"I agree. And the only reason I got involved is because Terry asked me to."

"He did?"

I nodded. "Several weeks ago. After Gabe showed up. After he began hanging around all the time."

I let that sink in for a minute. I gave Crawford time to speak. He remained silent.

"Terry feels threatened by your relationship with Gabe," I said.

"He shouldn't be."

"Terry doesn't understand what's going on."

Crawford's hands had been resting on the arms of his chair. Now I saw his fingers clench. "What do you mean?"

"I didn't get it at first either," I said, dodging his question. "It wasn't until I saw you and Gabe working side by side this past weekend that I realized the real nature of your connection."

Crawford stood up. He walked across the room with

stiff, angry, strides. When he'd reached his desk, he spun around to face me. "I am not one of your little mysteries to be solved, Melanie."

"No, of course not." I tried not to wince. The part about *little mysteries* definitely stung.

"My life isn't something for you to poke around in. Or ask questions about. Or form conclusions that may or may not be wrong."

"I don't think I'm wrong about this," I said quietly.

Crawford crossed his arms over his chest. "All right. Then why don't you go ahead and tell me what you think you know?"

"I understand why you're angry," I said.

"Do you? Because it doesn't sound that way to me."

I lifted my chin and stared up at him. "Rather than telling you what *I* think, let me tell you what Terry thinks."

Crawford lifted a brow and waited for me to continue.

"He thinks you've grown tired of him. He thinks Gabe is your new conquest, your shiny new boy toy."

Crawford's mouth sagged open. He snapped it shut. He glared at me incredulously. "That's ridiculous."

"It's not," I told him. "Terry watches you and Gabe when you're together. He sees how happy you are when Gabe is around. He's aware that you're teaching Gabe the very same things that you taught him when the two of you first became a couple."

Crawford had started to shake his head. With every sentence I uttered, the movement became faster and more deliberate. He could deny what I was saying all day long. Until Crawford decided to talk to me, I was going to keep going.

"Terry was particularly upset when you cooked Gabe dinner last week. He knows you'd only do that for someone who was special to you. He thinks you're besotted with Gabe."

That, of all things, was what finally made Crawford speak up. "Dinner was terrible. Just about inedible."

Now it was my turn to look incredulous. "I hope that isn't what you think this conversation is about."

"No, of course not," Crawford replied gruffly. "But I don't know where these things you're saying are coming from. Terry seems fine when Gabe is around. He's certainly never said anything to me about him."

"That's because he's an idiot," I muttered.

"Yes, but he's *my* idiot." Crawford paused to draw in a deep breath. "An idiot who ought to know better, damn it."

As I watched the play of emotion across his face, a lump rose in my throat.

He shook his head. "After all the time we've been together, how could he be so stupid as to think that I would ever let him go?"

No answer was needed. Instead, I turned away and let my gaze drift through the window and over the wide lawn outside. A minute passed before Crawford had himself back under control.

"So I guess you've figured out who Gabe is," he said.

"I think so. He's your son, isn't he?"

His head dipped in a brief nod. Maybe that was easier than confirming the relationship out loud.

"I don't understand," I said. "Why haven't you told Terry?"

"Because I didn't think I needed to." Crawford frowned. This time it looked as though he was angry at himself. "Gabe preferred that our relationship remain a secret. I figured it was his story to tell when he was ready. It looks like I was wrong."

He reached across the desk and pushed a button on an intercom. He had to push it twice before Terry's voice sounded through the small speaker.

"I'm in my office," Crawford said to him. "Come over here. Now."

"But I'm not finished—"

"I don't care. Put the dog away and get yourself over here."

There was a pause, then Terry asked, "Am I in trouble?"

"Yes!" Crawford shot back. He severed the connection, then turned back to me. Unexpectedly, he grinned. "That ought to bring him running."

Terry arrived at Crawford's office in less than five minutes. Since he would have had to make arrangements for a wet Standard Poodle, that seemed pretty quick. We'd heard the back door to the house open and close, followed by the sound of running feet.

There was a pause as Terry must have stopped to compose himself just outside the office. I pictured him straightening his shirt and running a hand through his tousled hair. A moment later, he stepped through the doorway looking calm and unruffled.

His gaze went quickly to Crawford. He offered his partner a tentative smile. Then Terry saw me. His surprise was evident.

"What are you doing here?" he asked.

"I'm having a conversation with Crawford," I told him. "Like you should have done a month ago."

"I don't know what you're talking about," Terry said nervously.

"Sure, you do," Crawford replied. "Don't bother denying it. That cat's way out of the bag. Have a seat." He gestured toward the armchair he'd recently vacated. "We need to talk about Gabe."

As Terry crossed the room, he turned his back to Crawford. *Is he going to kill me?* he mouthed silently.

I shook my head.

Is everything all right?

This time I nodded.

"What's going on with the two of you?" Crawford's gaze skimmed back and forth between us. "Is that some sort of secret code I don't know about?"

"It's nothing." Terry quickly sat down. "Nothing's going on." He smoothed his already smooth pants. "I'm ready now. Go ahead."

"I think you should go ahead," Crawford suggested. "I'd like to hear about the crazy ideas you've been cooking up in your head for the last month."

"Umm . . ." Terry cast about the room wildly.

I pretended not to notice. I wasn't about to help him.

"According to Melanie, you've been laboring under a misapprehension," Crawford announced. "A pretty sizeable one. I'd hate to think that I can't even make a new friend without you reading all sorts of things into it that aren't even there."

"Is that what Gabe is to you?" Terry asked. He suddenly looked hopeful. "A new friend?"

"No," Crawford replied. "He's my son."

Terry just about fell off his chair. He grabbed both arms to steady himself as if he couldn't believe what he'd just heard. Several second passed before he was able to speak. When he did, his voice emerged on a squeak. "How did that happen?"

"The usual way," Crawford said. When neither Terry nor I said a thing, he continued. "I guess you're going to want more explanation than that?"

We both nodded.

"This isn't something I talk about. Ever. So I guess maybe I should start by giving you a little history lesson." Crawford's eyes shifted Terry's way. "Back when I was growing up, times were less enlightened. Young men who were gay were encouraged—by their parents, by their churches, by society—to go against their natural instincts and deny their attraction to men. As if being gay was some kind of disease you could recover from if you applied yourself diligently enough."

Crawford grimaced. I shut my eyes briefly. Terry just sat in silence and listened.

"So like I was supposed to do, I applied myself. I had several relationships with girls. It was what was expected of me. In those days, boys were shown an inflexible mold and told to fit into it. So I tried to make it work."

"For how long?" Terry asked.

"Until I got older and realized that I needed to stop lying to myself about who I really was. Gabe was conceived in the last relationship I had with a woman. His mother and I weren't married; that idea wasn't even on the table. As the relationship developed I think she realized that I wouldn't have made good marriage material."

"That depends on your point of view," I said under my breath.

Crawford heard me. His lips quirked upward in a small smile before he continued. "Gabe's mother wanted a baby. She had a good job and I was willing to help out financially. She decided to raise Gabe as a single mother. Gabe wasn't even two when she married someone else. That man adopted Gabe and gave him his name. The two of them brought him up as their son."

"Why didn't you ever tell me any of this?" Terry asked plaintively.

"When?" Crawford wanted to know. "That relationship was over and done with years ago. It was a youthful folly that ended long before you and I even met. It's something I never talk about. Something that until recently, I mostly tried to not think about."

"Why?" I asked curiously.

"How would you feel knowing that you'd made a bone-headed choice that brought a child into the world, whom you were never going to be a real father to?"

Pretty bad, I thought. Just like Crawford had. "Did you have contact with Gabe over the years?"

"Some," Crawford admitted. "Not a lot. After his mother remarried, she didn't want me hanging around. She said her new husband was Gabe's father and that seeing me was confusing to him. Maybe I shouldn't have listened to her about that, but I did."

"So how did Gabe end up here?" asked Terry.

"I guess he finally got curious enough to want to know more about me. It was his decision that we should meet. Apparently his mother had told him I was some kind of glorified dog walker."

That broke the tension in the room. Despite the gravity of the subject, we all chuckled together.

"I watched you teach him how to do things. I thought you were grooming him to become your new assistant," Terry said. "And maybe more," he added under his breath.

"You have fluff where your brains ought to be," Crawford replied with a hint of exasperation. "I was showing Gabe stuff because I couldn't figure out what else to do with him. And because it's easier to talk when your hands are busy. And because maybe someday he'll actually become a handler himself. I didn't know ahead of time that Gabe was coming. He just showed up and said he was staying for a month, maybe longer. I was really happy to have a chance to get to know him. But four weeks is a long time for a visit."

I nodded.

Terry was busy doing calculations in his head. "His stay must be almost over."

"That's right," said Crawford. "It was great that Gabe and I had this opportunity. But he'll be heading home to upstate New York soon."

"Soon." Terry smiled. "That sounds good."

"It sounds good to me too," Crawford agreed.

The two of them were gazing at each other as if they'd forgotten that I was even there. I slipped out of my chair and sidled toward the door.

"I guess I'll be going now," I said.

Neither man responded. I didn't know what they were doing because I didn't look back. Besides, I knew my way out.

Chapter 26

"Gabe is Crawford's son," I said to Sam when I got home.

He turned and stared. "How did that happen?"

"The usual way," I told him with a laugh. It felt good to finally be able to laugh about the situation. Really good.

Sam was still curious, so I sat him down and told him everything. Then I swore him to secrecy. Maybe someday Crawford would feel comfortable sharing the story with his circle of friends. But until he made that decision, nobody other than Sam would hear about it from me.

That night I got an e-mail from Annette. The entire message was four words long. "Done. Now go away."

She'd sent the list as an attachment. I needed to download it, but my finger hovered uncertainly over the mouse. "I hope she didn't send me a virus," I said to Faith, who was sitting beside me.

Faith got up to have a look at the screen. She knows even less about computers than I do, but she likes to be included in the conversation. When she wagged her tail, I took that as confirmation that I should proceed.

A minute later, I'd printed out the list. It was even longer than I'd expected. Four pages of typed, single-spaced names were arranged in reverse chronological order. The list began with those who'd invested money recently and ended with those who had been with the company the longest.

Evan had not only noted who the individuals were, but also their contact information and the amounts they'd invested. Payouts, when applicable, were also listed.

The first page revealed nothing of interest. But midway down the second page, a familiar name caught my eye. Marge Brennan had opened an account with NEWealth three years earlier. The amount she'd invested wasn't nearly as large as some, but it still seemed sizeable to me. There was no record of the account having taken any returns.

I thought back to the previous book club meeting. Marge had admitted to recognizing Evan and knowing about his past history. But she certainly hadn't said anything about having money invested with his company.

Rush Landry's name appeared on page three. Some of the investors were listed as couples, but there was no mention of Vic on Rush's notation. As I recalled, Rush had talked about "their" investment when he was addressing the group. Vic had taken steps in the meantime to remedy her ignorance about their finances. I wondered if she was aware that her husband was using joint funds to open accounts that were solely in his name.

Rush had characterized the amount of money they'd invested as limited. But the number I saw beside his name on the page didn't look that way to me. From my point of view, it was big enough to take a chunk out of just about anyone's savings.

But was it big enough to cause someone to commit murder? I wondered. I supposed that depended on how angry Rush had been.

I could all too easily imagine him confronting Evan. Demanding that he make reparations. Evan would have refused—just as he'd refused his brother and his ex-wife.

I doubted there were many people who stood up to Rush. And I could see how Evan's defiance—compounded by Rush's humiliation at having been duped by a financial scheme so well known that its name was infamous—could have caused their encounter to spiral out of control.

I was about to pick up my phone and call Aunt Peg when it occurred to me that I should probably skim through the remainder of the list first. Just in case there was anything else interesting to see.

It was a good thing that I did. Page four held another surprise. One of NEWealth's earliest investors had a familiar last name: Celia Barrundy. The amount of money the woman had entrusted to the care of Evan's partners was large enough to make me gasp.

I grabbed my computer and pulled up a search engine. Within minutes I'd been able to confirm what I'd suspected. The Celia Barrundy named on Evan's list was Bella Barrundy's mother. Which meant she was also the woman who'd recently moved in with Bella and was—by several accounts—making her daughter's life miserable.

I stared at the number shown on the page. I counted the zeros twice.

With that much money on the line, the losses Celia Barrundy would have incurred when NEWealth went bankrupt had to have made a significant difference to her financial health. Perhaps a life changing difference. Maybe one that explained why mother and daughter now found themselves living together under the same unhappy roof.

I snatched up my phone and waited impatiently through the six rings it took Aunt Peg to pick up. Quickly I outlined everything I'd learned.

"How very interesting," she said at the end.

We were physically separated by at least a dozen miles. So maybe I was only imagining that I could hear the wheels turning in her head.

"I have an idea," Aunt Peg announced.

"Good," I replied. Because I was fresh out. I had plenty of suspicions and no way to prove any of them.

"I think I ought to call an emergency Bite Club meeting."

"What?" That wasn't at all what I'd expected her to say.

Aunt Peg rolled on enthusiastically. "Let's gather everyone together in one place and get to the bottom of this."

"We already tried that," I said. "People nearly came to blows when the topic was introduced."

"Yes, but now I'll be better prepared. I'll steer the conversation precisely where we wish it to go."

I was pretty sure she'd done that last time. With semi-disastrous results on my part. I tried another tack.

"You're forgetting something," I said.

"What's that?"

"Several of the people sitting in the room with us will be suspects."

I thought I'd made a good point. Aunt Peg just laughed.

"That's the whole idea. It's positively brilliant!"

"But—"

She ignored me and resumed planning. "We'll hold the meeting here, of course. Tomorrow night should suit quite well. It's Tuesday and that's our regular night. So everyone will be free."

"They're free on the nights we have a meeting scheduled," I pointed out. "That doesn't mean they'll be able to show up tomorrow."

"Oh pish," said Aunt Peg. "I'm giving them twenty-four-hours' notice. What more could they want? Of course they'll all show up. The fact that I've called it an emergency meeting will be enough to bring them running. That includes our suspects. They'll have no choice but to appear."

"They won't?"

"Certainly not. Staying away would make them look guilty. Plus, everyone would be bound to talk about them in their absence. Someone like Rush Landry would much rather be on hand to control the conversation—and to deflect suspicion away from himself."

She was probably right about that.

"I think I'll drop a little teaser into my e-mail," Aunt Peg decided. "I'll imply that we've turned up some juicy new information that they definitely don't want to miss."

"Juicy?"

Aunt Peg wasn't listening to me. That was nothing new. "Of course I'll need to order a cake or two. A nice sugar buzz is just what we need to put everyone on edge. That should stir things up nicely."

"Sugar buzz?" I gulped.

"This is such a splendid idea, I can't believe I didn't think of it sooner," Aunt Peg cried. "This is going to be such fun!"

"Fun?" I said weakly.

"Tomorrow night, seven o'clock," she told me. "Don't be late!"

The connection ended. Aunt Peg was finished with me. As I frowned at the phone, Faith nudged her head into my lap.

"That was Aunt Peg," I told her.

Faith *woofed* softly. She knew that.

"Once again she's taken control," I told the big Poodle. "I don't know why I ever thought that Bite Club was my book club. I must have been delusional. Aunt Peg was running things all along."

Faith *woofed* again in agreement. She knew that too.

Tuesday evening, I arrived at Aunt Peg's at six forty-five. I thought she might want help setting up—and I also wanted to confer with her about her plans for the meeting.

Aunt Peg was having none of it. Instead, she told me to take her Standard Poodle pack outside and run them around the fenced acre field that served as her backyard. She tried to make the job sound important, but we both knew perfectly well that the dogs were quite capable of exercising themselves.

I went anyway. It was easier than arguing.

Terry joined me out there a few minutes later.

"You're here early," I said.

"Of course I'm early." Terry grinned. "Aunt Peg called an *emergency* meeting. She's lucky I didn't show up this morning." He leaned closer and whispered, "I think she's up to something."

"Of course she's up to something," I said with a laugh. "She's always up to something."

The Poodles were racing in big happy circles around the perimeter of the yard. All former show dogs, they knew better than to pull on each other's hair. That meant Coral didn't need my attention, so I focused on Terry instead.

He looked good. No, better than good. He looked relaxed, maybe even content. He looked like the old Terry I knew and loved, the one I'd been missing recently.

The gang of Poodles came flying toward us. Terry turned and his gaze met mine. He tipped his head to one side as if he was considering something. I was pretty sure he was reading my mind.

He reached out and took my hand, then gave my fingers a squeeze. "Thank you."

"You're welcome. I'm glad you and Crawford are finally back on the same page."

"Not just the same *page*." Terry waggled his eyebrows suggestively.

"Stop that." I laughed. "I don't even want to know."

"Gabe's leaving at the end of the week," he said instead.

"That's a good thing, right?"

"It's a very good thing." He blew out a sigh of relief. "Crawford and I could use some time to ourselves. I'm sure Gabe will be back to visit again someday. But not for a while."

Together we walked up the steps to the wraparound porch. Tired and happy, the five Standard Poodles trailed along behind us. Once on the porch, we could see Aunt Peg's driveway. Several additional cars were now parked behind ours. Another was turning in from the road.

"This meeting was Aunt Peg's idea," I said. "I wasn't sure people would be able to come on such short notice."

"You're kidding, right? The crowd that Peg added to the group are all dog show people. They wouldn't dare say no."

I reached for the doorknob, but the back door was already opening from the other side. Aunt Peg was standing just inside her kitchen, staring at the two of us. It was clear that she'd been listening to our conversation.

"I told you they would be here," she said with satisfaction. "Dog show people like me. Bring the Poodles inside and let's get everyone a drink."

The dogs scrambled past us and headed for the water bowls. Bully had been lying on his bed, playing with a rope toy. He got up and went to join them.

"Some dog show people like you," Terry said. "And some pretend to like you because they're afraid of you."

"Afraid of me?" Aunt Peg spun around. "Why would anyone be afraid of me?"

Terry and I shared a look. I nearly smiled. The expression on Aunt Peg's face was enough to quell that idea.

"You can be a little intimidating," Terry pointed out.

"Oh, that." Aunt Peg sniffed. "That's entirely different. Some people deserve to be intimidated."

Which brought us back to why we were here.

"So," said Terry, "what's the emergency?"

Aunt Peg glanced around before replying. We could hear voices coming from the hallway, and no doubt there were people in the living room, but the three of us were alone in the kitchen. Except for the Poodles, of course. But I was pretty sure they wouldn't spill our secrets.

"Melanie and I believe that a murderer will be sitting among us tonight," she said in a low tone. "We've organized this meeting to flush him out."

Terry reared back in surprise. "That sounds like a job for the police."

"Give me a break," I said. "You should love this idea. You're the one who's always egging me on."

"That's *you*. Not me. I have a healthy appreciation for my own safety." Terry gave me a pointed look. "Something that you seem to be curiously lacking."

The dogs had finished drinking. Zeke walked to the doorway and peered out over the baby gate. Bully and the other Poodles lay down on the floor.

Aunt Peg waited until they were settled, then turned back to us. "Nobody needs to be concerned about their health or security. Except perhaps, for our killer, who will hopefully find tonight's proceedings quite uncomfortable. The rest of us won't be at risk. We'll have numbers on our side. I don't see how anything could go wrong."

She never did, I thought. That was the problem.

Terry looked reassured, even if I didn't. "What do you want me to do?" he asked.

"Just play along," Aunt Peg told him. "No matter what I say or do, lend your support. Act as if it makes perfect sense."

"I always do," Terry replied with a smirk.

"I thought you had a plan," I said to Aunt Peg. "Now it sounds like you're going to be improvising on the fly."

"Of course I have a plan," she replied with hauteur. "First, ply the participants with cake. Then tease them with the possibility of new and incriminating information. Next, throw out a few accusations. Finally . . . watch mayhem ensue."

"That sounds like fun," said Terry.

Okay, I had to admit it. It kind of did.

Besides, as plans went, I'd heard worse. I'd even used worse.

I gestured toward the doorway, ready to move along. "Let's get this party started," I said.

Chapter 27

W hile we'd been in the kitchen chatting, the rest of the
Bite Club members had arrived.

Aunt Peg had left her front door standing open. People
had come inside and gone straight to the living room, the
site of our previous meetings. A few were helping themselves to drinks and dessert. Most had already taken a
seat. Nobody seemed to be talking much.

While Aunt Peg closed the door, I paused at the entrance
to the living room and took a look around. Claire and
Alice were seated side by side. Claire had a plate holding a
large wedge of chocolate cake balanced on her lap. Alice
was sipping a glass of white wine. She gave me a little
wave and motioned to the empty chair beside her.

Toby Cane was on a loveseat. He'd brought his book
with him to our two previous meetings. He'd held it up as
a prop while he spoke. Now his hands were empty and he
looked as though he didn't know what to do with them.

Marge Brennan was seated beside him. She'd also taken
a piece of cake, but it sat untouched on her plate. She was
gazing around the room nervously as if she expected
someone to jump out and pounce on her.

Vic and Rush Landry were at opposite ends of the room.
Rush was standing near the fireplace, nursing a beer. Vic and
Felicity Barber were on the second loveseat. Heads tipped

toward each other, they were holding a whispered conversation. I wondered what they had to talk about.

Bella Barrundy was seated in a straight-backed chair near the sideboard. She had a piece of chocolate cake too. Unlike Marge, she was shoveling forkfuls into her mouth as fast as she could swallow. She didn't look like she wanted to speak to anyone.

Jeff Schwin had taken a chair with empty seats on either side. He wasn't eating, but he was drinking. He appeared distinctly uncomfortable. I recalled he'd been alarmed about belonging to a club with a member who'd been killed. Aunt Peg's labeling this meeting an emergency probably hadn't done anything to assuage his anxiety.

Terry sidled past me and took a seat. I entered the room and went to sit beside Alice. Aunt Peg waited until everyone was facing the doorway before making her entrance.

She opened her mouth to speak, but Rush beat her to it. He pushed himself away from the mantelpiece, straightened his shoulders, and said, "We've come as you ordered. All of us are here. It seems to me that we're due an explanation. What is the meaning of this?"

Heads were nodding in agreement. I didn't look around to see whose. I kept my eyes on Aunt Peg. She seemed unperturbed by Rush's outburst.

"Sit down, Rush," she said mildly, gesturing toward an empty chair. "You'll have your chance to speak soon enough. I hope everyone has helped themselves to cake?"

A titter of nervous laughter went around the room. Marge held up her plate and smiled. Rush just looked annoyed. There were two empty chairs left. He sat down, but not in the seat Aunt Peg had indicated. Vic looked at him across the room and frowned.

"Excellent," said Aunt Peg. "I've asked you here tonight because we, as a group, were the last community that Evan Major belonged to before his untimely death. And since I was the one who brought this group together—"

I cleared my throat. Loudly. Aunt Peg pretended not to notice.

"—I thought it only right that I do what I could to aid the cause of justice." She paused and looked around sternly. "I have known some of you longer and better than others. But I have thought of all of you as friends. Which is why it's painful for me to have to say that there are people in this room tonight who have misled us."

Aunt Peg's gaze stopped abruptly on Marge. Her voice rose. "Indeed, people who have lied to us about their involvement with Evan Major's company and with his subsequent death!"

"Why are you looking at me?" Marge protested. Color rose to her cheeks as all eyes turned her way. "I don't know what you're talking about."

"Oh, I think you do," Aunt Peg retorted. "But allow me to refresh your memory. At our last meeting, you admitted to recognizing Evan's name. You even said that you were fascinated by NEWealth's financial shenanigans."

"I was," Marge sputtered. "But that doesn't mean that I wished Evan ill."

"Then why did you hide the truth from us?" Aunt Peg demanded.

"Truth?" Marge looked surprised. "What truth?"

"What you neglected to say at the time—the information that you intentionally withheld from all of us—is that you weren't merely an interested bystander when Evan's company went belly up. No, you yourself had an important stake in the outcome."

"No, I didn't!"

"You did," Aunt Peg confirmed. "There's no point in lying to us again. Not now when we all know that you had money invested with NEWealth—money that you subsequently lost every penny of."

I wasn't the only Bite Club member who was watching this exchange with a sick feeling in the pit of my stomach.

Alice and Claire looked equally horrified by what they were witnessing. As did Felicity. Vic regarded the confrontation with an air of remove—as if she was watching actors recite lines in a play. Both Jeff and Toby seemed to be entertained. Perhaps they were enjoying the startling showdown taking place in front of them.

I didn't understand what Aunt Peg was doing. I'd thought she was going to try and wheedle a confession out of Rush—not assault Marge with both barrels blazing. Even worse, I was pretty sure that her attack was unwarranted. Yes, Marge had lost money with NEWealth. But the sum she'd invested had been paltry compared to the amounts lost by other investors.

I was about to speak up—and to try and redirect the conversation—when Aunt Peg marched across the room to stand in front of Marge's chair. She propped her hands on her hips and glared downward at the hapless woman.

"Tell us, Marge. How did it make you feel when you saw Evan Major sitting in our midst like just another mystery reader?" she demanded. "How badly did you want to leap up and seek revenge for what he had done to you?"

"I didn't!" Marge cried. Her voice hovered on the edge of hysteria. "You know I didn't. I would never do something like that!"

"That's enough!" Rush said sharply. His glare, directed at Aunt Peg, was enough to make her back away. "You have no right to treat Marge that way."

"I have every right," Aunt Peg replied evenly. "A terrible wrong has been committed. One that must be rectified. Evan Major lost his life. And his killer needs to be brought to justice."

"That doesn't mean that you get to act like some kind of avenging angel. Standing over Marge like that, accusing her of a horrible crime and scaring her half to death," Rush growled. "So she invested in Evan's company, so what? I did too. So did hundreds of other people."

"Hundreds of other people didn't join my book club," Aunt Peg shot back.

Rush frowned. "I guess that means you suspect me too."

"Yes," she replied evenly. "Especially as you've given me every reason to. Not only did Evan's company cost you a great deal of money, I've also been made aware that the only reason you joined this club was so that you could spy on him."

Rush's face darkened. I thought he was going to deny the accusation, but then he shrugged instead. "So what if I did?"

"Rush was spying on Evan?" Toby suddenly sounded outraged. "What the hell does that even mean?"

"It means that Evan's brother was trying to extract money from him," I said. "Money that Evan asserted he didn't have. His brother thought Rush could help."

"Help him do what?" asked Jeff.

"Find the missing money," Felicity guessed. "Is that right?"

I nodded.

"I didn't know about that," Bella spoke up. "If there's money to be had, I want my share too."

"This is all beside the point," Rush stated. "Just because we were angry at what happened doesn't mean that one of us wanted Evan dead."

"It wasn't just the money," said Aunt Peg. "There was also the embarrassment factor. Smart people, people who thought of themselves as top-notch investors"—she stared right at Rush—"falling prey to the oldest scheme in the book like rank novices? That had to have hurt."

"Of course it hurt," Rush snapped. "I never said it didn't. The whole episode was painful on a number of counts."

"That's why you struck back," Toby charged. Several people nodded in agreement. "A big, strong man like you. It probably wouldn't have taken much for you to overpower Evan."

Suddenly everyone was looking at Rush. They were all speaking at once. Terry was doing his best to whip everyone into a frenzy and there were too many conversations to follow. I kept my eyes on Vic, who looked to be on the verge of tears.

"Okay. All right." Rush held up a hand. "*Enough.* You're right, I was mad at Evan. Livid even. And I fell in with Mark's plan because I thought it might put some of the money I'd lost back in my pocket. I confronted Evan."

"You killed him," Toby accused.

"Maybe I wanted to hurt him." Rush hung his head briefly. "But I didn't. Evan and I talked about what had happened. He apologized."

"Big deal," said Jeff. "How did that help?"

"It didn't," Bella spoke up. "Evan apologized to me too. And it didn't help one damn bit."

"You had money invested in NEWealth too?" Marge asked.

"My mother did. It was her IRA. She lost every dollar of her savings. And do you know what Evan did about that?" she spat out. "*Nothing.* He said he was sorry but it wasn't his fault. Of course it was his fault. He was just as involved as those other guys who were running the company."

"Evan lived right down the road from you," Claire spoke up.

Bella nodded. "That made things even worse. Every day, I saw him puttering around over there. He was a reminder of everything we'd had—and lost. It just about drove my mother crazy."

"And your mother drove you crazy," I said. A suspicion was forming in my mind. "Crazy enough to make you want to do something about it."

"Oh, I did something about it all right," Bella said harshly. "I marched over to Evan's house and told him that he needed to make things right. My mother needed her money back. I wanted her out of my house, and out of my hair, and back in her own damn place."

"I thought Bella had a crush on Evan," Alice said under her breath.

"She did have a crush on him," Terry agreed. "I bet this isn't about her mother. She's probably just mad because Evan didn't return her interest."

Bella straightened in her chair. She glared at both of them. "That's not true. Evan was useless—he couldn't help with anything. I didn't care about him. I cared about my mother's missing IRA."

"Why are we talking about Bella?" Toby asked. "She can get another boyfriend. Rush is the one who matters. We all know he likes a fight. We've seen him in action—he treats dog shows like a blood sport. It doesn't surprise me that he attacked Evan. I bet he got the drop on him."

"That's not fair!" Bella interjected angrily. "I matter too. And Evan wasn't my boyfriend."

"That's not what they're saying," Jeff pointed out.

"They're wrong." Bella's voice rose. "You're *all* wrong."

"What difference does it make?" Toby scoffed. "A little woman like you, what could you possibly do?"

Bella was frustrated. And furious. "I could do plenty."

Toby started to laugh. Vic and Felicity were talking again. Rush was yelling at Jeff. Bella's eyes narrowed. Her face grew red. Nobody was taking her seriously. She looked ready to explode.

"You could do plenty," I said softly. "You could pick up a knife."

"Nah." Terry scoffed. "Probably not. She's not brave enough for that."

Bella's head whipped around. "The knife was already out. It was sitting on the counter."

"You picked it up." I encouraged her to continue.

She frowned. "No . . . somehow it came into my hand. Like it belonged there."

"Evan did something terrible to you," I goaded her. "He ruined your mother's life. He ruined *your* life. He deserved what happened next."

Bella nodded grimly. She stared past me, unseeing, as though her thoughts were turned inward. I wondered if she was reliving a memory.

"Evan deserved to die," she said through gritted teeth. "And then he did."

Terry drew in a sharp breath. "You're the one who killed Evan."

Bella blinked her eyes. She suddenly refocused. "No, I didn't. That's not true. I never said that."

"You just did," Terry told her.

"You're crazy." Bella jumped up from her seat. "And you're a liar too."

"Only sometimes," Terry allowed.

I glared at him.

"But not now," he added.

"I have to go." Bella's gaze flew wildly around the crowded room. "It's time for me to leave."

"So soon?" Aunt Peg was standing near the door. That far away, she'd missed our whole conversation. "Things were just getting interesting."

"Things are *already* interesting," I told her. "Bella just confessed to murdering Evan."

"I did not!" she shrieked.

Aunt Peg looked at me. I nodded.

"I think perhaps you shouldn't go anywhere just yet," Aunt Peg said calmly. "At least not until we have everything sorted out. Bella, please sit back down."

"I will *not*. I want to go home. You can't make me stay here."

Actually, I thought, *we probably could.* As Aunt Peg had pointed out earlier, numbers were on our side.

I was about to mention that when Bella suddenly leapt over to the sideboard where Aunt Peg had put out the refreshments. She cast a quick glance over the offerings, then snatched up the flower-sprigged china teapot. I was sure it was heavy. It looked like it was hot too, because Bella juggled it back and forth from hand to hand.

"You'd better get out of my way," she told Aunt Peg.

"Or what? You'll pour me a cup of tea?"

Apparently it wasn't the right time for levity. Certainly Bella didn't find the remark funny. She growled something under her breath. Then her arm lifted. She hefted the teapot back like it was a baseball and let fly.

I was too stunned by that unexpected turn of events to react quickly. Thank goodness Aunt Peg had better reflexes. She dodged nimbly to one side and the teapot went whistling past her head.

It crashed into the wall behind her and shattered. Tea sprayed backward toward the loveseat where Vic and Felicity were sitting. Both women jumped to their feet.

"What the hell!" cried Vic.

Those were pretty much my sentiments too.

"That's quite enough," Aunt Peg said firmly.

"Oh, I don't think so," Bella replied. She reached for the remains of the chocolate cake. "Move out of my way."

She wouldn't, I thought. *Would she?*

"Bella, don't be ridiculous. Whatever's going on here, I'm sure we can work things out." Jeff stood up and went to intercept her. When he grabbed for her arm, Bella swung to meet him. He got a face full of cake for his efforts.

Blinking and sputtering, Jeff retreated.

Rush sized up the situation and darted toward the buffet table from the other side. Quickly he grabbed up the wine bottles, then jumped back out of range. That was well done. Unfortunately he hadn't been able to save the pupcakes too.

Bella went for them next. The woman had quite an arm. She lobbed the small cakes like icing-covered missiles at anyone who dared to approach her.

Toby took a direct hit. Claire had a near miss. Several pupcakes splattered against the furniture. Two chairs and a loveseat bloomed with sticky chocolate blobs.

Bella was clearing the sideboard at an alarming rate. "We'd better watch out when she finds the knives," I said under my breath to Aunt Peg. I'd crossed the room to stand beside her.

"They're cake knives," she snapped. "There's a limit to the amount of damage they can do."

"Tell that to your teapot," I muttered. The wall near the doorway was stained with a large brown splotch of Earl Grey.

My comment had drawn Bella's attention. "This is all your fault!" she screamed. Seconds later a pupcake came flying toward my head.

I batted it away, then licked the frosting off my fingers. *Mmmm, buttercream.*

"You're enjoying this entirely too much," Aunt Peg accused.

"You're the one who set it in motion," I told her.

"Yes, but I didn't expect people to lose control—or all sense of decency."

"You could stop blocking the doorway and let her leave."

Aunt Peg propped her hands on her hips defiantly. "Never!"

So there we were. Bella was glaring across the cake-splattered living room at Aunt Peg and me. Aunt Peg was glaring right back. The remaining book club members were mostly huddled behind furniture, waiting to see what would happen next.

There was no point in trying to be a hero, I decided. The once full sideboard was now looking pretty empty. At the rate Bella was throwing things, she would be out of edible ammunition soon.

The same thought must have crossed Bella's mind. When she reached for another pupcake and came up with only a fistful of napkins, she began to look frantically around the room for another exit. I hoped she didn't decide to jump out a window.

And to think, I'd imagined Bella's mother was the difficult one.

Abruptly my heart sank as Bella turned and looked behind her.

A small alcove in the back of the living room held a closed door that was almost hidden from view. The door led to Aunt Peg's office, and it probably wasn't locked. If Bella retreated that way, she wouldn't find the exit she sought—but she might be able to do some serious damage inside the room before we were able to reach her.

When Bella spun around, I was already moving toward her. I'd expected Aunt Peg to follow. Instead, she remained in place. That seemed odd. Surely she must have seen the same threat I did.

Dodging between the circled chairs, I was only halfway across the room when Bella reached the door and yanked it open. She started to rush forward, then abruptly stopped.

I'd been looking down to watch where I was going, so I almost went barreling into her. Then I stumbled to a sudden stop myself. My gaze lifted and I saw what had halted Bella's progress.

Aunt Peg's office wasn't empty. Detective Sturgill was standing in the doorway.

I blinked once, then again, to make sure I wasn't imagining things. A lively babble of conversation erupted behind me.

Aunt Peg's voice rose above the rest. She addressed Detective Sturgill. "For pity's sake, what took you so long? Were you waiting for her to demolish my *entire* living room?"

Chapter 28

Once Detective Sturgill appeared, things got back to normal quickly. Or as normal as they could be in a room that was liberally festooned with cake. Presumably Sturgill had heard what was happening—but he didn't see the damage until he stepped out into the living room.

I could have sworn I saw him bite back a smile.

Bella remained in the alcove with a uniformed officer. Another officer stayed behind in Aunt Peg's office, bent over some equipment that was arrayed across her desk. Meanwhile most of the remaining Bite Club members were quickly making themselves scarce.

Terry was the nosiest man in the world. He and his big ears remained behind.

I was surprised that Sturgill allowed the other participants to leave. Since several had been witness to Bella's confession, I would have thought that he'd want to question them.

It turned out that wasn't necessary—the detective had had Aunt Peg's living room bugged. He stood in the back of the room and gave the walls and furniture a long, slow, look.

"This is going to take some cleaning up," he said.

"Never mind about that," Aunt Peg retorted. "Did you hear what Bella said?"

"Every word," Sturgill confirmed. "No sweat. The recording devices we use now could pick up a flea's sneeze."

Aunt Peg looked offended. "Not in this house they couldn't." She glanced over at Terry and me. "That's why I had you two wear out the Poodles. I had to stash them in the kitchen so they wouldn't sniff out the detective and his men and give the game away."

Terry raised a brow in my direction. He looked as befuddled as I felt. "Did you know about this?"

"Not a thing," I told him.

Marge came walking around the corner from the hall. Apparently she hadn't left with the others. She crossed the living room and went straight to Aunt Peg.

I grabbed Terry's arm. We both waited to see what Marge would do. Aunt Peg had treated her hideously this evening. I half expected Marge to throw a fit—one that Aunt Peg most assuredly deserved.

It seemed I was due for another surprise.

Marge opened her arms wide. She and Aunt Peg both began to laugh. The next thing I knew, the two women were hugging each other as though they were the best of friends. I thought I heard Marge congratulate Aunt Peg on a job well done.

What?

Terry turned and stared at me again. "Did you know about *that?*"

I shook my head. Suddenly I felt very foolish.

"But . . ." I sputtered.

"Do close your mouth, Melanie." Aunt Peg looked at me over Marge's shoulder. "You look ridiculous."

"Marge?" I said as the woman turned around. "You're not angry?"

"Angry? I don't know when I've had so much fun. You didn't know I was such a good actress, did you?"

Apparently I didn't know much of anything.

"So when Aunt Peg jumped on you earlier—that wasn't real?"

"Of course not," Aunt Peg replied. "It was just a ploy to get everyone all riled up. I knew Marge couldn't have been involved in Evan's murder, so I took her into my confidence. She and I staged a confrontation to get the conversation started."

"I was happy to help." Marge was still beaming.

My knees felt boneless and I sank down in the nearest chair. Once again, Aunt Peg had hatched one of her grand schemes. And once again, I'd been left out of the loop. I probably ought to have been used to that by now. But somehow I wasn't.

"How did you know that if you went after Marge, Rush would leap to her defense?" I asked Aunt Peg.

"I didn't. The plan was for Marge to deal with my outburst by deflecting the attention toward Rush. We hoped that would force him to say something brash about his own involvement."

"Neither of us had any idea that Rush possessed such chivalrous instincts," Marge said.

"Or that Bella possessed such murderous ones," Aunt Peg added darkly.

The technician had packed up his equipment. We watched in silence as the three policemen took their leave. Bella, hands cuffed in front of her, went with them. Detective Sturgill paused to have a word with Aunt Peg on his way out.

I sidled closer. Even then, I still couldn't overhear what was being said.

Terry and Marge departed together. I was ready to go too. But first I wanted to know what the detective had said to Aunt Peg.

"He thanked me for my assistance," she said happily. "He said he'd be willing to work with me anytime."

"With you," I repeated.

"Of course, me." Aunt Peg nodded. "He and I got along splendidly."

It figured.

I had one last interview with Detective Sturgill about a week later. It took place in his office at the Stamford police station. Having been upgraded from the little room off the lobby, I decided that perhaps I'd risen in his estimation too.

Not as far as Aunt Peg, of course. But still, it was something.

"There's one thing I don't understand," I said. "How did Bella Barrundy and Evan Major end up living right down the road from each other?"

"I wondered about that myself," Sturgill replied. "It seemed like quite a coincidence, but there turned out to be an explanation. Before she moved in with her daughter, Celia Barrundy lived in New Jersey, not far from where the Northeast Wealth Management office was located. An older lady like that, living alone, I guess she had some time on her hands. Apparently it wasn't unusual for her to stop by the office and visit the nice men who were taking care of her money."

Four busy money managers—all of them allegedly intent on hiding what they were doing from their clients. And none of them eager to answer any questions about their investments.

"They must have loved that." I smirked.

"You got it," he said with a nod. "It was just the five of them working there. The partners didn't want to waste their time entertaining Mrs. Barrundy. But Evan Major was docile and deferential enough. I guess he didn't mind listening to her talk."

I thought about the single conversation I'd had with

Celia Barrundy. "Either that or he couldn't figure out a way to make her go away."

"That too, probably." Sturgill grinned. "Apparently she used to talk about her daughter who lived in a lovely place called Flower Estates. Evan thought a spot with a name like that sounded like it must be nirvana. He remembered it when the time came for him to make a fresh start, and he came looking for it."

"He must have been disappointed," I said. Flower Estates was an older housing development in a growing metropolis. It was a nice place to live, but it was hardly the promised land.

"I don't know about that," Sturgill replied. "But I can tell you that Celia Barrundy just about blew a gasket when Evan showed up in her neighborhood. There she was—forced to live in what she thought of as "reduced circumstances"—and then one of the men she held responsible ended up right under her nose. She was not happy."

"And in turn Celia made Bella just as miserable as she was," I said.

"Those two are quite a pair." The detective reached over and straightened some papers next to his blotter. "I'm sure you'll hear about Ms. Barrundy's defense on the news. Especially since the lawyer she hired is the kind of guy who likes to play things up for the media."

What defense? I wondered. Bella had confessed. And Sturgill had it on tape.

"Is there going to be a trial?" I asked.

"It looks that way. Ms. Barrundy is now claiming that it was her mother who went to confront Evan. She says she only followed along to bring Celia back. And that she ended up getting involved in the altercation by accident. Her lawyer says she was defending herself from Evan when she struck the blow that killed him."

"Will she get away with it?" I asked.

The detective shrugged. "That part's not up to me, so I

guess it remains to be seen. I'll tell you this though. Bella Barrundy is a pretty sharp cookie. She admitted to us that the reason she went back to Evan's house to "discover" his body was so there'd be an excuse for her DNA to be at the crime scene. And sending us off in the wrong direction chasing after you? That was a good distraction on her part too."

I smiled tightly. "I'm sure you'll understand if I don't agree."

Detective Sturgill nodded. It was probably as much of an apology as I was going to get.

Mark Major ended up inheriting all his brother's worldly goods. There wasn't much. The house on Bluebell Lane was a rental. The furniture was mostly secondhand. As was Evan's car. The lawyers had already taken everything else.

Mark and I had a brief conversation about Bully. He didn't want the puppy and told me to dispose of him. That wasn't happening. Instead, I put Aunt Peg on the case.

It didn't take her long to come up with a solution. Within days, she'd delivered Bully to the new home Marge had found for him. The poor puppy had already been passed around too many times. Marge promised us that this home would stick.

Thankfully, everything was back to normal between Crawford and Terry. But for now, the handler and I were maintaining a civil distance from one another. I'd hoped that the happy ending would be enough to restore me to Crawford's good graces, but apparently not.

Terry was grateful for my intervention. Crawford wasn't. Sam had warned me that would be the case. And even without that, I'd known I was treading on thin ice. I've lost Crawford's trust and now I'm going to have to put in some serious work to regain it.

Alice was relieved to have Evan's murder resolved—even though the killer had turned out to be another neighbor. Over time, the local furor gradually died down. By the end of summer, the small subdivision was once again a peaceful place to live.

Alice held a pool party to celebrate the return to normalcy. We all sat around her backyard in beach chairs and drank plenty of wine. Some of the more adventurous adults ended the night sitting in the wading pool.

Since it seemed unlikely that Bite Club would survive the recent turmoil, we even spent some of the evening talking about books. Mystery novels, of course. Claire had a new list of reading suggestions.

I've looked over her selections and I can't wait to get started. Tracking down clues and coming up with answers is a daunting endeavor. It will be nice to let someone else do all the hard work for a change.